Jack Vance was born in 1920 and educated at the University of California, first as a mining engineer, then majoring in physics and finally in journalism. He has since had a varied career: his first story was written while he was serving in the US Merchant Marine during the Second World War. During the late 1940s and early 1950s, he contributed a variety of short stories to the science fiction and fantasy magazines of the time. His first published book was THE DYING EARTH (1950). Since then he has produced several series of novels — for example, the *Planet of Adventure*, *Durdane* and *Demon Princes* series — as well as various individual novels. THE DYING EARTH is in the same series as THE EYES OF THE OVERWORLD and CUGEL'S SAGA.

Jack Vance has won the two most coveted trophies of the science fiction world, the Hugo Award and the Nebula Award. He has also won the Edgar Award of the Mystery Writers of America for his novel THE MAN IN THE CAGE (1960). In addition, he has written scripts for television science fiction series.

Jack Vance's non-literary interests include blue-water sailing and early jazz. He lives in Oakland, California.

By the same author

The Five Gold Bands
Sons of the Tree
Vandals of the Void
To Live Forever
Big Planet
The Languages of Pao
The Man in the Cage
The Dragon Masters
The Houses of Iszm
Future Tense
The Moon Moth
The Blue World
The Last Castle
Emphyrio
Fantasms and Magics
Trullion: Alastor 2262
Marune: Alastor 993
Wyst: Alastor 1716
Showboat World
The Best of Jack Vance
Lyonesse

Demon Princes series
Star King
The Killing Machine
The Palace of Love
The Face
The Book Of Dreams

Planet of Adventure series
City of the Chasch
Servants of the Wankh
The Dirdir
The Pnume

Durdane series
The Anome
The Brave Free Man
The Asutra

The Dying Earth series
The Dying Earth
Cugel's Saga

JACK VANCE

The Eyes of
the Overworld

PANTHER
Granada Publishing

Panther Books
Granada Publishing Ltd
8 Grafton Street, London W1X 3LA

Published by Panther Books 1972
Reprinted 1975, 1985

ISBN 0-583-12127-6

Printed and bound in Great Britain by
Collins, Glasgow

Set in Times

CHAPTER ONE
The Overworld

On the heights above the river Xzan, at the site of certain ancient ruins, Iucounu the Laughing Magician had built a manse to his private taste: an eccentric structure of steep gables, balconies, sky-walks, cupolas, together with three spiral green glass towers through which the red sunlight shone in twisted glints and peculiar colors.

Behind the manse and across the valley, low hills rolled away like dunes to the limit of vision. The sun projected shifting crescents of black shadow; otherwise the hills were unmarked, empty, solitary. The Xzan, rising in the Old Forest to the east of Almery, passed below, then three leagues to the west made junction with the Scaum. Here was Azenomei, a town old beyond memory, notable now only for its fair, which attracted folk from all the region. At Azenomei Fair Cugel had established a booth for the sale of talismans.

Cugel was a man of many capabilities, with a disposition at once flexible and pertinacious. He was long of leg, deft of hand, light of finger, soft of tongue. His hair was the blackest of black fur, growing low down his forehead, coving sharply back above his eyebrows. His darting eye, long inquisitive nose and droll mouth gave his somewhat lean and bony face an expression of vivacity, candor, and affability. He had known many vicissitudes, gaining therefrom a suppleness, a fine discretion, a mastery of both bravado and stealth. Coming into the possession of an ancient lead coffin – after discarding the contents – he had formed a number of leaden lozenges. These, stamped with appropriate seals and runes, he offered for sale at the Azenomei Fair.

Unfortunately for Cugel, not twenty paces from his booth a certain Fianosther had established a larger booth with articles of greater variety and more obvious efficacy, so that whenever Cugel halted a passerby to enlarge upon the merits of his merchandise, the passerby would like as not display an article purchased from Fianosther and go his way.

On the third day of the fair Cugel had disposed of only four periapts, at prices barely above the cost of the lead itself, while Fianosther was hard put to serve all his customers. Hoarse from bawling futile inducements, Cugel closed down his booth and approached Fianosther's place of trade in order to inspect the mode of construction and the fastenings at the door.

Fianosther, observing, beckoned him to approach. 'Enter, my friend, enter. How goes your trade?'

'In all candor, not too well,' said Cugel. 'I am both perplexed and disappointed, for my talismans are not obviously useless.'

'I can resolve your perplexity,' said Fianosther. 'Your booth occupies the site of the old gibbet, and has absorbed unlucky essences. But I thought to notice you examining the manner in which the timbers of my booth are joined. You will obtain a better view from within, but first I must shorten the chain of the captive erb which roams the premises during the night.'

'No need,' said Cugel. 'My interest was cursory.'

'As to the disappointment you suffer,' Fianosther went on, 'it need not persist. Observe these shelves. You will note that my stock is seriously depleted.'

Cugel acknowledged as much. 'How does this concern me?'

Fianosther pointed across the way to a man wearing garments of black. This man was small, yellow of skin, bald as a stone. His eyes resembled knots in a plank; his mouth was wide and curved in a grin of chronic mirth. 'There stands Iucounu the Laughing Magician,' said Fianosther. 'In a short time he will come into my booth and attempt to buy a particular red libram, the casebook of Dibarcas Maior, who studied under Great Phandaal. My price is higher than he will pay, but he is a patient man, and will remonstrate for at least three hours. During this time his manse stands untenanted. It contains a vast collection of thaumaturgical artifacts, instruments, and activans, as well as curiosa, talismans, amulets and librams. I'm anxious to purchase such items. Need I say more?'

'This is all very well,' said Cugel, 'but would Iucounu leave his manse without guard or attendant?'

Fianosther held wide his hands. 'Why not? Who would dare steal from Iucounu the Laughing Magician?'

'Precisely this thought deters me,' Cugel replied. 'I am a man of resource, but not insensate recklessness.'

'There is wealth to be gained,' stated Fianosther. 'Dazzles and displays, marvels beyond worth, as well as charms, puissances, and elixirs. But remember, I urge nothing, I counsel nothing; if you are apprehended, you have only heard me exclaiming at the wealth of Iucounu the Laughing Magician! But here he comes. Quick: turn your back so that he may not see your face. Three hours he will be here, so much I guarantee!'

Iucounu entered the booth, and Cugel bent to examine a bottle containing a pickled homunculus.

'Greetings, Iucounu!' called Fianosther. 'Why have you delayed? I have refused munificent offers for a certain red libram, all on your account! And here – note this casket! It was found in a crypt near the site of old Karkod. It is yet

7

sealed and who knows what wonder it may contain? My price is a modest twelve thousand terces.'

'Interesting,' murmured Iucounu. 'The inscription – let me see . . . Hmm. Yes, it is authentic. The casket contains calcined fish-bone, which was used throughout Grand Motholam as a purgative. It is worth perhaps ten or twelve terces as a curio. I own caskets eons older, dating back to the Age of Glow.'

Cugel sauntered to the door, gained the street, where he paced back and forth, considering every detail of the proposal as explicated by Fianosther. Superficially the matter seemed reasonable: here was Iucounu; there was the manse, bulging with encompassed wealth. Certainly no harm could result from simple reconnaissance. Cugel set off eastward along the banks of the Xzan.

The twisted turrets of green glass rose against the dark blue sky, scarlet sunlight engaging itself in the volutes. Cugel paused, made a careful appraisal of the countryside. The Xzan flowed past without a sound. Nearby, half-concealed among black poplars, pale green larch, drooping pall-willow, was a village – a dozen stone huts inhabited by bargemen and tillers of the river terraces: folk engrossed in their own concerns.

Cugel studied the approach to the manse: a winding way paved with dark brown tile. Finally he decided that the more frank his approach the less complex need be his explanations, if such were demanded. He began the climb up the hillside, and Iucounu's manse reared above him. Gaining the courtyard, he paused to search the landscape. Across the river hills rolled away into the dimness, as far as the eye could reach.

Cugel marched briskly to the door, rapped, but evoked no response. He considered. If Iucounu, like Fianosther, maintained a guardian beast, it might be tempted to utter a sound if provoked. Cugel called out in various tones: growling, mewing, yammering.

8

Silence within.

He walked gingerly to a window and peered into a hall draped in pale grey, containing only a tabouret on which, under a glass bell jar, lay a dead rodent. Cugel circled the manse, investigating each window as he came to it, and finally reached the great hall of the ancient castle. Nimbly he climbed the rough stones, leapt across to one of Iucounu's fanciful parapets and in a trice had gained access to the manse.

He stood in a bed chamber. On a dais six gargoyles supporting a couch turned heads to glare at the intrusion. With two stealthy strides Cugel gained the arch which opened into an outer chamber. Here the walls were green and the furnishings black and pink. He left the room for a balcony circling a central chamber, light streaming through oriels high in the walls. Below were cases, chests, shelves and racks containing all manner of objects: Iucounu's marvelous collection.

Cugel stood poised, tense as a bird, but the quality of the silence reassured him: the silence of an empty place. Still, he trespassed upon the property of Iucounu the Laughing Magician, and vigilance was appropriate.

Cugel strode down a sweep of circular stairs into a great hall. He stood enthralled, paying Iucounu the tribute of unstinted wonder. But his time was limited; he must rob swiftly and be on his way. Out came his sack; he roved the hall, fastidiously selecting those objects of small bulk and great value: a small pot with antlers, which emitted clouds of remarkable gasses when the prongs were tweaked; an ivory horn through which sounded voices from the past; a small stage where costumed imps stood ready to perform comic antics; an object like a cluster of crystal grapes, each affording a blurred view into one of the demon-worlds; a baton sprouting sweetmeats of assorted flavour; an ancient ring engraved with runes; a black stone

9

surrounded by nine zones of impalpable color. He passed by hundreds of jars of powders and liquids, likewise forebore from the vessels containing preserved heads. Now he came to shelves stacked with volumes, folios and librams, where he selected with care, taking for preference those bound in purple velvet, Phandaal's characteristic color. He likewise selected folios of drawings and ancient maps, and the disturbed leather exuded a musty odor.

He circled back to the front of the hall past a case displaying a score of small metal chests, sealed with corroded bands of great age. Cugel selected three at random; they were unwontedly heavy. He passed by several massive engines whose purpose he would have liked to explore, but time was advancing, and best he should be on his way, back to Azenomei and the booth of Fianosther. . . .

Cugel frowned. In many respects the prospect seemed impractical. Fianosther would hardly choose to pay full value for his goods, or, more accurately, Iucounu's goods. It might be well to bury a certain proportion of the loot in an isolated place. . . . Here was an alcove Cugel had not previously noted. A soft light welled like water against the crystal pane, which separated alcove from hall. A niche to the rear displayed a complicated object of great charm. As best Cugel could distinguish, it seemed a miniature carousel on which rode a dozen beautiful dolls of seeming vitality. The object was clearly of great value, and Cugel was pleased to find an aperture in the crystal pane.

He stepped through, but two feet before him a second pane blocked his way, establishing an avenue which evidently led to the magic whirligig. Cugel proceeded confidently, only to be stopped by another pane which he had not seen until he bumped into it. Cugel retraced his steps and to his gratification found the doubtlessly correct entrance a few feet back. But this new avenue led him by several right angles to another blank pane. Cugel decided to forego acquisition of the carousel and depart the castle. He turned, but discovered himself to be a trifle confused. He had come from his left – or was it his right?

. . . Cugel was still seeking egress when in due course Iucounu returned to his manse.

Pausing by the alcove, Iucounu gave Cugel a stare of humorous astonishment. 'What have we here? A visitor? And I have been so remiss as to keep you waiting! Still, I see you have amused yourself, and I need feel no mortification.' Iucounu permitted a chuckle to escape his lips. He then pretended to notice Cugel's bag. 'What is this? You have brought objects for my examination? Excellent! I am always anxious to enhance my collection, in order to keep pace with the attrition of the years. You would be astounded to learn of the rogues who seek to despoil me! That merchant of claptrap in his tawdry little booth, for instance – you could not conceive his frantic efforts in this regard! I tolerate him because to date he has not been bold enough to venture himself into my manse. But come, step out here into the hall, and we will examine the contents of your bag.'

Cugel bowed graciously. 'Gladly. As you assume, I have indeed been waiting for your return. If I recall correctly, the exit is by this passage . . .' He stepped forward, but again was halted. He made a gesture of rueful amusement. 'I seem to have taken a wrong turning.'

'Apparently so,' said Iucounu. 'Glancing upward, you will notice a decorative motif upon the ceiling. If you heed the flexion of the lunules you will be guided to the hall.'

'Of course!' And Cugel briskly stepped forward in accordance with the directions.

'One moment!' called Iucounu. 'You have forgotten your sack!'

11

Cugel reluctantly returned for the sack, once more set forth, and presently emerged into the hall.

Iucounu made a suave gesture. 'If you will step this way I will be glad to examine your merchandise.'

Cugel glanced reflectively along the corridor toward the front entrance. 'It would be a presumption upon your patience. My little knickknacks are below notice. With your permission I will take my leave.'

'By no means!' declared Iucounu heartily. 'I have a few visitors, most of whom are rogues and thieves. I handle them severely, I assure you! I insist that you at least take some refreshment. Place your bag on the floor.'

Cugel carefully set down the bag. 'Recently I was instructed in a small competence by a sea-hag of White Alster. I believe you will be interested. I require several ells of stout cord.'

'You excite my curiosity!' Iucounu extended his arm; a panel in the wainscoting slid back; a coil of rope was tossed to his hand. Rubbing his face as if to conceal a smile, Iucounu handed the rope to Cugel, who shook it out with great care.

'I will ask your cooperation,' said Cugel. 'A small matter of extending one arm and one leg.'

'Yes, of course.' Iucounu held out his hand, pointed a finger. The rope coiled around Cugel's arms and legs, pinning him so that he was unable to move. Iucounu's grin nearly split his great soft head. 'This is a surprising development! By error I called forth Thief-taker! For your own comfort, do not strain, as Thief-taker is woven of wasp-legs. Now then, I will examine the contents of your bag.' He peered into Cugal's sack and emitted a soft cry of dismay. 'You have rifled my collection! I note certain of my most treasured valuables!'

Cugal grimaced. 'Naturally! But I am no thief; Fianosther sent me here to collect certain objects, and therefore—'

12

Iucounu held up his hand. 'The offense is far too serious for flippant disclaimers. I have stated my abhorrence for plunderers and thieves, and now I must visit upon you justice in its most unmitigated rigor – unless, of course, you can suggest an adequate requital.'

'Some such requital surely exists,' Cugel averred. 'This cord however rasps upon my skin, so that I find cogitation impossible.'

'No matter. I have decided to apply the Charm of Forlorn Encystment, which constricts the subject in a pore some forty-five miles below the surface of the earth.'

Cugel blinked in dismay. 'Under these conditions, re-quital could never be made.'

'True,' mused Iucounu. 'I wonder if after all there is some small service which you can perform for me.'

'The villain is as good as dead!' declared Cugel. 'Now remove these abominable bonds!'

'I had no specific assassination in mind,' said Iucounu. 'Come.'

The rope relaxed, allowing Cugel to hobble after Iucounu into a side chamber hung with intricately embroidered tapestry. From a cabinet Iucounu brought a small case and laid it on a floating disk of glass. He opened the case and gestured to Cugel, who perceived that the box showed two indentations lined with scarlet fur, where reposed a single small hemisphere of filmed violet glass.

'As a knowledgeable and traveled man,' suggested Iucounu, 'you doubtless recognize this object. No? You are familiar, of course, with the Cutz Wars of the Eighteenth Aeon? No?' Iucounu hunched up his shoulders in astonishment. 'During these ferocious events the demon Unda-Hrada – he listed as 16–04 Green in Thrump's Almanac – thought to assist his principals, and to this end thrust certain agencies up from the sub-world La-Er. In order that they might perceive, they were tipped

13

with cusps similar to the one you see before you. When events went amiss, the demon snatched himself back to La-Er. The hemispheres were dislodged and broadcast across Cutz. One of these, as you see, I own. You must procure its mate and bring it to me, whereupon your trespass shall be overlooked.'

Cugel reflected. 'The choice, if it lies between a sortie into the demon-world La-Er and the Spell of Forlorn Encystment, is moot. Frankly, I am at a loss for decision.'

Iucounu's laugh almost split the big yellow bladder of his head. 'A visit to La-Er perhaps will prove unnecessary. You may secure the article in that land once known as Cutz.'

'If I must, I must,' growled Cugel, thoroughly displeased by the manner in which the day's work had ended. 'Who guards this violet hemisphere? What is its function? How do I go and how return? What necessary weapons, talismans and other magical adjuncts do you undertake to fit me out with?'

'All in good time,' said Iucounu. 'First I must ensure that, once at liberty, you conduct yourself with unremitting loyalty, zeal and singleness of purpose.'

'Have no fear,' declared Cugel. 'My word is my bond.'

'Excellent!' cried Iucounu. 'This knowledge represents a basic security which I do not in the least take lightly. The act now to be performed is doubtless supererogatory.'

He departed the chamber and after a moment returned with a covered glass bowl containing a small white creature, all claws, prongs, barbs and hooks, now squirming angrily. 'This,' said Iucounu, 'is my friend Firx, from the star Achernar, who is far wiser than he seems. Firx is annoyed at being separated from his comrade with whom he shares a vat in my work-room. He will assist you in the expeditious discharge of your duties.' Iucounu stepped close, deftly thrust the creature against Cugel's abdomen.

14

It merged into his viscera, and took up a vigilant post clasped around Cugel's liver.

Iucounu stood back, laughing in that immoderate glee which had earned him his cognomen. Cugel's eyes bulged from his head. He opened his mouth to utter an objurgation, but instead clenched his jaw and rolled up his eyes.

The rope uncoiled itself. Cugel stood quivering, every muscle knotted.

Iucounu's mirth dwindled to a thoughtful grin. 'You spoke of magical adjuncts. What of those talismans whose efficacy you proclaimed from your booth in Azenomei? Will they not immobilize enemies, dissolve iron, impassion virgins, confer immortality?'

'These talismans are not uniformly dependable,' said Cugel. 'I will require further competences.'

'You have them,' said Iucounu, 'in your sword, your crafty persuasiveness and the agility of your feet. Still, you have aroused my concern and I will help you to this extent.' He hung a small square tablet about Cugel's neck. 'You now may put aside all fear of starvation. A touch of this potent object will induce nutriment into wood, bark, grass, even discarded clothing. It will also sound a chime in the presence of poison. So now – there is nothing to delay us! Come, we will go. Rope? Where is Rope?'

Obediently the rope looped around Cugel's neck, and Cugel was forced to march along behind Iucounu.

They came out upon the roof of the antique castle. Darkness had long since fallen over the land. Up and down the valley of the Xzan faint lights glimmered, while the Xzan itself was an irregular width darker than dark.

Iucounu pointed to a cage. 'This will be your conveyance. Inside.'

Cugel hesitated. 'It might be preferable to dine well, to sleep and rest, to set forth tomorrow refreshed.'

15

'What?' spoke Iucounu in a voice like a horn. 'You dare stand before me and state preferences? You, who came skulking into my house, pillaged my valuables and left all in disarray? Do you understand your luck? Perhaps you prefer the Forlorn Encystment?'

'By no means!' protested Cugel nervously. 'I am anxious only for the success of the venture!'

'Into the cage, then.'

Cugel turned despairing eyes around the castle roof, then slowly went to the cage and stepped within.

'I trust you suffer no deficiency of memory,' said Iucounu. 'But even if this becomes the case, and if you neglect your prime responsibility, which is to say, the procuring of the violet cusp, Firx is on hand to remind you.'

Cugel said, 'Since I am now committed to this enterprise, and unlikely to return, you may care to learn my appraisal of yourself and your character. In the first place—'

But Iucounu held up his hand. 'I do not care to listen; obloquy injures my self-esteem and I am sceptical of praise. So now – be off!' He drew back, stared up into the darkness, then shouted that invocation known as Thasdrubal's Laganetic Transfer. From high came a thud and a buffet, a muffled bellow of rage.

Iucounu retreated a few steps, shouting up words in an archaic language; and the cage with Cugel crouching within was snatched aloft and hurled through the air.

Cold wind bit Cugel's face. From above came a flapping and creaking of vast wings and dismal lamentation; the cage swung back and forth. Below all was dark, a blackness like a pit. By the disposition of the stars Cugel perceived that the course was to the north, and presently he sensed the thrust of the Maurenron Mountains below;

16

and then they flew over that wilderness known as the Land of the Falling Wall. Once or twice Cugel glimpsed the lights of an isolated castle, and once he noted a great bonfire. For a period a winged sprite came to fly alongside the cage and peer within. It seemed to find Cugel's plight amusing, and when Cugel sought information as to the land below, it merely uttered raucous cries of mirth. It became fatigued and sought to cling to the cage, but Cugel kicked it away, and it fell off into the wind with a scream of envy.

The east flushed the red of old blood, and presently the sun appeared, trembling like an old man with a chill. The ground was shrouded by mist; Cugel was barely able to see that they crossed a land of black mountains and dark chasms. Presently the mist parted once more to reveal a leaden sea. Once or twice he peered up, but the roof of the cage concealed the demon except for the tips of the leathern wings.

At last the demon reached the north shore of the ocean. Swooping to the beach, it vented a vindictive croak, and allowed the cage to fall from a height of fifteen feet.

Cugel crawled from the broken cage. Nursing his bruises, he called a curse after the departing demon, then plodded back through sand and dank yellow spinifex, and climbed the slope of the foreshore. To the north were marshy barrens and a far huddle of low hills, to east and west ocean and dreary beach. Cugel shook his fist to the south. Somehow, at some time, in some manner, he would visit revenge upon the Laughing Magician! So much he vowed.

A few hundred yards to the west was the trace of an ancient sea-wall. Cugel thought to inspect it, but hardly moved three steps before Firx clamped prongs into his liver. Cugel, rolling up his eyes in agony, reversed his direction and set out along the shore to the east.

17

Presently he hungered, and bethought himself of the charm furnished by Iucounu. He picked up a piece of driftwood and rubbed it with the tablet, hoping to see a transformation into a tray of sweetmeats or a roast fowl. But the driftwood merely softened to the texture of cheese, retaining the flavor of driftwood. Cugel ate with snaps and gulps. Another score against Iucounu! How the Laughing Magician would pay!

The scarlet globe of the sun slid across the southern sky. Night approached, and at last Cugel came upon human habitation: a rude village beside a small river. The huts were like birds'-nests of mud and sticks, and smelled vilely of ordure and filth. Among them wandered a people as unlovely and graceless as the huts. They were squat, brutish and obese; their hair was a coarse yellow tangle; their features were lumps. Their single noteworthy attribute – one in which Cugel took an instant and keen interest – was their eyes: blind-seeming violet hemispheres, similar in every respect to that object required by Iucounu.

Cugel approached the village cautiously but the inhabitants took small interest in him. If the hemisphere coveted by Iucounu were identical to the violet eyes of these folk, then a basic uncertainty of the mission was resolved, and procuring the violet cusp became merely a matter of tactics.

Cugel paused to observe the villagers, and found much to puzzle him. In the first place, they carried themselves not as the ill-smelling loons they were, but with a remarkable loftiness and a dignity which verged at times upon hauteur. Cugel watched in puzzlement: were they a tribe of dotards? In any event, they seemed to pose no threat, and he advanced into the main avenue of the village, walking gingerly to avoid the more noxious heaps of refuse. One of the villagers now deigned to notice him, and

18

addressed him in grunting guttural voice. 'Well, sirrah: what is your wish? Why do you prowl the outskirts of our city Smolod?'

'I am a wayfarer,' said Cugel. 'I ask only to be directed to the inn, where I may find food and lodging.'

'We have no inn; travelers and wayfarers are unknown to us. Still, you are welcome to share our plenty. Yonder is a manse with appointments sufficient for your comfort.' The man pointed to a dilapidated hut. 'You may eat as you will; merely enter the refectory yonder and select what you wish; there is no stinting at Smolod.'

'I thank you gratefully,' said Cugel, and would have spoken further except that his host had strolled away.

Cugel gingerly looked into the shed, and after some exertion cleaned out the most inconvenient debris, and arranged a trestle on which to sleep. The sun was now at the horizon and Cugel went to that storeroom which had been identified as the refectory. The villager's description of the bounty available, as Cugel had suspected, was in the nature of hyperbole. To one side of the storeroom was a heap of smoked fish, to the other a bin containing lentils mingled with various seeds and cereals. Cugel took a portion to his hut, where he made a glum supper.

The sun had set; Cugel went forth to see what the village offered in the way of entertainment, but found the streets deserted. In certain of the huts lamps burned, and Cugel peering through the cracks saw the residents dining upon smoked fish or engaged in discourse. He returned to his shed, built a small fire against the chill and composed himself for sleep.

The following day Cugel renewed his observation of the village Smolod and its violet-eyed folk. None, he noticed, went forth to work, nor did there seem to be fields near at hand. The discovery caused Cugel dissatisfaction. In order to secure one of the violet eyes, he would be obliged to kill

19

its owner, and for this purpose freedom from officious interference was essential.

He made tentative attempts at conversation among the villagers, but they looked at him in a manner which presently began to jar at Cugel's equanimity: it was almost as if they were gracious lords and he the ill-smelling lout!

During the afternoon he strolled south, and about a mile along the shore came upon another village. The people were much like the inhabitants of Smolod, but with ordinary-seeming eyes. They were likewise industrious; Cugel watched them till fields and fish the ocean.

He approached a pair of fishermen on their way back to the village, their catch slung over their shoulders. They stopped, eyeing Cugel with no great friendliness. Cugel introduced himself as a wayfarer and asked concerning the lands to the east, but the fishermen professed ignorance other than the fact that the land was barren, dreary and dangerous.

'I am currently guest at the village Smolod,' said Cugel. 'I find the folk pleasant enough, but somewhat odd. For instance, why are their eyes as they are? What is the nature of their affliction? Why do they conduct themselves with such aristocratic self-assurance and suavity of manner?'

'The eyes are magic cusps,' stated the older of the fishermen in a grudging voice. 'They afford a view of the Overworld; why should not the owners behave as lords? So will I when Radkuth Vomin dies, for I inherit his eyes.'

'Indeed!' exclaimed Cugel, marveling. 'Can these magic cusps be detached at will and transferred as the owner sees fit?'

'They can, but who would exchange the Overworld for this?' The fisherman swung his arm around the dreary landscape. 'I have toiled long and at last it is my turn to taste the delights of the Overworld. After this there is nothing, and the only peril is death through a surfeit of bliss.'

'Vastly interesting!' remarked Cugel. 'How might I qualify for a pair of these magic cusps?'

'Strive as do all the others of Grodz: place your name on the list, then toil to supply the lords of Smolod with sustenance. Thirty-one years have I sown and reaped lentils and emmer and netted fish and dried them over slow fires, and now the name of Bubach Angh is at the head of the list, and you must do the same.'

'Thirty-one years,' mused Cugel. 'A period of not negligible duration.' And Firx squirmed restlessly, causing Cugel's liver no small discomfort.

The fishermen proceeded to their village Grodz; Cugel returned to Smolod. Here he sought out that man to whom he had spoken upon his arrival at the village. 'My lord,' said Cugel, 'as you know, I am a traveler from a far land, attracted here by the magnificence of the city Smolod.'

'Understandable,' grunted the other. 'Our splendor cannot help but inspire emulation.'

'What then is the source of the magic cusps?'

The elder turned the violet hemispheres upon Cugel as if seeing him for the first time. He spoke in a surly voice. 'It is a matter we do not care to dwell upon, but there is no harm in it, now that the subject has been broached. At a remote time the demon Underherd sent up tentacles to look across Earth, each tipped with a cusp. Simbilis the Sixteenth pained the monster, which jerked back to his subworld and the cusps became dislodged. Four hundred and twelve of the cusps were gathered and brought to Smolod, then as splendid as now it appears to me. Yes, I realize that I see but a semblance, but so do you, and who is to say which is real?'

'I do not look through magic cusps,' said Cugel.

21

'True.' The elder shrugged. 'It is a matter I prefer to overlook. I dimly recall that I inhabit a sty and devour the coarsest of food – but the subjective reality is that I inhabit a glorious palace and dine on splendid viands among the princes and princesses who are my peers. It is explained thus: the demon Underherd looked from the sub-world to this one; we look from this to the Overworld, which is the quintessence of human hope, visionary longing, and beatific dream. We who inhabit this world – how can we think of ourselves as other than splendid lords? This is how we are.'

'It is inspiring!' exclaimed Cugel. 'How may I obtain a pair of these magic cusps?'

'There are two methods. Underherd lost four hundred and fourteen cusps; we control four hundred and twelve. Two were never found, and evidently lie on the floor of the ocean's deep. You are at liberty to secure these. The second means is to become a citizen of Grodz, and furnish the lords of Smolod with sustenance till one of us dies, as we do infrequently.'

'I understand that a certain Lord Radkuth Vomin is ailing.'

'Yes, that is he.' The elder indicated a potbellied old man with a slack, drooling mouth, sitting in filth before his hut. 'You see him at his ease in the pleasaunce of his palace. Lord Radkuth strained himself with a surfeit of lust, for our princesses are the most ravishing creations of human inspiration, just as I am the noblest of princes. But Lord Radkuth indulged himself too copiously, and thereby suffered a mortification. It is a lesson for us all.'

'Perhaps I might make special arrangements to secure his cusps?' ventured Cugel.

'I fear not. You must go to Grodz and toil as do the others. As did I, in a former existence which now seems dim and inchoate . . . To think I suffered so long! But you are young; thirty or forty or fifty years is not too long a time to wait.'

Cugel put his hand to his abdomen to quiet the fretful stirrings of Firx. 'In the space of so much time, the sun may well have waned. Look!' He pointed as a black flicker crossed the face of the sun and seemed to leave a momentary crust. 'Even now it ebbs!'

'You are over-apprehensive,' stated the elder. 'To us who are lords of Smolod, the sun puts forth a radiance of exquisite colors.'

'This may well be true at the moment,' said Cugel, 'but when the sun goes dark, what then? Will you take an equal delight in the gloom and the chill?'

But the elder no longer attended him. Radkuth Vomin had fallen sideways into the mud, and appeared to be dead.

Toying indecisively with his knife, Cugel went to look down at the corpse. A deft cut or two – no more than the work of a moment – and he would have achieved his goal. He swayed forward, but already the fugitive moment had passed. Other lords of the village had approached to jostle Cugel aside; Radkuth Vomin was lifted and carried with the most solemn nicety into the ill-smelling precincts of his hut.

Cugel stared wistfully through the doorway, calculating the chances of this ruse and that.

'Let lamps be brought!' intoned the elder. 'Let a final effulgence surround Lord Radkuth on his gem-encrusted bier! Let the golden clarion sound from the towers; let the princesses don robes of samite; let their tresses obscure the faces of delight Lord Radkuth loved so well! And now we must keep vigil! Who will guard the bier?'

Cugel stepped forward. 'I would deem it honor indeed.'

23

The elder shook his head. 'This is a privilege reserved for his peers. Lord Maulfag, Lord Glus: perhaps you will act in this capacity.' Two of the villagers approached the bench on which Lord Radkuth Vomin lay.

'Next,' declared the elder, 'the obsequies must be proclaimed, and the magic cusps transferred to Bubach Angh, that most deserving squire of Grodz. Who, again, will go to notify this squire?'

'Again,' said Cugel, 'I offer my services, if only to requite in some small manner the hospitality I have enjoyed at Smolod.'

'Well spoken!' intoned the elder. 'So, then, at speed to Grodz; return with that squire who by his faith and dutiful toil deserves advancement.'

Cugel bowed, and ran off across the barrens toward Grodz. As he approached the outermost fields he moved cautiously, skulking from tussock to copse, and presently found that which he sought: a peasant turning the dank soil with a mattock.

Cugel crept quietly forward and struck down the loon with a gnarled root. He stripped off the best garments, the leather hat, the leggings and foot-gear; with his knife he hacked off the stiff straw-colored beard. Taking all and leaving the peasant lying dazed and naked in the mud, he fled on long strides back toward Smolod. In a secluded spot he dressed himself in the stolen garments. He examined the hacked-off beard with some perplexity, and finally, by tying up tufts of the coarse yellow hair and tying tuft to tuft, contrived to bind enough together to make a straggling false beard for himself. That hair which remained he tucked up under the brim of the flapping leather hat.

Now the sun had set; plum-colored gloom obscured the land. Cugel returned to Smolod. Oil lamps flickered before the hut of Radkuth Vomin, where the obese and misshaped village women wailed and groaned.

24

Cugel stepped cautiously forward, wondering what might be expected of him. As for his disguise it would either prove effective or it would not. To what extent the violet cusps befuddled perception was a matter of doubt; he could only hazard a trial.

Cugel marched boldly up to the door of the hut. Pitching his voice as low as possible, he called, 'I am here, revered princes of Smolod: Squire Bubach Angh of Grodz, who for thirty-one years has heaped the choicest of delicacies into the Smolod larders. Now I appear, beseeching elevation to the estate of nobility.'

'As is your right,' said the Chief Elder. 'But you seem a man different from that Bubach Angh who so long has served the princes of Smolod.'

'I have been transfigured – through grief at the passing of Prince Radkuth Vomin and through rapture at the prospect of elevation.'

'This is clear and understandable. Come, then – prepare yourself for the rites.'

'I am ready as of this instant,' said Cugel. 'Indeed, if you will but tender me the magic cusps I will take them quietly aside and rejoice.'

The Chief Elder shook his head indulgently. 'This is not in accord with the rites. To begin with you must stand naked here on the pavilion of this mighty castle, and the fairest of the fair will anoint you in aromatics. Then comes the invocation to Eddith Bran Maur. And then—'

'Revered,' stated Cugel, 'allow me one boon. Before the ceremonies begin, fit me with the magic cusps so that I may understand the full portent of the ceremony.'

The Chief Elder considered. 'The request is unorthodox but reasonable. Bring forth the cusps!'

There was a wait, during which Cugel stood first on one foot then the other. The minutes dragged; the garments and the false beard itched intolerably. And now at the outskirts of the village he saw the approach of several new figures, coming from the direction of Grodz. One was almost certainly Bubach Angh, while another seemed to have been shorn of his beard.

The Chief Elder appeared, holding in each hand a violet cusp. 'Step forward!'

Cugel called loudly, 'I am here, sir.'

'I now apply the potion which sanctifies the junction of magic cusp to right eye.'

At the back of the crowd Bubach Angh raised his voice. 'Hold! What transpires?'

Cugel turned, pointed. 'What jackal is this that interrupts solemnities? Remove him: hence!'

'Indeed!' called the Chief Elder peremptorily. 'You demean yourself and the dignity of the ceremony.'

Bubach Angh crouched back, momentarily cowed.

'In view of the interruption,' said Cugel, 'I had as lief merely take custody of the magic cusps until these louts can properly be chastened.'

'No,' said the Chief Elder. 'Such a procedure is impossible.' He shook drops of rancid fat in Cugel's right eye. But now the peasant of the shorn beard set up an outcry: 'My hat! My blouse! My beard! Is there no justice?'

'Silence!' hissed the crowd. 'This is a solemn occasion!'

'But I am Bu—'

Cugel called, 'Insert the magic cusp, lord; let us ignore these louts.'

'A lout, you call me?' roared Bubach Angh. 'I recognize you now, you rogue. Hold up proceedings!'

The Chief Elder said inexorably, 'I now invest you with the right cusp. You must temporarily hold this eye closed to prevent a discord which would strain the brain, and cause stupor. Now the left eye.' He stepped forward with the ointment, but Bubach Angh and the beardless peasant no longer would be denied.

26

'Hold up proceedings! You ennoble an impostor! I am Bubach Angh, the worthy squire! He who stands before you is a vagabond!'

The Chief Elder inspected Bubach Angh with puzzlement. 'For a fact you resemble that peasant who for thirty-one years has carted supplies to Smolod. But if you are Bubach Angh, who is this?'

The beardless peasant lumbered forward. 'It is the soulless wretch who stole the clothes from my back and the beard from my face.'

'He is a criminal, a bandit, a vagabond—'

'Hold!' called the Chief Elder. 'The words are ill-chosen. Remember that he has been exalted to the rank of prince of Smolod.'

'Not altogether!' cried Bubach Angh. 'He has one of my eyes. I demand the other!'

'An awkward situation,' muttered the Chief Elder. He spoke to Cugel: 'Though formerly a vagabond and cut-throat, you are now a prince, and a man of responsibility. What is your opinion?'

'I suggest a hiding for these obstreperous louts. Then—'

Bubach Angh and the beardless peasant, uttering shouts of rage, sprang forward. Cugel, leaping away, could not control his right eye. The lid flew open; into his brain crashed such a wonder of exaltation that his breath caught in his throat and his heart almost stopped from astonishment. But concurrently his left eye showed the reality of Smolod. The dissonance was too wild to be tolerated; he stumbled and fell against a hut. Bubach Angh stood over him with mattock raised high, but now the Chief Elder stepped between.

'Do you take leave of your senses? This man is a prince of Smolod!'

'A man I will kill, for he has my eye! Do I toil thirty-one years for the benefit of a vagabond?'

27

'Calm yourself, Bubach Angh, if that be your name, and remember the issue is not yet entirely clear. Possibly an error has been made – undoubtedly an honest error, for this man is now a prince of Smolod, which is to say, justice and sagacity personified.'

'He was not that before he received the cusp,' argued Bubach Angh, 'which is when the offense was committed.'

'I cannot occupy myself with casuistic distinctions,' replied the elder. 'In any event, your name heads the list and on the next fatality—'

'Ten or twelve years hence?' cried Bubach Angh. 'Must I toil yet longer, and receive my reward just as the sun goes dark? No, no, this cannot be!'

The beardless peasant made a suggestion: 'Take the other cusp. In this way you will at least have half of your rights, and so prevail the interloper from cheating you totally.'

Bubach Angh agreed. 'I will start with my one magic cusp; I will then kill that knave and take the other, and all will be well.'

'Now then,' said the Chief Elder haughtily. 'This is hardly the tone to take in reference to a prince of Smolod!'

'Bah!' snorted Bubach Angh. 'Remember the source of your viands! We of Grodz will not toil to no avail.'

'Very well,' said the Chief Elder. 'I deplore your uncouth bluster, but I cannot deny that you have a measure of reason on your side. Here is the left cusp of Radkuth Vomin. I will dispense with the invocation, annointment and the congratulatory paean. If you will be good enough to step forward and open your left eye – so.'

As Cugel had done, Bubach Angh looked through both eyes together and staggered back in a daze. But clapping his hand to his left eye he recovered himself, and advanced upon Cugel. 'You now must see the futility of your

28

trick. Extend me that cusp and go your way, for you will never have the use of the two.'

'It matters very little,' said Cugel. 'Thanks to my friend Firx I am well content with the one.'

Bubach Angh ground his teeth. 'Do you think to trick me again? Your life has approached its end: not just I but all Grodz goes warrant for this!'

'Not in the precincts of Smolod!' warned the Chief Elder. 'There must be no quarrels among the princes: I decree amity! You who have shared the cusps of Radkuth Vomin must also share his palace, his robes, appurtenances, jewels and retinue, until that hopefully remote occasion when one or the other dies, whereupon the survivor shall take all. This is my judgment; there is no more to be said.'

'The moment of the interloper's death is hopefully near at hand,' rumbled Bubach Angh. 'The instant he sets foot from Smolod will be his last! The citizens of Grodz will maintain a vigil of a hundred years, if necessary!'

Firx squirmed at this news and Cugel winced at the discomfort. In a conciliatory voice he addressed Bubach Angh. 'A compromise might be arranged: to you shall go the entirety of Radkuth Vomin's estate: his palace, appurtenances, retinue. To me shall devolve only the magic cusps.'

But Bubach Angh would have none of it. 'If you value your life, deliver that cusp to me this moment.'

'This cannot be done,' said Cugel.

Bubach Angh turned away and spoke to the beardless peasant, who nodded and departed. Bubach Angh glowered at Cugel, then went to Radkuth Vomin's hut and sat on the heap of rubble before the door. Here he experimented with his new cusp, cautiously closing his right eye, opening the left to stare in wonder at the Overworld. Cugel thought to take advantage of his absorption and sauntered off toward the edge of town. Bubach Angh appeared not to notice. Ha! thought Cugel. It was to be so easy, then! Two more strides and he would be lost into the darkness!

Jauntily he stretched his long legs to take those two strides. A slight sound – a grunt, a scrape, a rustle of clothes – caused him to jerk aside; down swung a mattock blade, cutting the air where his head had been. In the faint glow cast by the Smolod lamps Cugel glimpsed the beardless peasant's vindictive countenance. Behind him Bubach Angh came loping, heavy head thrust forward like a bull. Cugel dodged, and ran with agility back into the heart of Smolod.

Slowly and in vast disappointment Bubach Angh returned, to seat himself once more. 'You will never escape,' he told Cugel. 'Give over the cusp and preserve your life!'

'By no means,' replied Cugel with spirit. 'Rather fear for your own sodden vitality, which goes in even greater peril!'

From the hut of the Chief Elder came an admonitory call. 'Cease the bickering! I am indulging the exotic whims of a beautiful princess and must not be distracted.'

Cugel, recalling the oleaginous wads of flesh, the leering slab-sided visages, the matted verminous hair, the wattles and wens and evil odors which characterized the women of Smolod, marveled anew at the power of the cusps. Bubach Angh was once more testing the vision of his left eye. Cugel composed himself on a bench and attempted the use of his right eye, first holding his hand before his left . . .

Cugel wore a shirt of supple silver scales, tight scarlet trousers, a dark blue cloak. He sat on a marble bench before a row of spiral marble columns overgrown with dark foliage and white flowers. To either side the palaces of Smolod towered into the night, one behind the other, with soft lights accenting the arches and windows. The sky was a soft dark blue, hung with great glowing stars: among the palaces were gardens of cypress, myrtle, jasmine, sphade, thyssam; the air was pervaded with the perfume of flowers and flowing water. From somewhere came a wisp of music: a murmur of soft chords, a sigh of melody. Cugel took a deep breath and rose to his feet. He stepped forward, moving across the terrace. Palaces and gardens shifted perspective; on a dim lawn three girls in gowns of white gauze watched him over their shoulders.

Cugel took an involuntary step forward, then, recalling the malice of Bubach Angh, paused to check on his whereabouts. Across the plaza rose a palace of seven stories, each level with its terrace garden, with vines and flowers trailing down the walls. Through the windows Cugel glimpsed rich furnishings, lustrous chandeliers, the soft movement of liveried chamberlains. On the pavilion before the palace stood a hawk-featured man with a cropped golden beard in robes of ocher and black, with gold epaulettes and black buskins. He stood one foot on a stone griffin, arms on bent knee, gazing toward Cugel with an expression of brooding dislike. Cugel marveled: could this be the pig-faced Bubach Angh? Could the magnificent seven-tiered palace be the hovel of Radkuth Vomin?

Cugel moved slowly off across the plaza, and now came upon a pavilion lit by candelabra. Tables supported meats, jellies and pastries of every description; and Cugel's belly, nourished only by driftwood and smoked fish, urged him forward. He passed from table to table, sampling morsels from every dish, and found all to be of the highest quality.

'Smoked fish and lentils I may still be devouring,' Cugel told himself, 'but there is much to be said for the enchantment by which they become such exquisite delicacies. Indeed, a man might do far worse than spend the rest of his life here in Smolod.'

Almost as if Firx had been anticipating the thought, he instantly inflicted upon Cugel's liver a series of agonizing pangs, and Cugel bitterly reviled Iucounu the Laughing Magician and repeated his vows of vengeance.

Recovering his composure, he sauntered to that area where the formal gardens surrounding the palaces gave way to parkland. He looked over his shoulder, to find the hawk-faced prince in ocher and black approaching, with manifestly hostile intent. In the dimness of the park Cugel noted other movement and thought to spy a number of armored warriors.

Cugel returned to the plaza and Bubach Angh followed once more to stand glowering at Cugel in front of Radkuth Vomin's palace.

'Clearly,' said Cugel aloud, for the benefit of Firx, 'there will be no departure from Smolod tonight. Naturally I am anxious to convey the cusp to Iucounu, but if I am killed then neither the cusp nor the admirable Firx will ever return to Almery.'

Firx made no further demonstration. Now, thought Cugel, where to pass the night? The seven-tiered palace of Radkuth Vomin manifestly offered ample and spacious accommodation for both himself and Bubach Angh. In essence, however, the two would be crammed together in a one-roomed hut, with a single heap of damp reeds for a couch. Thoughtfully, regretfully, Cugel closed his right eye, opened his left.

Smolod was as before. The surly Bubach Angh crouched before the door to Radkuth Vomin's hut. Cugel stepped forward and kicked Bubach Angh smartly. In surprise and shock, both Bubach Angh's eyes opened, and the rival impulses colliding in his brain induced paralysis.

32

Back in the darkness the beardless peasant roared and came charging forward, mattock on high, and Cugel relinquished his plan to cut Bubach Angh's throat. He skipped inside the hut, closed and barred the door.

He now closed his left eye and opened his right. He found himself in the magnificent entry hall of Radkuth Vomin's palace, the portico of which was secured by a portcullis of forged iron. Without, the golden-haired prince in ocher and black, holding his hand over one eye, was lifting himself in cold dignity from the pavement of the plaza. Raising one arm in noble defiance, Bubach Angh swung his cloak over his shoulder and marched off to join his warriors.

Cugel sauntered through the palace, inspecting the appointments with pleasure. If it had not been for the importunities of Firx, there would haved been no haste in trying the perilous journey back to the Valley of the Xzan.

Cugel selected a luxurious chamber facing to the south, doffed his rich garments for satin nightwear, settled upon a couch with sheets of pale blue silk, and instantly fell asleep.

In the morning there was a degree of difficulty remembering which eye to open, and Cugel thought it might be well to fashion a patch to wear over that eye not currently in use.

By day the palaces of Smolod were more grand than ever, and now the plaza was thronged with princes and princesses, all of utmost beauty.

Cugel dressed himself in handsome garments of black, with a jaunty green cap and green sandals. He descended to the entry hall, raised the portcullis with a gesture of command, and went forth into the plaza.

There was no sign of Bubach Angh. The other inhabitants of Smolod greeted him with courtesy and the princesses displayed noticeable warmth, as if they found him good address. Cugel responded politely, but without fervor: not even the magic cusp could persuade him against the sour wads of fat, flesh, grime and hair which were the Smolod women.

He breakfasted on delightful viands at the pavilion, then returned to the plaza to consider his next course of action. A cursory inspection of the parklands revealed Grodz warriors on guard. There was no immediate prospect of escape.

The nobility of Smolod applied themselves to their diversions. Some wandered the meadows; others went boating upon the delightful waterways to the north. The Chief Elder, a prince of sagacious and noble visage, sat alone on an onyx bench, deep in reverie.

Cugel approached; the Chief Elder aroused himself and gave Cugel a salute of measured cordiality. 'I am not easy in my mind,' he declared. 'In spite of all judiciousness, and allowing for your unavoidable ignorance of our customs, I feel a certain inequity has been done, and I am at a loss as how to repair it.'

'It seems to me,' said Cugel, 'that Squire Bubach Angh, though doubtless a worthy man, exhibits a lack of discipline unfitting the dignity of Smolod. In my opinion he would be all the better for a few years more seasoning at Grodz.'

'There is something in what you say,' replied the elder. 'Small personal sacrifices are sometimes essential to the welfare of the group. I feel certain that you, if the issue arose, would gladly offer up your cusp and enroll anew at Grodz. What are a few years? They flutter past like butterflies.'

Cugel made a suave gesture. 'Or a trial by lot might be arranged, in which all who see with two cusps participate, the loser of the trial donating one of his cusps to Bubach Angh. I myself will make do with one.'

The elder frowned. 'Well – the contingency is remote. Meanwhile you must participate in our merrymaking. If I may say so, you cut a personable figure and certain of the princesses have been casting sheep's eyes in your direction. There, for instance, the lovely Udela Narshag – and there, Zokoxa of the Rose-Petals, and beyond the vivacious Ilviu Lasmal. You must not be backward; here in Smolod we live an uncircumscribed life.'

'The charm of these ladies has not escaped me,' said Cugel. 'Unluckily I am bound by a vow of continence.'

'Unfortunate man!' exclaimed the Chief Elder. 'The princesses of Smolod are nonpareil! And notice – yet another soliciting your attention!'

'Surely it is you she summons,' said Cugel, and the elder went to confer with the young woman in question, who had come riding into the plaza in a magnificent boat-shaped car which walked on six swan-feet. The princess reclined on a couch of pink down and was beautiful enough to make Cugel rue the fastidiousness of his recollection, which projected every matted hair, mole, dangling underlip, sweating seam and wrinkle of the Smolod women to the front of his memory. This princess was indeed the essence of a daydream: slender and supple, with skin like still cream, a delicate nose, lucent brooding eyes, a mouth of delightful flexibility. Her expression intrigued Cugel, for it was more complex than that of the other princesses: pensive, yet willful; ardent yet dissatisfied.

Into the plaza came Bubach Angh, accoutered in military wise, with corselet, morion and sword. The Chief Elder went to speak to him; and now to Cugel's irritation the princess in the walking boat signaled to him.

He went forward. 'Yes, princess; you saluted me, I believe?'

The princess nodded. 'I speculate on your presence up here in these northern lands.' She spoke in a soft clear voice like music.

Cugel said, 'I am here on a mission; I stay but a short while at Smolod, and then must continue east and south.'

'Indeed!' said the princess. 'What is the nature of your mission?'

'To be candid, I was brought here by the malice of a magician. It was by no means a yearning of my own.'

The princess laughed softly. 'I see few strangers. I long for new faces and new talk. Perhaps you will come to my palace and we will talk of magic and the strange circumstances which throng the dying earth.'

Cugel bowed stiffly. 'Your offer is kind. But you must seek elsewhere; I am bound by a vow of continence. Control your displeasure, for it applies not only to you but to Udela Narshag yonder, to Zokoxa, and to Ilviu Lasmal.'

The princess raised her eyebrows, sank back on her down-covered couch. She smiled faintly. 'Indeed, indeed. You are a harsh man, a stern relentless man, thus to refuse yourself to so many imploring women.'

'This is the case, and so it must be.' Cugel turned away to face the Chief Elder, who approached with Bubach Angh at his back.

'Sorry circumstances,' announced the Chief Elder in a troubled voice. 'Bubach Angh speaks for the village of Grodz. He declares that no more victuals will be furnished until justice is done, and this they define as the surrender of your cusp to Bubach Angh, and your person to a punitive committee who waits in the parkland yonder.'

Cugel laughed uneasily. 'What a distorted view! You assured them of course that we of Smolod would eat grass and destroy the cusps before agreeing to such detestable provisions?'

'I fear that I temporized,' stated the Chief Elder. 'I feel that the others of Smolod favor a more flexible course of action.'

The implication was clear, and Firx began to stir in exasperation. In order to appraise circumstances in the most forthright manner possible, Cugel shifted the patch to look from his left eye.

Certain citizens of Grodz, armed with scythes, mattocks and clubs, waited at a distance of fifty yards: evidently the punitive committee to which Bubach Angh had referred. To one side were the huts of Smolod; to the other the walking boat and the princess of such – Cugel stared in astonishment. The boat was as before, walking on six bird-legs, and sitting in the pink down was the princess – if possible, more beautiful than ever. But now her expression, rather than faintly smiling, was cool and still.

Cugel drew a deep breath and took to his heels. Bubach Angh shouted an order to halt, but Cugel paid no heed. Across the barrens he raced, with the punitive committee in pursuit.

Cugel laughed gleefully. He was long of limb, sound of wind; the peasants were stumpy, knot-muscled, phlegmatic. He could easily run two miles to their one. He paused, and turned to wave farewell. To his dismay two legs from the walking boat detached themselves and leapt after him. Cugel ran for his life. In vain. The legs came bounding past, one on either side. They swung around and kicked him to a halt.

Cugel sullenly walked back, the legs hopping behind. Just before he reached the outskirts of Smolod he reached under the patch and pulled loose the magic cusp. As the punitive committee bore down on him, he held it aloft. 'Stand back – or I break the cusp to fragments!'

'Hold! Hold!' called Bubach Angh. 'This must not be! Come, give me the cusp and accept your just deserts.'

'Nothing has yet been decided,' Cugel reminded him. 'The Chief Elder has ruled for no one.'

The girl rose from her seat in the boat. 'I will rule; I am Derwe Coreme, of the House of Domber. Give me the violet glass, whatever it is.'

'By no means,' said Cugel. 'Take the cusp from Bubach Angh.'

'Never!' exclaimed the squire from Grodz.

'What? You both have a cusp and both want two? What are these precious objects? You wear them as eyes? Give them to me.'

Cugel drew his sword. 'I prefer to run, but I will fight if I must.'

'I cannot run,' said Bubach Angh. 'I prefer to fight.' He pulled the cusp from his own eye. 'Now then, vagabond, prepare to die.'

'A moment,' said Derwe Coreme. From one of the legs of the boat thin arms reached to seize the wrists of both Cugel and Bubach Angh. The cusps fell to earth; that of Bubach Angh struck a stone and shivered to fragments. He howled in anguish and leapt upon Cugel, who gave ground before the attack.

Bubach Angh knew nothing of swordplay; he hacked and slashed as if he were cleaning fish. The fury of his attack, however, was unsettling and Cugel was hard put to defend himself. In addition to Bubach Angh's sallies and slashes, Firx was deploring the loss of the cusp.

Derwe Coreme had lost interest in the affair. The boat started off across the barrens, moving faster and ever faster. Cugel slashed out with his sword, leapt back, leapt back once more, and for the second time fled across the barrens, and the folk of Smolod and Grodz shouted curses after him.

The boat-car jogged along at a leisurely rate. Lungs throbbing, Cugel gained upon it, and with a great bound leapt up, caught the downy gunwhale and pulled himself astride.

It was as he expected. Derwe Coreme had looked through the cusp and lay back in a daze. The violet cusp reposed in her lap.

Cugel seized it, then for a moment stared down into the exquisite face and wondered if he dared more. Firx thought not. Already Derwe Coreme was sighing and moving her head.

Cugel leapt from the boat, and only just in time. Had she seen him? He ran to a clump of reeds which grew by a pond, and flung himself into the water. From here he saw the walking-boat halt while Derwe Coreme rose to her feet. She felt through the pink down for the cusp, then she looked all around the countryside. But the blood-red light of the low sun was in her eyes when she looked toward Cugel, and she saw only the reeds and the reflection of sun on water.

Angry and sullen as never before, she set the boat into motion. It walked, then cantered, then loped to the south.

Cugel emerged from the water, inspected the magic cusp, tucked it into his pouch, and looked back toward Smolod. He started to walk south, then paused. He took the cusp from his pocket, closed his left eye, and held the cusp to his right. There rose the palaces, tier on tier, tower above tower, the gardens hanging down the terraces . . . Cugel would have stared a long time, but Firx became restive.

Cugel returned the cusp to his pouch, and once again set his face to the south, for the long journey back to Almery.

CHAPTER TWO

Cil

Sunset across the northern wastelands was a mournful process, languid as the bleeding of a dead animal; twilight came to find Cugel toiling across a salt-marsh. The dark red light of afternoon had deceived him; starting across a low-lying barrens, he first found dankness underfoot, then a soggy softness, and now on all sides were mud, bog-grass, a few larches and willows, puddles and sloughs reflecting the leaden purple of the sky.

To the east were low hills; toward these Cugel proceeded, jumping from tussock to tussock, running delicately over the crusted slime. At times he missed his footing, to sprawl into mud or rotting reeds, whereupon his threats and imprecations in regard to Iucounu the Laughing Magician reached a maximum of rancor.

Dusk held until, tottering with fatigue, he reached the slope of the eastern hills, where his condition was worsened rather than improved. Certain half-human bandits had noted his approach, and now they set upon him. A vile reek reached Cugel even before the sound of their footsteps; fatigue forgotten, he sprang away, and was pursued up the slope.

A shattered tower rose against the sky. Cugel clambered over moldering stones, drew his sword and stepped into the gap which once had served as doorway. Within was silence, the odor of dust and damp stone; Cugel dropped to his knee and against the skyline saw the three grotesque shapes come to a halt at the edge of the ruins.

Odd, thought Cugel, though gratifying – if coincidentally somewhat ominous. The creatures apparently feared the tower.

The last vestige of twilight departed; by various portents Cugel came to understand that the tower was haunted. Near the middle of night a ghost appeared, wearing pale robes and a silver fillet supporting twenty moonstones on long silver stalks. It swirled close to Cugel, staring down with vacant eye-sockets into which a man might lose his thoughts. Cugel pressed back against the wall so that his bones creaked, unable to move a muscle.

The ghost spoke: 'Demolish this fort. While stone joins stone I must stay, even while Earth grows cold and swings through darkness.'

'Willingly,' croaked Cugel, 'if it were not for those outside who seek my life.'

'To the back of the hall is a passage. Use stealth and strength, then do my behest.'

'The fort is as good as razed,' declared Cugel fervently. 'But what circumstances bound you to so unremitting a post?'

'They are forgotten; I remain. Perform my charge, or I curse you with an everlasting tedium like my own!'

Cugel awoke in the dark, aching with cold and cramp. The ghost had vanished: how long had he slept? He looked through the door to find the eastern sky colored by the approach of dawn.

After an interminable wait the sun appeared, sending a flaming ray through the door and to the back of the hall. Here Cugel found a stone stairway descending to a dusty passage, which after five minutes of slow groping returned him to the surface. From concealment he surveyed the ground and saw the three bandits, at separate points, each hidden behind a tumbled pillar.

Cugel unsheathed his sword and with great caution stole forth. He reached the first prone figure, and thrust steel

41

into the corded neck. The creature flung out its arms, groped at the ground and died.

Cugel wrenched free his blade and wiped it on the leather of the corpse. With the deftest and most facile stealth he came up behind the second bandit, which in its dying made a sound of distress. The third bandit came to investigate.

Springing from concealment, Cugel ran it through. The bandit screamed, drew its own dagger and lunged, but Cugel leapt back and hurled a heavy stone which felled it to the ground. Here it lay, grimacing in hate.

Cugel came cautiously forward. 'Since you face death, tell me what you know of hidden treasure.'

'I know of none,' said the bandit. 'Were there such you, would be the last to learn, for you have killed me.'

'This is no fault of mine,' said Cugel. 'You pursued me, not I you. Why did you do so?'

'To eat, to survive, though life and death are equally barren and I despise both equally.'

Cugel reflected. 'In this case you need not resent my part in the transition which you now face. The question regarding hidden valuables again becomes relevant. Perhaps you have a final word on this matter?'

'I have a final word. I display my single treasure.' The creature groped in its pouch and withdrew a round white pebble. 'This is the skull-stone of a grue, and at this moment trembles with force. I use this force to curse you, to bring upon you the immediate onset of cankerous death.'

Cugel hastily killed the bandit, then heaved a dismal sigh. The night had brought only difficulty. 'Iucounu, if I survive, there shall be a reckoning indeed!'

Cugel turned to examine the fort. Certain of the stones would fall at a touch; others would require much more effort. He might well not survive to perform the task.

What were the terms of the bandit's curse? '—immediate onset of cankerous death.' Sheer viciousness. The ghost-king's curse was no less oppressive: how had it gone? '—everlasting tedium.'

Cugel rubbed his chin and nodded gravely. Raising his voice, he called, 'Lord ghost, I may not stay to do your bidding: I have killed the bandits and now I depart. Farewell and may the eons pass with dispatch.'

From the depths of the fort came a moan, and Cugel felt the pressure of the unknown. 'I activate my curse!' came a whisper to Cugel's brain.

Cugel strode quickly away to the southeast. 'Excellent; all is well. The "everlasting tedium" exactly countervenes the "immediate onset of death" and I am left only with the "canker" which, in the person of Firx, already afflicts me. One must use his wits in dealing with maledictions.'

He proceeded over the barrens until the fort was beyond vision, and presently came once more to the sea. Mounting the foreshore, he looked up and down the beach, to see a dark headland to east and another to west. He descended to the beach, and set off to the east. The sea, sluggish and gray, sent listless surf against the sand, which was smooth, unmarked by footprint.

Ahead Cugel spied a dark blot, which a moment later proved to be an aged man on his knees, passing the sand of the beach through a sieve.

Cugel halted to watch. The old man gave him a dignified nod and proceeded with his work.

Cugel's curiosity at last prompted him to speak. 'What do you seek so assiduously?'

The old man put down his sieve and rubbed his arms. 'Somewhere along the beach an amulet was lost by the father of my great-grandfather. During his entire life he sifted sand, hoping to find that which he had lost. His son, and after him my grandfather, then my father and now I, the last of my line, have done likewise. All the way from Cil we have sifted sand, but there is yet six leagues to Benbadge Stull.'

'These names are unknown to me,' said Cugel. 'What place is Bendage Stull?'

The old man indicated the headland to the west. 'An ancient port, though now you will find only a crumbled breakwater, an old jetty, a hut or two. Yet barques from Benbadge Stull once plied the sea to Falgunto and Mell.'

'Again, regions beyond my knowledge,' said Cugel. 'What lies beyond Benbadge Stull?'

'The land dwindles into the north. The sun hangs low over marsh and bog; there are none to be found here but a few forlorn outcasts.'

Cugel turned his attention to the east. 'And what place is Cil?'

'This entire domain is Cil, which my ancestor forfeited to the House of Domber. All grandeur is gone; there remains the ancient palace and a village. Beyond, the land becomes a dark and dangerous forest, so much has our realm dwindled.' The old man shook his head and returned to his sieving.

Cugel stood watching a moment, then, kicking idly in the sand, uncovered a glint of metal. Stooping, he picked up a bracelet of black metal shining with a purple luster. Around the circumference were thirty studs in the form of carbuncles, each circled by a set of engraved runes. 'Ha!' exclaimed Cugel, displaying the bracelet. 'Notice this fine object: a treasure indeed!'

The old man put down scoop and sieve, rose slowly to his knees, then to his feet. He lurched forward, blue eyes round and staring. He held forth his hand. 'You have uncovered the amulet of my ancestors, the House of Slaye! Give it to me!'

Cugel stepped back. 'Come, come, you make a flagrantly unreasonable request!'

'No no! The amulet is mine; you do wrong by withholding it. Do you wish to vitiate the work of my lifetime and of four lifetimes before mine?'

'Why do you not rejoice that the amulet has been found?' demanded Cugel peevishly. 'You are now relieved from further search. Explain, if you will, the potency of this amulet. It exhales a heavy magic. How does it profit the owner?'

'The owner is myself,' groaned the old man. 'I implore you, be generous!'

'You put me in an uncomfortable position,' said Cugel. 'My property is too small to admit of largesse but I cannot consider this a failure of generosity. If you had found the amulet, would you have given it to me?'

'No, since it is mine!'

'Here we disagree. Assume, if you will, that your conviction is incorrect. Your eyesight will attest that the amulet is in my hands, under my control, and, in short, my property. I would appreciate, therefore, any information upon its capabilities and mode of employment.'

The old man threw his arms in the air, kicked his sieve with such wild emotion that he burst out the mesh, and the sieve went trundling down the beach to the water's edge. A wave swept in and floated the sieve; the old man made an involuntary motion to retrieve it, then once more threw up his hands and tottered up the foreshore. Cugel gave his head a shake of grave disapproval, and turned to continue east along the beach.

Now occurred an unpleasant altercation with Firx, who was convinced that the most expeditious return to Almery lay west through the port of Benbadge Stull. Cugel clasped his hands to his belly in distress. 'There is but one feasible route! By means of the lands which lie to the

45

south and east. What if the ocean offers a more direct route? There are no boats to hand; it is not possible to swim so great a distance!'

Firx administered a few dubious pangs, but finally permitted Cugel to continue eastward along the shore. Behind, on the ridge of the foreshore, sat the old man, scoop dangling between his legs, staring out to sea.

Cugel proceeded along the beach, well pleased with the events of the morning. He examined the amulet at length: it exuded a rich sense of magic, and in addition was an object of no small beauty. The runes, incised with great skill and delicacy, unfortunately were beyond his capacity to decipher. He gingerly slipped the bracelet on his wrist, and in so doing pressed one of the carbuncles. From somewhere came an abysmal groan, a sound of the deepest anguish. Cugel stopped short, and looked up and down the beach. Gray sea, pallid beach, foreshore with clumps of spinifex. Benbadge Stull to west, Cil to east, gray sky above. He was alone. Whence had come the great groan?

Cautiously Cugel touched the carbuncle again, and again evoked the stricken protest.

In fascination Cugel pressed another of the carbuncles, this time bringing forth a wail of piteous despair in a different voice. Cugel was puzzled. Who along this sullen shore manifested so frivolous a disposition? Each carbuncle in turn he pressed and caused to be produced a whole concert of outcries, ranging the gamut of anguish and pain. Cugel examined the amulet critically. Beyond the evocation of groans and sobs it displayed no obvious power and Cugel presently tired of the occupation.

The sun reached its zenith. Cugel appeased his hunger with seaweed, which he rendered nutritious by rubbing it with the charm Iucounu had provided for this purpose. As he ate he seemed to hear voices and careless prattling laughter, so indistinct that it might have been the sound of the surf. A tongue of rock protruded into the ocean nearby; listening carefully, Cugel discovered the voices to be coming from this direction. They were clear and childlike, and rang with innocent gaiety.

He went cautiously out upon the rock. At the far end, where the ocean surged and dark water heaved, four large shells had attached themselves. These now were open; heads looked forth, attached to naked shoulders and arms. The heads were round and fair, with soft cheeks, blue-gray eyes, tufts of pale hair. The creatures dipped their fingers in the water, and from the drops they pulled thread which they deftly wove into a fine soft fabric. Cugel's shadow fell on the water; instantly the creatures clamped themselves into their shells.

'How so?' exclaimed Cugel jocularly. 'Do you always lock yourselves apart at the sight of a strange face? Are you so timorous then? Or merely surly?'

The shells remained closed. Dark water swirled over the fluted surfaces.

Cugel came a step closer, squatted on his haunches and cocked his head askew. 'Or perhaps you are proud? So that you withdraw yourselves in disdain? Or is it that you lack grace?'

Still no response. Cugel remained as before, and began to whistle, trilling a tune he had heard at the Azenomei Fair.

Presently the shell at the far edge of the rock opened a crack, and eyes peered at him. Cugel whistled another bar or two, then spoke once more. 'Open your shells! Here waits a stranger, anxious to learn the road to Cil, and other matters of import!'

Another shell opened a crack; another set of eyes glistened from the dark within.

'Perhaps you are ignorant,' scoffed Cugel. 'Perhaps you know nothing save the color of fish and the wetness of water.'

The shell of the farthest opened further, enough to show the indignant face within. 'We are by no means ignorant!'

47

'Nor indolent, nor lacking in grace, nor disdainful,' shouted the second.

'Nor timorous!' added a third.

Cugel nodded sagely. 'This well may be. But why do you withdraw so abruptly at my mere approach?'

'Such is our nature,' said the first shell-creature. 'Certain creatures of the sea would be happy to catch us unaware, and it is wise to retreat first and investigate second.'

All four of the shells were now ajar, though none stood as fully wide as when Cugel had approached.

'Well then,' he said, 'what can you tell me of Cil? Are strangers greeted with cordiality, or driven off? Are inns to be found, or must the wayfarer sleep in a ditch?'

'Such matters lie beyond our specific knowledge,' said the first shell-creature. It fully opened its shell, and extruded pale arms and shoulders. 'The folk of Cil, if rumor of the sea goes correctly, are withdrawn and suspicious, even to their ruler, who is a girl, no more, of the ancient House of Domber.'

'There walks old Slaye now,' said another. 'He returns early to his cabin.'

Another tittered. 'Slaye is old; never will he find his amulet, and thus the House of Domber will rule Cil till the sun goes out.'

'What is all this?' asked Cugel ingenuously. 'Of what amulet do you speak?'

'As far as memory can return,' one of the shell-creatures explained, 'old Slaye has sifted sand, and his father before him, and yet other Slayes across the years. They seek a metal band, by which they hope to regain their ancient privileges.'

'A fascinating legend!' said Cugel with enthusiasm. 'What are the powers of the amulet, and how are they activated?'

48

'Slaye possibly would provide this information,' said one dubiously.

'No, for he is dour and crabbed,' declared another. 'Consider his petulant manner when he sieves a scoop of sand to no avail!'

'Is there no information elsewhere?' Cugel demanded anxiously. 'No rumor of the sea? No ancient tablet or set of glyphs?'

The shell-creatures laughed in merriment. 'You ask so earnestly that you might be Slaye himself. Such lore is unknown to us.'

Concealing his dissatisfaction, Cugel asked further questions, but the creatures were artless and unable to maintain their attention upon any single matter. As Cugel listened they discussed the flow of the ocean, the flavor of pearl, the elusive disposition of a certain sea-creature they had noted the day previously. After a few minutes Cugel once more turned the conversation to Slaye and the amulet, but again the shell-creatures were vague, almost childlike in the inconsequence of their talk. They seemed to forget Cugel, and, dipping their fingers in the water, drew pallid threads from the drops. Certain conches and whelks had aroused their disapproval through impudence, and they discussed a great urn lying on the off-shore seabottom.

Cugel finally tired of the conversation and rose to his feet, at which the shell-creatures once more gave him their attention. 'Must you fare forth so soon? Just when we were about to inquire the reason for your presence; passers-by are few along Great Sandy Beach, and you seem a man who has journeyed far.'

'This is correct,' said Cugel, 'and I must journey yet farther. Notice the sun: it starts down the western curve, and tonight I wish to house myself at Cil.'

One of the shell-creatures lifted up its arms and displayed a fine garment it had woven from water-threads. 'This garment we offer as a gift. You seem a sensitive man and so may require protection from wind and cold.' It tossed the garment to Cugel. He examined it, marveling at the suppleness of the cloth and its lucent shimmer.

'I thank you indeed,' said Cugel. 'This is generosity beyond my expectation.' He wrapped himself in the garment, but at once it reverted to water and Cugel was drenched. The four in the shells shouted loud in mischievous glee, and as Cugel stepped wrathfully forward they snapped their shells shut.

Cugel kicked the shell of the creature which had tossed him the garment, bruising his foot and exacerbating his rage. He seized a heavy rock and dashed it down upon the shell, crushing it. Snatching forth the squealing creature, Cugel hurled it far up the beach, where it lay staring at him, head and small arms joined to pale entrails.

In a faint voice it asked, 'Why did you treat me so? For a prank you have taken my life from me, and I have no other.'

'And thereby you will be prevented from further pranks,' declared Cugel. 'Notice you have drenched me to the skin!'

'It was merely an act of mischief; a small matter surely.' The shell-creature spoke in a fading voice. 'We of the rocks know little magic, yet I am given the power to curse, and this I now pronounce: may you lose your heart's-desire, whatever its nature; you shall be bereft before a single day is gone.'

'Another curse?' Cugel shook his head in displeasure. 'Two curses already I have voided this day; am I now inflicted with another?'

'This curse you shall not void,' whispered the shell-creature. 'I make it the final act of my life.'

'Malice is a quality to be deplored,' said Cugel fretfully. 'I doubt the efficacy of your curse; nevertheless, you would be well-advised to clear the air of its odium and so regain my good opinion.'

But the shell-creature said no more. Presently it collapsed into a cloudy slime which was absorbed into the sand.

Cugel set off down the beach, considering how best to avert the consequences of the shell-creature's curse. 'One must use his wits in dealing with maledictions,' Cugel said for the second time. 'Am I known as Cugel the Clever for nothing?' No stratagem came to mind, and he proceeded along the beach pondering the matter in all its aspects.

The headland to the east grew distinct. Cugel saw it to be cloaked in tall dark trees, through which appeared glimpses of white buildings.

Slaye showed himself once more, running back and forth across the beach like one departed of his senses. He approached Cugel and fell on his knees. 'The amulet, I beg of you! It belongs to the House of Slaye; it conferred upon us the rule of Cil! Give it to me and I will fulfill your heart's-desire!'

Cugel stopped short. Here was a pretty paradox! If he surrendered the amulet, Slaye evidently would betray him, or at the very least fail to make good his promise – assuming the potency of the curse. On the other hand, if Cugel retained the amulet, he would lose his heart's-desire to no less a degree – assuming the potency of the curse – but the amulet would yet be his.

Slaye misinterpreted the hesitation as a sign of pliancy. 'I will make you grandee of the realm!' he cried in a fervent voice. 'You shall have a barge of carved ivory, and two hundred maidens shall serve your wants; your enemies shall be clamped into a rotating cauldron – only give me the amulet!

'The amulet confers so much power?' inquired Cugel. 'It is possible to achieve all this?'

'Indeed, indeed!' cried Slaye, 'when one can read the runes!'

'Well then,' said Csugel, 'what is their import?'

Slaye gazed at him in woeful injury. 'That I cannot say; I must have the amulet!'

Cugel flourished his hand in a contemptuous gesture. 'You refuse to gratify my curiosity; in my turn I denounce your arrogant ambitions!'

Slaye turned to look toward the headland, where white walls gleamed among the trees. 'I understand all. You intend to rule Cil in your own right!'

There were less desirable prospects, thought Cugel, and Firx, appreciating something of this, performed a small monitory constriction. Regretfully Cugel put aside the scheme; nevertheless, it suggested a means to nullify the shell-creature's curse. 'If I am to be deprived of my heart's-desire,' Cugel told himself, 'I would be wise to fix upon a new goal, a fervent new enthusiasm, for at least the space of a day. I shall therefore aspire to the rule of Cil, which now becomes my heart's-desire.' So as not to arouse the vigilance of Firx, he said aloud, 'I intend to use this amulet to achieve highly important ends. Among them may well be the lordship of Cil, to which I believe I am entitled by virtue of my amulet.'

Slaye gave a wild sardonic laugh. 'First you must convince Derwe Coreme of your authority. She is of the House of Domber, gloomy and fitful; she looks little more than a girl, but she manifests the brooding carelessness of a forest grue. Beware of Derwe Coreme; she will order you and my amulet plunged into the ocean's deep!'

'If you fear to this extent,' said Cugel with asperity, 'instruct me in the use of the amulet, and I will prevent that calamity.'

But Slaye mulishly shook his head. 'The deficiencies of Derwe Coreme are known; why exchange them for the outlandish excesses of a vagabond?'

For his outspokenness Slaye received a buffet which sent him staggering. Cugel then proceeded along the shore. The sun wallowed low upon the sea; he hastened his steps, anxious to find shelter before dark.

He came at last to the end of the beach. The headland loomed above, with the tall dark trees standing still higher. A balustrade surrounding the gardens showed intermittently through the foliage; somewhat below, a colonnaded rotunda overlooked the ocean to the south. Grandeur indeed! thought Cugel, and he examined the amulet with a new attentiveness. His temporary heart's-desire, sovereignty over Cil, had become no longer felicitious. And Cugel wondered if he should not fix upon a new heart's-desire – an aspiration to master the lore of animal husbandry, for instance, or a compelling urge to excel at acrobatic feats. . . Reluctantly Cugel dismissed the scheme. In any event, the cogency of the shell-creature's curse was not yet certain.

A path left the beach, to wind up among bushes and odorous shrubs: dymphian, heliotrope, black quince, olus, beds of long-stemmed stardrops, shade ververica, flowering amanita. The beach became a ribbon fading into the maroon blur of sunset, and the headland at Benbadge Stull could no longer be seen. The path became level, traversed a dense grove of bay trees, and issued upon a weed-grown oval, at one time a parade ground or exercise field.

Along the left boundary was a tall stone wall, broken by a great ceremonial portico which held aloft a heraldic device of great age. The gates stood wide upon a marble-flagged promenade a mile in length leading to the palace: this a richly detailed structure of many tiers, with a green

53

bronze roof. A terrace extended along the front of the palace; promenade and terrace were joined by a flight of broad steps. The sun had now disappeared; gloom descended from the sky. With no better shelter in prospect, Cugel set off toward the palace.

The promenade at one time had been a work of monumental elegance, but now all was in a state of dilapidation which the twilight invested with a melancholy beauty. To right and left were elaborate gardens now untended and overgrown. Marble urns festooned with garlands of carnelian and jade flanked the promenade; down the center extended a line of pedestals somewhat taller than the height of a man. Each of these supported a bust, identified by an inscription in runes which Cugel recognized as similar to those carved on the amulet. The pedestals were five paces apart, and proceeded the entire mile to the terrace. The carving of the first was softened by wind and rain until the faces were barely discernible; as Cugel proceeded the features became more keen. Pedestal after pedestal, bust after bust; each face stared briefly at Cugel as he marched toward the palace. The last of the series, obscure in the fading light, depicted a young woman. Cugel stopped short: this was the girl of the walking boat, whom he had encountered in the land to the north: Derwe Coreme, of the House of Domber, ruler of Cil!

Beset by misgivings, Cugel paused to consider the massive portal. He had not departed from Derwe Coreme in amity; indeed she might be expected to harbor resentment. On the other hand, at their first encounter she had invited him to her palace, using language of unmistakable warmth; possibly her resentment had disappeared, leaving only the warmth. And Cugel, recalling her remarkable beauty, found the prospect of a second meeting stimulating.

But what if she were still resentful? She must be impressed by the amulet, provided she did not insist that Cugel demonstrate its use. If only he knew how to read the runes, all would be simplicity itself. But since the knowledge was not to be derived from Slaye, he must seek it elsewhere, which in practicality meant within the palace.

He stood before a reach of shallow steps leading up to the terrace. The marble treads were cracked; the balustrade along the terrace was stained by moss and lichen: a condition which the murk of twilight invested with a mournful grandeur. The palace behind seemed in somewhat better repair. An extremely tall arcade rose from the terrace, with slender fluted columns and an elaborately carved entablature, the pattern of which Cugel could not discern through the gloom. At the back of the arcade were tall arched windows, showing dim lights, and the great portal.

Cugel mounted the steps, beset by renewed doubts. What if Derwe Coreme laughed at his pretensions, defied him to do his worst? What then? Groans and outcries might not be enough. He crossed the terrace on lagging steps, optimism waning as he went, and halted under the arcade; perhaps after all, it might be wise to seek shelter elsewhere. But looking back over his shoulder, he thought to see a tall still shape standing among the pedestals. Cugel thought no more of seeking shelter elsewhere, and walked quickly to the tall door: if he presented himself in humble guise he might escape the notice of Derwe Coreme. There was a stealthy sound on the steps. With great urgency Cugel plied the knocker. The sound reverberated inside the palace.

A minute passed, and Cugel thought to hear further sounds behind him. He rapped again, and again the sound echoed within. A peephole opened and an eye inspected

Cugel with care. The eye moved up; a mouth appeared. 'Who are you?' spoke the mouth. 'What do you wish?' The mouth slid away, to reveal an ear.

'I am a wayfarer, I wish shelter for the night, and with haste for a creature of dread approaches.'

The eye reappeared, looked carefully across the terrace, then returned to focus on Cugel. 'What are your qualities, where are your certifications?'

'I have none,' said Cugel. He glanced over his shoulder. 'I much prefer to discuss the matter within, since the creature step by step mounts to the terrace.'

The peephole slammed shut. Cugel stared at the blank door. He banged on the knocker, peering back into the gloom. With a scrape and a creak the portal opened. A small stocky man wearing purple livery motioned to him. 'Inside, with haste.'

Cugel slipped smartly through the door, which the footman at once heaved shut and bolted with three iron pegs. Even as he did so there came a creak and a pressure upon the door.

The footman struck the door smartly with his fist. 'I have thwarted the creature again,' he said with satisfaction. 'Had I been less swift, it would have been upon you, to my distress as well as yours. This is now my chief amusement, depriving the creature of its pleasures.'

'Indeed,' said Cugel, breathing heavily. 'What manner of being is it?'

The footman signified his ignorance. 'Nothing definite is known. It has only appeared of late, to lurk by night among the statues. Its behavior is both vampirish and unnaturally lustful, and several of my associates have had cause to complain; in fact, all are dead by its odious acts. So now, to divert myself, I taunt the creature and cause it dissatisfaction.' The footman stood back, to survey Cugel with attention. 'What of yourself? Your manner, the tilt of your head, the swing of your eyes from side to side denotes recklessness and unpredictability. I trust you will hold this quality in abeyance, if indeed it exists.'

'At this moment,' said Cugel, 'my wants are simple: an alcove, a couch, a morsel of food for my supper. If I am provided these, you will find me benevolence personified; indeed I will assist you in your pleasures; together we will contrive stratagems to bait the ghoul.'

The footman bowed. 'Your needs can be fulfilled. Since you are a traveler from afar, our ruler will wish to speak to you, and indeed may extend a bounty far more splendid than your minimal requirements.'

Cugel hurriedly disavowed any such ambition. 'I am of low quality; my garments are soiled, my person reeks; my conversation consists of insipid platitudes. Best not to disturb the ruler of Cil.'

'We will repair what deficiencies we may,' said the footman. 'Follow, if you will.'

He took Cugel along corridors lit by cressets, finally turning into a set of apartments. 'Here you may wash; I will brush your garments and find fresh linen.'

Cugel reluctantly divested himself of his clothes. He bathed, trimmed the soft black mat of his hair, shaved his beard, rubbed his body with pungent oil. The footman brought fresh garments, and Cugel, much refreshed, dressed himself. Donning his jacket he chanced to touch the amulet at his wrist, pressing one of the carbuncles. From deep under the floor came a groan of the most profound anguish.

The footman sprang about in terror, and his eye fell upon the amulet. He stared in gape-mouthed astonishment, then became obsequious. 'My dear sir, had I realized your identity, I would have conducted you to apartments of state, and brought forth the finest robes.'

'I make no complaints,' said Cugel, 'though for a fact the linens were a trifle stale.' In jocular emphasis he tapped a carbuncle at his wrist, and the responsive groan caused the servitor's knees to knock together.

'I beseech your understanding,' he quavered.

'Say no more,' said Cugel. 'Indeed it was my hope to visit the palace incognito, so to speak, that I might see how affairs were conducted.'

'This is judicious,' agreed the servitor. 'Undoubtedly you will wish to discharge both Sarman the chamberlain and Bilbab the under-cook when their peccancies come to light. As for myself, when your lordship restores Cil to its ancient grandeur, perhaps there will be a modest sinecure for Yodo, the most loyal and cooperative of your servants.'

Cugel made a gracious gesture. 'If such an event comes to pass – and it is my heart's desire – you shall not be neglected. For the present I shall remain quietly in this apartment. You may bring hither a suitable repast, with a variety of choice wines.'

Yodo performed a sweeping bow. 'As your lordship desires.' He departed. Cugel relaxed upon the most comfortable couch of the chamber and fell to studying the amulet which had so promptly aroused Yodo's fidelity. The runes, as before, were inscrutable; the carbuncles produced only groans, which, while diverting, were of small practical utility. Cugel attempted every exhortation, compulsion, rigor and enjoinment his smattering of wizardry provided, to no avail.

Yodo returned to the apartment, but without the repast Cugel had ordered.

'Your lordship,' stated Yodo, 'I have the honor to convey to you an invitation from Derwe Coreme, erstwhile ruler of Cil, to attend her at the evening banquet.'

'How is this possible?' demanded Cugel. 'She has had no information of my presence; as I recall, I gave you specific instructions in this regard.'

Yodo performed another sweeping bow. 'Naturally I obeyed your lordship. The wiles of Derwe Coreme exceed my understanding. By some device she learned of your presence and so has issued the invitation which you have just heard.'

'Very well,' said Cugel glumly. 'Be so good as to lead the way. You mentioned my amulet to her?'

'Derwe Coreme knows all,' was Yodo's ambiguous reply. 'This way, your lordship, if you please.'

He led Cugel along the old corridors, finally through a tall narrow arch into a great hall. To either side stood a row of what appeared to be men-at-arms in brass armor with helmets of checkered bone and jet; there were forty in all, but only six suits of armor were occupied by living men, the others being supported on racks. Telamons of exaggerated elongation and grotesquely distorted visage supported the smoky beams; a rich rug of green concentric circles on a black ground covered the floor.

Derwe Coreme sat at the end of a circular table, this so massive as to give her the seeming of a girl, a sullen brooding girl of the most delicate beauty. Cugel approached with a confident mien, halted and bowed curtly. Derwe Coreme inspected him with gloomy resignation, her eyes dwelling upon the amulet. She drew a deep breath. 'Who do I have the privilege to address?'

'My name is of no consequence,' said Cugel. 'You may address me as "Exalted".'

Derwe Coreme shrugged indifferently. 'As you will. I seem to recall your face. You resemble a vagabond whom lately I ordered whipped.'

'I am that vagabond,' said Cugel. 'I cannot say that your conduct has failed to leave a residue of resentment and I

59

am now here to demand an explanation.' And Cugel touched a carbuncle, evoking so desolate and heartfelt a groan that the crystalware rattled on the table.

Derwe Coreme blinked and her mouth sagged. She spoke ungraciously. 'It appears that my actions were poorly conceived. I failed to perceive your exalted condition, and thought you only the ill-conditioned scapegrace your appearance suggests.'

Cugel stepped forward, put his hand under the small pointed chin and turned up the exquisite face. 'Yet you besought me to visit you at your palace. Do you recall this?'

Derwe Coreme gave a grudging nod.

'Just so,' said Cugel. 'I am here.'

Derwe Coreme smiled, and for a brief period became winsome. 'So you are, and knave, vagabond, or whatever your nature, you wear the amulet by which the House of Slaye ruled across two hundred generations. You are of this house?'

'In due course you will know me well,' said Cugel. 'I am a generous man, though given to caprice, and were it not for a certain Firx . . . Be that as it may, I hunger, and now I invite you to share the banquet which I have ordered the excellent Yodo to set before me. Kindly be good enough to move a place or two aside, and I will be seated.'

Derwe Coreme hesitated, whereupon Cugel's hand went suggestively toward the amulet. She moved with alacrity and Cugel settled himself into the seat she had vacated. He rapped on the table: 'Yodo? Where is Yodo?'

'I am here, Exalted!'

'Bring forth the banquet: the finest fare the palace offers!'

Yodo bowed, scuttled away, and presently a line of footmen appeared bearing trays and flagons, and a banquet more than meeting Cugel's specifications was arranged on the table.

Cugel brought forth the periapt provided by Iucounu the Laughing Magician, which not only converted organic waste to nourishment, but also chimed warning in the presence of noxious substances. The first few courses were salubrious and Cugel ate with gusto. The old wines of Cil were as beneficial, and Cugel drank freely, from goblets of black glass, carved cinnabar and ivory inlaid with turquoise and mother-of-pearl.

Derwe Coreme toyed with her food and sipped her wine, watching Cugel thoughtfully all the while. Further delicacies were brought and now Derwe Coreme leaned forward. 'You truly plan to rule Cil?'

'Such is my heart's-desire!' declared Cugel with fervor.

Derwe Coreme moved close to him. 'Do you then take me as your consort? Say yes; you will be more than content.'

'We will see, we will see,' said Cugel expansively. 'Tonight is tonight, tomorrow is tomorrow. Many changes will be made, this is certain.'

Derwe Coreme smiled faintly, and nodded to Yodo. 'Bring the most ancient of our vintages – we will drink the health of the new Lord of Cil.'

Yodo bowed, and brought a dull flagon webbed and dusty, which he decanted with utmost solicitude, and poured into crystal goblets. Cugel raised his goblet, and the charm purred warning. Cugel abruptly set down the goblet, and watched as Derwe Coreme raised hers to her lips. He reached forth, took the goblet, and again the charm purred. Poison in both? Strange. Perhaps she had not intended to drink. Perhaps she had already ingested an antidote.

Cugel signaled Yodo. 'Another goblet, if you please . . . and the decanter.' Cugel poured a third measure and again the charm signified direness. Cugel said, 'Though my acquaintance with the excellent Yodo is of short duration, I hereby elevate him to the post of Major-Domo of the Palace!'

'Exalted,' stammered Yodo, 'this is a signal honor indeed.'

'Drink then of the ancient vintage, to solemnize this new dignity!'

Yodo bowed low. 'With the most heartfelt gratitude, Exalted.' He raised the goblet and drank. Derwe Coreme watched indifferently. Yodo put down the goblet, frowned, gave a convulsive jerk, turned a startled glance at Cugel, fell to the rug, cried out, twitched and lay still.

Cugel frowningly inspected Derwe Coreme. She appeared as startled as had Yodo. Now she turned to look at him. 'Why did you poison Yodo?'

'It was your doing,' said Cugel. 'Did you not order poison in the wine?'

'No.'

'You must say "No, Exalted".'

'No, Exalted.'

'If you did not – who?'

'I am perplexed. The poison perhaps was meant for me.'

'Or both of us.' Cugel signaled one of the footmen. 'Remove the corpse of Yodo.'

The footman signaled a pair of hooded under-servants, who carried off the unfortunate major-domo.

Cugel took the crystal goblets and stared down into the amber liquid, but did not communicate his thoughts. Derwe Coreme leaned back in her chair, and contemplated him at length. 'I am puzzled,' she said presently. 'You are a man past the teaching of my experience. I cannot decide upon the color of your soul.'

Cugel was charmed by the quaint turn of phrase. 'You see souls in color, then?'

'Indeed. It was the birth-gift of a lady sorceress, who also provided me my walking boat. She is dead and I am alone, with no friend nor any who thinks of me with love. And so I have ruled Cil with little joy. And now you are here, with a soul which flickers through many colors, like that of no human man to come before me.'

Cugel forebore to mention Firx, whose own spiritual exhalation, mingling with that of Cugel's, undoubtedly caused the variegation Derwe Coreme had noted. 'There is a reason for this effect,' said Cugel, 'which in due course will be one shining with the purest ray imaginable.'

'I will try to keep this in mind, Exalted.'

Cugel frowned. In Derwe Coreme's remarks and the poise of her head he noted barely concealed insolence, which he found exasperating. Still, there was ample time to correct the matter after learning the use of the amulet, a business of prime urgency. Cugel leaned back into the cushions, and spoke as one who muses idly: 'Everywhere at this time of Earth's dying exceptional circumstances are to be noted. Recently, at the manse of Iucounu the Laughing Magician, I saw a great libram which indexed all the writings of magic, and all styles of thaumaturgical rune. Perhaps you have similar volumes in your library!'

'It well may be,' said Derwe Coreme. 'The Fourteenth Garth Haxt of Slaye was a diligent collator, and compiled a voluminous pandect on the subject.'

Cugel clapped his hands together. 'I wish to see this important work at once?'

Derwe Coreme looked at him in wonder. 'Are you then such a bibliophile? A pity, because The Eighth Rubel Zaff ordered this particular compendium submerged off Cape Horizon.'

Cugel made a sour face. 'Are no other treatises at hand?'

'Doubtless,' said Derwe Coreme. 'The library occupies the whole of the north wing. But will not tomorrow suffice for your research?' And stretching in languid warmth, she contrived to twist her body into first one luxurious position, then another.

Cugel drank deep from a black glass goblet. 'Yes, there is no haste in this matter. And now—' He was interrupted by a woman of middle age in voluminous brown garments, evidently one of the under-servants, who at this moment rushed into the hall. She was shouting hysterically and several footmen sprang forward to support her. Between racking sobs she made clear the source of her anguish: an abominable act only just now committed by the ghoul upon her daughter.

Derwe Coreme gracefully indicated Cugel. 'Here is the new Lord of Cil; he has vast powers of magic and will order the ghoul destroyed. Will you not, Exalted?'

Cugel thoughtfully rubbed his chin. A dilemma indeed. The woman and all the servitors fell down upon their knees. 'Exalted, if you control this corrosive magic, employ it instantly to destroy the vile ghoul!'

Cugel winced, and turning his head met Derwe Coreme's thoughtful gaze. He jumped to his feet. 'What need I of magic when I can wield a sword? I will hack the creature organ from organ!' He signaled the six men-at-arms who stood by in their brass armor. 'Come! Bring torches! We fare forth to dismember the ghoul!'

The men-at-arms obeyed without enthusiasm. Cugel herded them toward the great portal. 'When I fling wide the doors, rush forth with the torches, to create a blaze which will illuminate the evil being! Have swords drawn so that when I send him reeling you may strike the coup de grace!'

The men-at-arms each with torch and drawn sword stood before the portal. Cugel slid back the bolts and flung wide the portals. 'Out! Shine upon the ghoul the last light of his existence.'

The men-at-arms raced desperately forth, with Cugel swaggering after, flourishing his sword. The men-at-arms paused at the head of the steps, to look uncertainly out over the promenade, from which a quite horrid sound could be heard.

Cugel looked over his shoulder to see Derwe Coreme watching attentively from the doorway. 'Forward!' he shouted. 'Surround this wretched creature, whose death is now upon him!'

The men-at-arms gingerly descended the steps, with Cugel marching to the rear. 'Hack with a will!' he called. 'There is ample glory for all! The man who fails to deal a stroke I blast by magic!'

The flickering lights shone on the pedestals, ranging in a long line to merge at last with the darkness. 'Forward!' cried Cugel. 'Where is this bestial being? Why does he not appear to receive his deserts?' And Cugel peered through the wavering shadows, hoping the ghoul by now would have taken alarm and fled.

At his side came a small sound. Turning, Cugel saw a tall pale shape standing quietly. The men-at-arms gasped, and fled incontinently up the broad stones. 'Slay the beast by magic, Exalted!' called the sergeant. 'The most expeditious method is often the best!'

The ghoul came forward; Cugel stumbled back. The ghoul took a quick step forward. Cugel sprang behind a pedestal. The ghoul swung out its arm; Cugel hacked with his sword, sprang to the protection of another pedestal, then raced with great ability back across the terrace. The door was already closing; Cugel flung himself through the dwindling aperture. He heaved the door shut, and thrust home the bolts. The ghoul's weight slammed against the timbers and the bolts creaked in protest.

Cugel turned to meet the bright-eyed appraisal of Derwe Coreme. 'What ensued?' she asked. 'Why did you not slay the ghoul?'

'The warriors decamped with the torches,' said Cugel. 'I could see neither where to hack nor where to hew.'

'Strange,' mused Derwe Coreme. 'There seemed ample illumination for so negligible an exercise. Why did you not employ the power of the amulet or rend the ghoul limb from limb?'

'So simple and quick a death is unsuitable,' stated Cugel with dignity. 'I must cogitate at length, and decide how he may best expiate his crimes.'

'Indeed,' said Derwe Coreme. 'Indeed.'

Cugel strode back into the great hall. 'Back to the banquet! Let the wine flow! Everyone must drink to the accession of the new Lord of Cil!'

Derwe Coreme said in a silky voice, 'If you please, Exalted, make some display of the power of the amulet, to gratify our curiosity!'

'Certainly!' And Cugel touched carbuncle after carbuncle, producing rumbles and groans of grievous woe, with occasionally a wail or scream.

'Can you do more?' inquired Derwe Coreme, smiling the soft smile of an impish child.

'Indeed, should I so choose. But enough! Drink one and all!'

Derwe Coreme signaled the sergeant of the guard. 'Take sword and strike off the fool's arm; bring me the amulet.'

'With pleasure, Great Lady.' The sergeant advanced with bared blade.

Cugel shouted, 'Stay! One more step and magic will turn each of your bones at right angles!'

The sergeant looked at Derwe Coreme, who laughed. 'As I bade you, or fear my revenge, which is as you know.'

The sergeant winced, and marched forward again. But now an under-servitor rushed to Cugel, and under his hood Cugel saw the seamed face of old Slaye. 'I will save you. Show me the amulet!'

Cugel allowed the eager fingers to grope among the carbuncles. Slaye pressed one of these, and called something in a voice so exultant and shrill that the syllables were lost. There was a great fluttering, and an enormous black shape stood at the back of the hall. 'Who torments me?' it moaned. 'Who will give me surcease?'

'I!' cried Slaye. 'Advance through the hall, kill all but myself!'

'No!' cried Cugel. 'It is I who possess the amulet! I whom you must obey! Kill all but me!'

Derwe Coreme clutched at Cugel's arm, striving to see the amulet. 'It avails nothing unless you call him by name. We are all lost!'

'What is his name!' cried Cugel. 'Counsel me!'

'Hold back!' declared Slaye. 'I have considered—'

Cugel dealt him a blow and sprang behind the table. The demon was approaching, pausing to pluck up the men-at-arms and dash them against the walls. Derwe Coreme ran to Cugel. 'Let me see the amulet; do you know nothing whatever? I will order him!'

'By no means!' said Cugel. 'Am I Cugel the Clever for nothing? Show me which carbuncle, recite me the name.'

Derwe Coreme bent her head, read the rune, thrust out to press a carbuncle, but Cugel knocked her arm aside. 'What name? Or we all die!'

'Call on Vanille! Press here, call on Vanille!'

Cugel pressed the carbuncle. 'Vanille! Halt this strife.'

The black demon heeded not at all. There was a second great sound, and a second demon appeared. Derwe Coreme cried out in terror. 'It was not Vanille; show me the amulet once more!'

But there was insufficient time; the black demon was upon them.

'Vanille!' bellowed Cugel. 'Destroy this black monster!'

Vanille was low and broad, and of a swimming green color, with eyes like scarlet lights. It flung itself upon the first demon, and the terrible bellow of the encounter stunned the ears, and eyes could not follow the frenzy of the fight. The walls shuddered as the great forces struck and rebounded. The table splintered under great splayed feet; Derwe Coreme was flung into a corner. Cugel crawled after, to find her crumpled and staring, half-conscious but bereft of will. Cugel thrust the amulet before her eyes. 'Read the runes! Call forth the names; each I will try in turn! Quick, to save our lives!'

But Derwe Coreme merely made a soft motion with her lips. Behind, the black demon, mounted astride Vanille, was methodically clawing up handfuls of his substance and casting it aside, while Vanille bellowed and screamed and turned his ferocious head this way and that, snapping and snarling, striking with great green arms. The black demon plunged its arms deep, seized some central node and Vanille became a sparkling green slime of a myriad parts, each gleam and sparkle flitting and quivering and dissolving into the stone.

Slaye stood grinning above Cugel. 'Do you wish your life? Hand here the amulet and I spare you. Delay one instant and you are dead!'

Cugel divested himself of the amulet, but could not bring himself to relinquish it. He said with sudden cunning, 'I can give the amulet to the demon.'

Slaye glared down at him. 'And then we all are dead. To me it does not matter. Do so. I defy you. If you want life – the amulet.'

Cugel looked down at Derwe Coreme. 'What of her?'

'Together you shall be banished. The amulet, for here is the demon.'

The black demon towered above; Cugel hastily handed the amulet to Slaye, who uttered a sharp cry and touched a carbuncle. The demon whimpered, involuted and disappeared.

Slaye stood back, grinning in triumph. 'Now away with you and the girl. I keep my word to you, no more. You have your miserable lives: depart.'

'Grant me one desire!' pled Cugel. 'Transport us to Almery, to the Valley of the Xzan, where I may rid myself of a canker called Firx!'

'No,' said Slaye. 'I deny your heart's-desire. Go at once.'

Cugel lifted Derwe Coreme to her feet. Still dazed, she stared at the wreckage of the hall. Cugel turned to Slaye. 'The ghoul waits in the promenade.'

Slaye nodded. 'This may well be true. Tomorrow I shall chastise him. Tonight I call sub-world artisans to repair the hall and restore the glory of Cil. Hence! Do you think I care how you fare with the ghoul?' His face became suffused and his hand strayed toward the carbuncles of the amulet. 'Hence, at once!'

Cugel took Derwe Coreme's arm and led her from the hall to the great front portal. Slaye stood with feet apart, shoulders hunched, head bent forward, eyes following Cugel's every move. Cugel eased back the bolts, opened the door and stepped out upon the terrace.

There was silence along the promenade. Cugel led Derwe Coreme down the steps and off to the side, into the rank growth of the old garden. Here he paused to listen. From the palace came sounds of activity: rasping and scraping, hoarse shouts and bellows, the flash of many-colored lights. Down the center of the promenade came a tall white shape, stepping from the shadow of one pedestal to the next. It paused to listen to the sounds and watch the flaring lights in wonder. While it was so absorbed Cugel led Derwe Coreme away behind the dark banks of foliage, and so off into the night.

CHAPTER THREE

The Mountains of Magnatz

Shortly after sunrise Cugel and Derwe Coreme emerged from the hillside byre where they had huddled the night. The air was chill and the sun, a wine-colored bubble behind high mist, produced no warmth. Cugel clapped his arms and jigged back and forth, while Derwe Coreme stood pinch-faced and limp beside the old byre.

Cugel presently became irritated by her posture, which implied a subtle disparagement of himself. 'Fetch wood,' he told her curtly. 'I will strike a fire; we will breakfast in comfort.'

Without a word the erstwhile princess of Cil went to gather furze. Cugel turned to inspect the dim expanse to the east, voicing an automatic curse upon Iucounu the Laughing Magician, whose rancor had flung him into this northern wasteland.

Derwe Coreme returned with an armful of twigs; Cugel gave a nod of approval. For a brief period after their expulsion from Cil she had carried herself with an inappropriate hauteur, which Cugel had tolerated with a quiet smile for himself. Their first couching had been both eventful and taxing; thereafter Derwe Coreme had modified at least her overt behaviour. Her face, delicate and clear of feature, had lost little of its brooding melancholy, but the arrogance had altered, as milk becomes cheese, to a new and wakeful appreciation of reality.

The fire crackled cheerfully; they ate a breakfast of rampion and pulpy black gallberries, while Cugel put questions regarding the lands to the east and south. Derwe Coreme could return only small information, none

70

of which was optimistic. 'The forest is said to be endless. I have heard it called several names: the Great Erm, the Forest of the East, the Lig Thig. To the south you see the Mountains of Magnatz, which are reputedly dreadful.'

'In what respect?' demanded Cugel. 'The knowledge is of importance; we must cross these mountains on our way to Almery.'

Derwe Coreme shook her head. 'I have heard only hints, and paid no great heed, as never did I expect to visit the region.'

'Nor I,' grumbled Cugel. 'Were it not for Iucounu I would be elsewhere.'

A spark of interest animated the listless face. 'Who is this Iucounu?'

'A detestable wizard of Almery. He has a boiled squash for a head, and flaunts a mindless grin. In every way he is odious, and displays the spite of a scalded eunuch.'

Derwe Coreme's mouth moved in a small cool smile. 'And you antagonized this wizard.'

'Bah! It was nothing. For a trivial slight he flung me north on an impossible mission. I am not Cugel the Clever for nothing! The mission is achieved and now I return to Almery.'

'And what of Almery – is this a pleasant land?'

'Pleasant enough, compared to this desolation of forest and mist. Still, imperfections exist. Wizardry is rife, and justice is not invariable, as I have intimated.'

'Tell me more of Almery. Are there cities? Are there folk other than rogues and wizards?'

Cugel frowned. 'Certain cities exist, sad shadows of bygone glory. There is Azenomei, where the Xzan joins Scaum Flow, and Kaiin in Ascolais, and others along the shore opposite Kauchique, where the folk are of great subtlety.'

Derwe Coreme nodded thoughtfully. 'I will go to

Almery. In your company, from which I can soon recover.'

Cugel glanced at her sidewise, not liking the flavor of the remark, but before he could particularize, she asked, 'What lands lie between us and Almery?'

'They are wide and dangerous and peopled by gids, erbs, and deodands, as well as leucomorphs, ghouls and grues. Otherwise I am ignorant. If we survive the journey, it will be a miracle indeed.'

Derwe Coreme looked wistfully back toward Cil, then shrugged and became silent.

The frugal meal was at its end. Cugel leaned back against the byre, to enjoy the warmth of the fire, but Firx would allow no respite, and Cugel, grimacing, jumped to his feet. 'Come; we must set forth. The spite of Iucounu permits no less.'

Down the slope they walked, following what appeared to be an old road. The landscape changed. Heath gave way to a damp bottomland; presently they came to the forest. Cugel eyed the gloomy shadows with distrust. 'We must go quietly, and hope to arouse nothing baneful. I will watch ahead, and you behind, to ensure that nothing follows to leap on our backs.'

'We will lose our way.'

'The sun hangs in the south: this is our guide.'

Derwe Coreme shrugged once more; they plunged forward into the shade. The trees stood tall overhead and the sunlight, filtered through the foliage, only exaggerated the gloom. Coming upon a stream, they walked along its banks and presently entered a glade where flowed a brimming river.

On the bank near a moored raft sat four men in ragged garments. Cugel looked Derwe Coreme over critically, and took the jeweled buttons from her garments. 'These by all odds are bandits and we must lull their cupidity, even though they seem a poor lot.'

'Better that we avoid them,' said Derwe Coreme. 'They are animals, no better.'

Cugel demurred. 'We need their raft and their guidance, which we must command; if we supplicate, they will believe themselves to have a choice, and become captious.' He strode forward and Derwe Coreme willy-nilly was forced to follow.

The rogues did not improve upon closer view. Their hair was long and matted, their faces gnarled, with eyes like beetles and mouths showing foul yellow teeth. Withal, their expressions were mild enough, and they watched Cugel and Derwe Coreme approach with wariness rather than belligerence. One of them, it so appeared, was a woman, though this was hardly evident from garments, face or refinement of manner. Cugel gave them a salute of lordly condescension, at which they blinked in puzzlement.

'What people are you?' asked Cugel.

'We call ourselves Busiacos,' responded the oldest of the men. 'It is both our race and our family; we make no differentiation, being somewhat polyandrous by habit.'

'You are denizens of the forest, familiar with its routes and trails?'

'Such is a fair description,' admitted the man, 'though our knowledge is local. Remember, this is the Great Erm, which sweeps on league after league without termination.'

'No matter,' said Cugel. 'We require only transfer across the river, then guidance upon a secure route to the lands of the south.'

The man consulted the others of his group; all shook their heads. 'There is no such route; the Mountains of Magnatz lie in the way.'

'Indeed,' said Cugel.

'If I were to ferry you across the river,' continued the old Busiaco, 'you would be as good as dead, for the region is haunted by erbs and grues. Your sword would be useless,

73

and you carry only the weakest magic – this I know for we Busiacos smell magic as an erb sniffs out meat.'

'How then may we achieve our destination?' demanded Cugel.

The Busiacos showed little interest in the question. But the man next in age to the eldest, glancing at Derwe Coreme, had a sudden idea, and looked across the river as if pondering. The effort presently overwhelmed him, and he shook his head in defeat.

Cugel, observing carefully, asked, 'What baffles you?'

'A problem of no great complexity,' replied the Busiaco. 'We have small practice in logic and any difficulty thwarts us. I only speculated as to which of your belongings you would exchange for guidance through the forest.'

Cugel laughed heartily. 'A good question. But I own only what you see: namely garments, shoes, cape and sword, all of which are necessary to me. Though, for a fact, I know an incantation which can produce a jeweled button or two.'

'These would be small inducement. In a nearby crypt jewels are heaped as high as my head.'

Cugel rubbed his jaw reflectively. 'The generosity of the Busiacos is everywhere known; perhaps you will lead us past this crypt.'

The Busiaco made a gesture of indifference. 'If you wish, although it is adjacent to the den of a great mother gid, now in oestrus.'

'We will proceed directly toward the south,' said Cugel. 'Come, let us depart at once.'

The Busiaco maintained his stubborn crouch. 'You have no inducement to offer?'

'Only my gratitude, which is no small matter.'

'What of the woman? She is somewhat gaunt, but not unappealing. Since you must die in the Mountains of Magnatz, why waste the woman?'

74

'True.' Cugel turned to look at Derwe Coreme. 'Perhaps we can come to terms.'

'What?' she gasped in outrage. 'Do you dare suggest such a thing? I will drown myself in the river!'

Cugel took her aside. 'I am not called Cugel the Clever for nothing,' he hissed in her ear. 'Trust me to outwit this moon-calf!'

Derwe Coreme surveyed him with distrust, then turned away, tears of bitter anger streaming down her cheeks. Cugel addressed the Busiaco. 'Your proposal is clearly the better part of wisdom; so now, let us be off.'

'The woman may remain here,' said the Busiaco, rising to his feet. 'We walk an enchanted path and rigid discipline is necessary.'

Derwe Coreme took a determined stride toward the river. 'No!' cried Cugel hastily. 'She is of sentimental temperament, and wishes to see me safely on my way to the Mountains of Magnatz, even though it means my certain death.'

The Busiaco shrugged. 'It is all one.' He led them aboard the raft, cast off the rope, and poled across the river. The water seemed shallow, the pole never descending more than a foot or two. It seemed to Cugel that wading across would have been simplicity itself.

The Busiaco, observing, said, 'The river swarms with glass reptiles, and an unwary man, stepping forth, is instantly attacked.'

'Indeed!' said Cugel, eying the river dubiously.

'Indeed. And now I must caution you as to the path. We will meet all manner of persuasions, but as you value your life, do not step aside from where I lead.'

The raft reached the opposite bank; the Busiaco stepped ashore and made it fast to a tree. 'Come now, after me.' He plunged confidently off among the trees. Derwe Coreme followed, with Cugel coming in the rear.

The trail was so faint that Cugel could not distinguish it from the untrodden forest, but the Busiaco never faltered. The sun, hanging low behind the trees, could be glimpsed only infrequently, and Cugel was never certain of the direction they traveled. So they proceeded, through sylvan solitudes where not so much as a bird-call could be heard.

The sun, passing its zenith, began to descend, and the trail became no more distinct. Cugel at last called ahead, 'You are certain of the trail? It seems that we veer left and right at random.'

The Busiaco stopped to explain. 'We of the forest are an ingenuous folk, but we have this peculiar facility.' He tapped his splayed nose significantly. 'We can smell out magic. The trail we follow was ordained at a time too remote to be recalled, and yields its direction only to such as ourselves.'

'Possibly so,' said Cugel petulantly. 'But it seems overly circuitous, and where are the fearsome creatures you mentioned? I have seen only a vole, and nowhere have I sensed the distinctive odor of the erb.'

The Busiaco shook his head in perplexity. 'Unaccountably they have taken themselves elsewhere. Surely you do not complain? Let us proceed, before they return.' And he set forth once again, by a track no less indistinguishable than before.

The sun sank low. The forest thinned somewhat; scarlet rays slanted along the aisles, burnishing gnarled roots, gilding fallen leaves. The Busiaco stepped into a clearing, where he swung about with an air of triumph. 'I have successfully achieved our goal!'

'How so?' demanded Cugel. 'We are still deep in the forest.'

The Busiaco pointed across the clearing. 'Notice the four well-marked and distinct trails?'

'This seems to be the case,' Cugel admitted grudgingly.

'One of these leads to the southern verge. The others plunge into the forest depths, branching variously along the way.'

Derwe Coreme, peering through the branches, uttered a sharp ejaculation. 'There, fifty paces yonder, is the river and the raft.'

Cugel turned the Busiaco a dire look. 'What of all this?'

The Busiaco nodded solemnly. 'Those fifty paces lack the protection of magic. I would have been scamping my responsibility to convey us here by the direct route. And now—' He advanced to Derwe Coreme, took her arm, then turned back to Cugel. 'You may cross the glade, whereupon I will instruct you as to which trail leads to the southern verge.' And he busied himself fixing a cord about Derwe Coreme's waist. She resisted with a fervor and was only subdued by a blow and a curse. 'This is to prevent any sudden leaps or excursions,' the Busiaco told Cugel with a sly wink. 'I am not too fleet of foot and when I wish the woman I do not care to pursue her here and there. But are you not in haste? The sun declines, and after dark the leucomorphs appear.'

'Well then, which of the trails leads to the southern verge?' Cugel asked in a frank manner.

'Cross the clearing and I will so inform you. Of course, if you distrust my instructions, you may make your own choice. But remember, I have vigorously exerted myself for a waspish, gaunt and anemic woman. As of now we are at quits.'

Cugel looked dubiously across the clearing, then to Derwe Coreme, who watched in sick dismay. Cugel spoke cheerfully. 'Well, it seems to be for the best. The Mountains of Magnatz are notoriously dangerous. You are at least secure with this uncouth rogue.'

'No!' she screamed. 'Let me free of this rope! He is a cheat; you have been duped! Cugel the Clever? Cugel the Fool!'

'Such language is vulgar,' stated Cugel. 'The Busiaco and I struck a bargain, which is to say, a sacred covenant, which must be discharged.'

'Kill the brute!' cried Derwe Coreme. 'Employ your sword! The edge of the forest cannot be far away!'

'An incorrect trail might lead into the heart of the Great Erm,' argued Cugel. He raised his arm in farewell. 'Far better to drudge for this hirsute ruffian than risk death in the Mountains of Magnatz!'

The Busiaco grinned in agreement, and gave the line a proprietary jerk. Cugel hurried across the clearing with Derwe Coreme's imprecations ringing in his ears, until she was silenced by some means Cugel did not observe. The Busiaco called, 'By chance you are approaching the correct path. Follow and you shall presently come to an inhabited place.'

Cugel returned a final salute and set forth. Derwe Coreme gave a scream of hysterical mirth: 'Cugel the Clever he calls himself! What an extravagant joke!'

Cugel proceeded quickly along the trail, somewhat troubled. 'The woman is a monomaniac!' he told himself. 'She lacks clarity and perceptiveness; how could I have done else, for her welfare and my own? I am rationality personified; it is unthinking to insist otherwise!'

Scarcely a hundred paces from the clearing the trail emerged from the forest. Cugel stopped short. Only a hundred paces? He pursed his lips. By some curious coincidence three other trails likewise left the forest nearby, all converging to one near where he stood. 'Interesting,' said Cugel. 'It is almost tempting to return to seek out the Busiaco and exact some sort of explanation. . .'

He fingered his sword thoughtfully, and even took a step or two back toward the forest. But the sun was low and shadows filled the gaps between the gnarled trunks. As Cugel hesitated, Firx impatiently drew several of his prongs and barbs across Cugel's liver, and Cugel abandoned the project of returning into the forest.

The trail led across a region of open land, with mountains riding across the southern sky. Cugel strode along at a smart pace, conscious of the dark shadow of the forest behind, and not completely settled in his mind. From time to time, at some particularly unsettling thought, he slapped his thigh sharply. But what folly! He had obviously managed affairs to their optimum! The Busiaco was gross and stupid; how could he have hoped to trick Cugel? The concept was untenable. As for Derwe Coreme, no doubt she would soon come to terms with her new life. . .

As the sun dropped behind the Mountains of Magnatz he came upon a rude settlement and a tavern beside the crossroads. This was a staunch structure of stone and timber, with round windows each formed of a hundred blue bull's eyes. Cugel paused at the door and took stock of his resources, which were scant. Then he remembered the jeweled buttons he had taken from Derwe Coreme, and congratulated himself on his forethought.

He pushed through the door, into a long room hung with old bronze lamps. The publican presided at a short buffet where he poured grogs and punches to the three men who were his present customers. All turned to stare as Cugel entered the room.

The publican spoke politely enough. 'Welcome, wanderer; what is your pleasure?'

'First a cup of wine, then supper and a night's lodging, and finally such knowledge regarding the road south as you can provide.'

The publican set forth a cup of wine. 'Supper and lodging in due course. As to the road south, it leads into the realm of Magnatz, which is enough to know.'

'Magnatz then is a creature of dread?'

The publican gave his head a dour shake. 'Men have fared south never to return. No man in memory has come north. I can vouch for only so much.'

The three men who sat drinking nodded in solemn coroboration. Two were peasants of the region, while the third wore the tall black boots of a professional witch-chaser. The first peasant signaled the publican: 'Pour this unfortunate a cup of wine, at my expense.'

Cugel accepted the cup with mixed feelings. 'I drink with thanks, though I specifically disavow the appellation "unfortunate" lest the virtue of the word project upon my destiny.'

'As you will,' responded the peasant indifferently, 'though in these melancholy times, who is otherwise?' And for a space the peasants argued the repair of the stone fence which separated their lands.

'The work is arduous, but the advantages great,' declared one.

'Agreed,' stated the other, 'but my luck is such that no sooner would we complete the task than the sun would go black, with all the toil for naught.'

The first flourished his arms in derisive rejection of the argument. 'This is a risk we must assume. Notice: I drink wine, though I may not live to become drunk. Does this deter me? No! I reject the future; I drink now, I become drunk as circumstances dictate.'

The publican laughed and pounded the buffet with his fist. 'You are as crafty as a Busiaco, of whom I hear there is an encampment nearby. Perhaps the wanderer met them?' And he looked questioningly at Cugel, who nodded grudgingly.

'I encountered such a group: crass rather than crafty, in my opinion. In reference once more to the road south, can anyone here supply specific advice?'

The witch-chaser said gruffly, 'I can: avoid it. You will

80

first encounter deodands avid for your flesh. Beyond is the realm of Magnatz, beside whom the deodands appear as angels of mercy, if a tenth of the rumors are true.'

'This is discouraging news,' said Cugel. 'Is there no other route to the lands of the south?'

'Indeed there is,' said the witch-chaser, 'and I recommend it. Return north along the trail to the Great Erm, and proceed eastward across the extent of the forest, which becomes even denser and more dread. Needless to say, you will need a stout arm and feet with wings to escape the vampires, grues, erbs and leucomorphs. After penetrating to the remote edge of the forest you must swing south to the Vale of Dharad, where according to rumor an army of basilisks besieges the ancient city Mar. Should you win past the raging battle, the Great Central Steppe lies beyond, where is neither food nor water and which is the haunt of the pelgrane. Crossing the steppe, you turn your face back to the west, and now you wade a series of poisonous swamps. Beyond lies an area of which I know nothing except that it is named the Land of Evil Recollection. After crossing this region you will find yourself at a point to the south of the Mountains of Magnatz.'

Cugel mused a moment or two. 'The route which you delineate, while it may be safer and less taxing than the direct way south, seems of inordinate length. I am disposed to risk the Mountains of Magnatz.'

The first peasant inspected him with awe. 'I surmise you to be a noted wizard, seething with spells.'

Cugel gave his head a smiling shake. 'I am Cugel the Clever; no more, no less. And now – wine!'

The landlord presently brought forth supper: a stew of tentils and land-crabs garnished with wild ramp and bilberries.

81

After the meal the two peasants drunk a final cup of wine and departed, while Cugel, the host and the witch-chaser sat before the fire discussing various aspects of existence. The witch-chaser finally arose to retire to his chamber. Before departing he approached Cugel, and spoke in a frank manner. 'I have noticed your cloak, which is of quality rarely seen in this backward region. Since you are as good as dead, why do you not bestow this cloak upon me, who has need of it?'

Cugel tersely rejected the proposal and went to his own chamber.

During the night he was aroused by a scraping sound near the foot of his bed. Leaping to his feet, he captured a person of no great stature. When hauled out into the light, the intruder proved to be the pot-boy, still clutching Cugel's shoes, which he evidently had intended to purloin. 'What is the meaning of this outrage?' demanded Cugel, cuffing the lad. 'Speak! How dare you attempt such an act!'

The pot-boy begged Cugel to desist. 'What difference does it make? A doomed man needs no such elegant footwear!'

'I will be the judge of that.' said Cugel. 'Do you expect me to walk barefoot to my death in the Mountains of Magnatz? Be off with you!' And he sent the wretched lad sprawling down the hall.

In the morning at breakfast he spoke of the incident to the landlord, who showed no great interest. When it came time to settle his score, Cugel tossed one of the jeweled buttons upon the counter. 'Fix, if you will, a fair value upon this gem, subtract the score and give me my change in gold coins.'

The landlord examined the ornament, pursed his lips and cocked his head to the side. 'The total of the charges to your account exactly equals the worth of this trinket – there is no change forthcoming.'

'What?' stormed Cugel. 'This clear aquamarine flanked by four emeralds? For a cup or two of poor wine, a porridge and sleep disturbed by the villainy of your pot-boy? Is this a tavern or a bandit lair?'

The landlord shrugged. 'The charges are somewhat in excess of the usual fee, but money moldering in the pockets of a corpse serves no one.'

Cugel at last extracted several gold coins from the land-lord together with a parcel of bread, cheese, and wine. The landlord came to the door and pointed. 'There is but a single trail, that leading south. The Mountains of Magnatz rise before you. Farewell.'

Not without foreboding, Cugel set off to the south. For a space the trail led past the tillage of local peasants; then as the foothills bulked to either side the trail became first a track, then a trace winding along a dry riverbed beside thickets of prickle-bush, spurge, yarrow, asphodel. Along the crest of the hill paralleling the trail grew a tangle of stunted oak, and Cugel, thinking to improve his chances for going unobserved, climbed to the ridge and continued in the shelter of the foliage.

The air was clear, the sky a brilliant dark blue. The sun wallowed up to the zenith and Cugel bethought himself of the food he carried in his pouch. He seated himself, but as he did so the motion of a skipping dark shadow caught his eye. His blood chilled. The creature surely meant to leap upon his back.

Cugel pretended not to notice, and presently the shadow moved forward again: a deodand, taller and heavier than himself, black as midnight except for shining white eyes, white teeth and claws, wearing straps of leather to support a green velvet shirt.

Cugel debated his best course of action. Face to face, chest to chest, the deodand would tear him to pieces. With his sword ready, Cugel might hack and stab and hold the

creature at bay until its frenzy for blood overcame its fear
of pain and it flung itself forward regardless of hurt.
Possibly Cugel was more fleet, and might out-distance the
creature, but only after a long and dogged pursuit . . . It
slipped forward again, to stand behind a crumbling outcrop twenty paces downslope from where Cugel sat. As
soon as it had disappeared, Cugel ran to the outcrop and
jumped to the top. Here he lifted a heavy stone and, as
the deodand came skulking below, threw it down upon the
creature's back. It toppled and lay kicking, and Cugel
jumped down to deliver the death-stroke.

The deodand had pulled himself against the rock and
hissed in horror at the sight of Cugel's naked blade.
'Hold your stroke,' it said. 'You gain nothing by my
death.'

'Only the satisfaction of killing one who planned to
devour me.'

'A sterile pleasure!'

'Few pleasures are otherwise,' said Cugel. 'But while
you live, inform me regarding the Mountains of Magnatz.'

'They are as you see: stern mountains of ancient black
rock.'

'And what of Magnatz?'

'I have no knowledge of any such entity.'

'What? The men to the north shudder at the very word!'

The deodand pulled himself slightly more erect. 'This
well may be. I have heard the name, and consider it no
more than a legend of old.'

'Why do travelers go south and none go north?'

'Why should anyone seek to travel north? As for those
coming south, they have provided food for myself and my
fellows.' And the deodand inched himself up. Cugel
picked up a great stone, held it aloft and dashed it down
upon the black creature, which fell back, kicking freely.
Cugel picked up another stone.

84

'Hold!' called the deodand in a faint voice. 'Spare me, and I will aid you to life.'

'How is this?' asked Cugel.

'You seek to travel south; others like me inhabit caves along the way: how can you escape them unless I guide you by ways they do not frequent?'

'You can do this?'

'If you undertake to spare my life.'

'Excellent. But I must take safeguards; in your lust for blood you might ignore the agreement.'

'You have maimed me; what further security do you need?' cried the deodand. Cugel nevertheless bound the creature's arms and arranged a halter around the thick black neck.

In such fashion they proceeded, the deodand limping and hopping, and directing Cugel by a circuitous route above certain caves.

The mountains lifted higher; winds boomed and echoed down the stone canyons. Cugel continued to question the deodand regarding Magnatz, but elicted only the opinion that Magnatz was a creature of fable.

At last they came to a sandy flat high above the lowlands, which the deodand declared beyond the zone of his particular sept.

'What lies beyond?' asked Cugel.

'I have no knowledge; this is the limit of my wandering. Now release me and go your way, and I will return to my people.'

Cugel shook his head. 'Night is not too far distant. What is to prevent you from following to attack me once again? Best that I kill you.'

The deodand laughed sadly. 'Three others follow us. They have kept their distance only because I waved them back. Kill me and you will never wake to see the morning sun.'

'We will travel further together,' said Cugel.

'As you wish.'

Cugel led the way south, the deodand limping to the boulders, and looking back Cugel saw black shapes moving among the shadows. The deodand grinned meaningfully at Cugel. 'You would do well to halt at once; why wait until dark? Death comes with less horror while the light shines.'

Cugel made no response, but pressed forward with all speed. The trail left the valley, climbing to a high meadow where the air blew cool. Larch, kaobab and balm-cedar grew to either side, and a stream ran among grasses and herbs. The deodand began to evince uneasiness, jerking at its halter, limping with exaggerated debility. Cugel could see no reason for the display: the countryside, except for the presence of the deodands, seemed without threat. Cugel became impatient. 'Why do you delay? I hope to find a mountain hospice before the coming of dark. Your lagging and limping discommode me.'

'You should have considered this before you maimed me with a rock,' said the deodand. 'After all, I do not accompany you of my own choice.'

Cugel looked behind. The three deodands who previously had skulked among the rocks now followed quite casually. 'You have no control over the grisly appetites of your fellows?' Cugel demanded.

'I have no control over my own,' responded the deodand. 'Only the fact of my broken limbs prevents me from leaping at your throat.'

'Do you wish to live?' asked Cugel, putting his hand significantly to sword-hilt.

'To a certain extent, though with not so fervent a yearning as do true men.'

'If you value life even an iota, order your fellows to turn back, to give over their sinister pursuit.'

'It would be a futile exercise. And in any event what is life to you? Look, before you tower the Mountains of Magnatz!'

'Ha!' muttered Cugel. 'Did you not claim the repute of the region to be purely fabulous?'

'Exactly; but I did not enlarge upon the nature of the fable.'

As they spoke there came a swift sigh in the air; looking about, Cugel saw that the three deodands had fallen, transfixed by arrows. From a nearby grove stepped four young men in brown hunting costume. They were of a fair, fresh complexion, brown hair, good stature, and seemed of good disposition.

The foremost called out, 'How is it that you come from the uninhabited north? And why do you walk with this dire creature of the night?'

'There is no mystery to either of your questions,' said Cugel. 'First, the north is not uninhabited; some hundreds of men yet remain alive. As to this black hybrid of demon and cannibal, I employed it to lead me safely through the mountains, but I am dissatisfied with its services.'

'I did all expected of me,' declared the deodand. 'Release me in accordance with our pact.'

'As you will,' said Cugel. He released the halter which secured the creature's throat, and it limped away glaring over its shoulder. Cugel made a sign to the leader of the huntsmen; he spoke a word to his fellows; they raised their bows and shot the deodand with arrows.

Cugel gave a curt nod of approval. 'What of yourselves? And what of Magnatz who reputedly makes the mountains unsafe for travel?'

The huntsmen laughed. 'A legend merely. At one time a terrible creature named Magnatz did indeed exist, and in deference to the tradition we of Vull Village still appoint one of our number to serve as Watchman. But this is all the credit to be given the tale.'

'Strange,' said Cugel, 'that the tradition wields so wide an influence.'

The huntsmen shrugged indifferently. 'Night approaches; it is time to turn back. You are welcome to join us, and at Vull there is a tavern where you may rest the night.'

'I gladly avail myself of your company.'

The group set off up the trail. As they marched Cugel made inquiry regarding the road to the south, but the huntsmen were of little assistance. 'Vull Village is situated on the shores of Lake Vull, which is unnavigable for its whirlpools, and a few of us have explored the mountains to the south. It is said that they are barren and drop off into an inhospitable gray waste.'

'Possibly Magnatz roams the mountains across the lake?' inquired Cugel delicately.

'Tradition is silent on this score,' replied the huntsman.

After an hour's march the group reached Vull, a village of an affluence surprising to Cugel. The dwellings were solidly constructed of stone and timber, the streets neatly laid-out and well-drained; there was a public market, a granary, a hall, a repository, several taverns, a number of modestly luxurious mansions. As the huntsmen marched up the main street, a man called out to them. 'Important news! The Watchman has perished!'

'Indeed?' inquired the leader of the huntsmen with keen interest. 'Who serves in the interim?'

'It is Lafel, son to the hetman – who else?'

'Who else indeed?' remarked the huntsman, and the group passed on.

'Is the post of Watchman held in such high esteem then?' asked Cugel.

The huntsman shrugged. 'It is best described as a ceremonial sinecure. A permanent functionary will no doubt be chosen tomorrow. But notice in the door of the hall!' And he pointed to a stocky broad-shouldered man wearing brown fur-trimmed robes and a black bifold hat. 'That is Hylam Wiskode, the hetman himself. Ho, Wiskode! We have encountered a traveler from the north!'

Hylam Wiskode approached, and saluted Cugel with courtesy. 'Welcome! Strangers are a novelty; our hospitality is yours!'

'I thank you indeed,' said Cugel. 'I had expected no such affability in the Mountains of Magnatz, which all the world holds in dread.'

The hetman chuckled. 'Misapprehensions are common everywhere; you may well find certain of our notions quaint and archaic, like our Watch for Magnatz. But come! here is our best tavern. After you have established yourself we will sup.'

Cugel was taken to a comfortable chamber, furnished various conveniences, and presently, clean and refreshed, he rejoined Hylam Wiskode in the common room. An appetizing supper was set before him, together with a flagon of wine.

After the meal the hetman conducted Cugel on a tour of the town, which enjoyed a pleasant aspect above the lake.

Tonight seemed to be a special occasion: everywhere cressets threw up plumes of flame, while the folk of Vull walked the streets, pausing to confer in small knots and groups. Cugel inquired the reason for the obvious perturbation. 'Is it because your watchman has died?'

'This is the case,' said the hetman. 'We treat our traditions with all earnestness, and the selection of a new Watchman is a matter for public debate. But observe: here is the public repository, where the common wealth is collected. Do you care to look within?'

'I abide your pleasure,' said Cugel. 'If you wish to inspect the communal gold, I will be glad to join you.'

The hetman threw back the door. 'Here is much more than gold! In this bin are jewels; that rack holds antique coins. Those bales contain fine silks and embroidered damask; to the side are cases of precious spice, even more precious liquors, and subtle pastes without value. But I should not use these terms on you, a traveler and man of experience, who has looked upon real wealth.'

Cugel insisted that the riches of Vull were by no means to be deprecated. The hetman bowed appreciatively and they proceeded to an esplanade beside the lake, now a great dark expanse illuminated by feeble starlight.

The hetman indicated a cupola supported five hundred feet in the air by a slender pillar. 'Can you guess the function of that structure?'

'It would seem to be the post of the Watchman,' said Cugel.

'Correct! You are a man of discernment. A pity you are in such haste and can not linger in Vull!'

Cugel, considering his empty wallet and the riches of the storehouse, made a suave gesture. 'I would not be averse to such a sojourn, but in all candor, I travel in penury, and would be forced to seek some sort of gainful employment. I wonder regarding the office of Watchman, which I understand to be a post of some prestige.'

'Indeed it is,' said the hetman. 'My own son stands watch tonight. Still, there is no reason why you should not be a suitable candidate for the position. The duties are by no means arduous; indeed the post is something of a sinecure.'

Cugel became conscious of Firx's fretful stirrings. 'And as to the emoluments?'

'They are excellent. The Watchman enjoys great prestige here in Vull, since, in a purely formal sense, he protects us all from danger.'

'They are specifically, what?'

The hetman paused to reflect, and ticked off the points on his fingers. 'First, he is provided a comfortable watch-tower, complete with cushions, an optical device whereby distant objects are made to seem close at hand, a brazier to provide heat and an ingenious communications system. Next, his food and drink are of the highest quality and provided free of charge, at his pleasure and to his order. Next, he is generally granted the subsidiary title "Guardian of the Public Repository," and to simplify matters he is invested with full title to, and powers of dispensation over, the total wealth of Vull. Fourth, he may select as his spouse that maiden who seems to him the most attractive. Fifthly, he is accorded the title of "Baron" and must be saluted with profound respect.'

'Indeed, indeed,' said Cugel. 'The position appears worthy of consideration. What responsibilities are entailed?'

'They are as the nomenclature implies. The Watchman must keep watch, for this is one of the old-fashioned customs we observe. The duties are hardly onerous, but they must not be scamped, because that would signify farce, and we are serious folk, even in connection with our quaint traditions.'

Cugel nodded judiciously. 'The conditions are straightforward. The Watchman watches; nothing could be more clearly expressed. But who is Magnatz, in what direction should he be apprehended, and how may he be recognized?'

'These questions are of no great application,' said the hetman, 'since the creature, in theory, has no existence.'

Cugel glanced up at the tower, across the lake, back toward the public repository. 'I hereby make application for the position, providing all is as you state.'

91

Firx instantly impinged a series of racking pangs upon Cugel's vitals. Cugel bent double, clasped his abdomen, straightened, and making excuses to the perplexed hetman, moved to the side. 'Patience!' he implored Firx. 'Temperance! Have you no concept of realities? My purse is empty; there are long leagues ahead! To travel with any degree of expedition, I must restore my strength and replenish my wallet. I plan to work at this office only long enough to do both, then it is post-haste to Almery!'

Firx reluctantly diminished the demonstrations, and Cugel returned to where the hetman waited.

'All is as before,' said Cugel. 'I have taken counsel with myself and believe I can adequately fulfill the obligations of the job.'

The hetman nodded. 'I am pleased to hear this. You will find my presentation of the facts to be accurate in every essential aspect. I likewise have been reflecting, and I can safely say that no other person of the town aspires to so august a position, and I hereby pronounce you Watchman of the Town!' Ceremoniously the hetman brought forth a golden collar, which he draped around Cugel's neck.

They returned toward the tavern, and as they went, the folk of Vull, noting the golden collar, pressed upon the hetman with eager questions. 'Yes,' was his answer. 'This gentleman has demonstrated his capabilities, and I have pronounced him Watchman of the Town!'

At the news the folk of Vull became generously expansive, and congratulated Cugel as if he had been a resident the whole of his life.

All repaired to the tavern; wine and spiced meat were set out; pipers appeared and there was decorous dancing and merrymaking.

During the course of the evening Cugel spied an extremely beautiful girl dancing with a young man who had been part of the hunting party. Cugel nudged the hetman, directed his attention to the girl.

'Ah yes: the delightful Marlinka! She dances with the lad whom I believe she plans to espouse.'

'Her plans possibly are subject to alteration?' inquired Cugel meaningfully.

The hetman winked slyly. 'You find her attractive?'

'Indeed, and since this is a prerequisite of my office, I hereby declare this delightful creature my bride-elect. Let the ceremonies be performed at once!'

'So swiftly?' inquired the hetman. 'Ah, well, the hot blood of youth brooks no delay.' He signaled the girl and she danced merrily over to the table. Cugel arose and performed a deep bow. The hetman spoke. 'Marlinka, the Watchman of the Town finds you desirable and wishes you for his spouse.'

Marlinka seemed first surprised, then amused. She glanced roguishly at Cugel, and performed an arch curtsy. 'The Watchman does me great honor.'

'Further,' intoned the hetman, 'he requires that the marital ceremonies be performed on the instant.'

Marlinka looked dubiously at Cugel, then over her shoulder at the young man with whom she had been dancing. 'Very well,' she said. 'As you will.'

The ceremony was performed, and Cugel found himself espoused to Marlinka, whom, on closer examination, he saw to be a creature of delightful animation, charming manners and exquisite appearance. He put his arm around her waist. 'Come,' he whispered, 'let us slip away for a period and solemnize the connubiality.'

'Not so soon,' whispered Marlinka. 'I must have time to order myself; I am overexcited!' She released herself, and danced away.

There was further feasting and merrymaking, and to his vast displeasure Cugel noted Marlinka again dancing with

93

the youth to whom she formerly had been betrothed. As he watched she embraced this young man with every evidence of ardor. Cugel marched forward, halted the dance, and took his bride aside. 'Such an act is hardly appropriate; you have only been married an hour!'

Marlinka, both surprised and nonplussed, laughed, then frowned, then laughed again and promised to behave with greater decorum. Cugel attempted to lead her to his chamber, but she once again declared the moment unsuitable.

Cugel drew a deep sigh of vexation, but was consoled by the recollection of his other perquisites: the freedom of the repository, for instance. He leaned over to the hetman. 'Since now I am titular guardian to the public repository, it is only prudent that I acquaint myself in detail with the treasure I am charged with guarding. If you will be so good as to turn over the keys, I will go to make a quick inventory.'

'Even better,' said the hetman. 'I will accompany you, and do what I can in the way of assistance.'

They crossed to the repository. The hetman unlocked the door and held a light. Cugel entered and examined the valuables. 'I see that all is in order, and perhaps it is advisable to wait till my head is settled before undertaking a detailed inventory. But in the meantime—' Cugel went to the jewel bin, selected several gems, and began to tuck them into his pouch.

'A moment,' said the hetman. 'I fear you inconvenience yourself. Shortly you will be fitted with garments of rich cloth deserving of your rank. The wealth is most conveniently kept here in the treasury; why trouble yourself with the weight, or incur the possibility of loss?'

'There is something in what you say,' remarked Cugel, 'but I wish to order the construction of a mansion overlooking the lake and I will need wealth to pay the costs of construction.'

'In due time, in due time. The actual work can hardly commence until you have examined the countryside and chosen the most felicitous site.'

'True,' agreed Cugel. 'I can see that there are busy times ahead. But now – back to the tavern! My spouse is overmodest and now I will brook no further delay!'

But upon their return Marlinka was nowhere to be found. 'Doubtless she has gone to array herself in seductive garments,' suggested the hetman. 'Have patience!'

Cugel compressed his lips in displeasure, and was further annoyed to find that the young huntsman had likewise departed.

The merrymaking waxed apace, and after many toasts, Cugel became a trifle fuddled, and was carried up to his chamber.

Early in the morning the hetman rapped at the door, and entered at Cugel's summons. 'We must now visit the watchtower,' said the hetman. 'My own son guarded Vull this last night, since our tradition demands incessant vigilance.'

With poor grace Cugel dressed himself and followed the hetman out into the cool air of morning. They walked to the watchtower, and Cugel was astounded both by its height and by the elegant simplicity of its construction, the slender stem rearing five hundred feet into the air to support the cupola.

A rope ladder was the only means of ascent. The hetman started up and Cugel came below, the ladder swaying and jiggling in such a fashion as to cause Cugel vertigo.

They gained the cupola in safety and the hetman's weary son descended. The cupola was furnished in rather less luxury than Cugel had expected, and indeed seemed almost austere. He pointed out this fact to the hetman, who stated that the deficiencies were readily repaired. 'Merely state your requirements: they shall be met!'

'Well then: I will want a heavy rug for the floor – tones of green and gold might be the most felicitous. I require a more elegant couch, of greater scope than that disreputable pallet I see against the wall, as my spouse Marlinka will be spending much of her time here. A cabinet for gems and valuables there, a compartment for sweetmeats there, a tray for perfume essences there. At this location I will require a taboret with provision for chilling wines.'

The hetman assented readily to all. 'It shall be as you say. But now we must discuss your duties, which are so simple as almost to require no elaboration: you must keep watch for Magnatz.'

'This I understand, but as before a corollary thought occurs to me: in order to work at optimum efficiency I should know what or whom I am to watch for. Magnatz might stalk unhindered along the esplanade were I unable to recognize him. What then is his semblance?'

The hetman shook his head. 'I cannot say; the information is lost in the fog of ages. The legend reports only that he was tricked and baffled by a sorcerer, and taken away.' The hetman went to the observation post. 'Notice: here is an optical device. Working by an ingenious principle, it bloats and augments those scenes toward which you direct it. From time to time you may choose to inspect landmarks of the area. Yonder is Mount Temus; below is Lake Vull, where no one can sail for vortices and whirlpools. In this direction is Padagar Pass, leading eastward into the land of Merce. You can barely discern that commemorative cairn decreed by Guzpah the Great when he brought eight armies to attack Magnatz. Magnatz erected another cairn – see that great mound to the north? – in order to cover their mangled corpses. And there is the notch Magnatz broke through the mountains

so that cooling air might circulate through the [...]
Across the lake lie certain titanic ruins, where Ma[...]
had his palace.'

Cugel inspected the various landmarks through [...]
optical device. 'Magnatz was by all accounts a creature [...]
vast potency.'

'So the legends assert. Now, a final matter. If Magnatz
appears – a laughable whimsy, of course – you must pull
this rod, which rings the great gong. Our laws stringently
forbid ringing the gong, except at the sight of Magnatz.
The penalty for such a crime is intensely severe; in fact,
the last Watchman betrayed his high office by wantonly
ringing the gong. Needless to say, he was judged harshly,
and after he had been torn to bits by a criss-cross of chains
his fragments were cast into a whirlpool.'

'What an idiotic fellow!' remarked Cugel. 'Why forfeit
so much wealth, good cheer and honor for a footling
amusement?'

'We are all of like opinion,' stated the hetman.

Cugel frowned. 'I am puzzled by his act. Was he a
young man, to yield so readily to a frivolous whim?'

'Not even this plea can be made in his behalf. He was a
sage of four-score years, three-score of which he had
served the town as Watchman.'

'His conduct becomes all the more incredible,' was
Cugel's wondering comment.

'All of Vull feel the same.' The hetman rubbed his
hands briskly. 'I believe that we have discussed all the
essentials; I will now depart and leave you to the enjoyment of your duties.'

'One moment,' said Cugel. 'I insist upon certain
alterations and improvements: the rug, the cabinet, the
cushions, the tray, the couch.'

'Of course,' said the hetman. He bent his head over the
rail, shouted instructions to those below. There was no

nstant response, and the hetman became exasperated. 'What a nuisance!' he exclaimed. 'It appears I must see to the matter myself.' He began to climb down the rope ladder.

Cugel called after him, 'Be good enough to send up my spouse Marlinka, as there are certain matters I wish to take up with her.'

'I shall seek her out at once,' called the hetman over his shoulder.

Several minutes later there was a creaking of the great pulley; the ladder was lowered at the end of the rope which supported it. Looking over the side, Cugel saw that the cushions were about to be raised. The heavy rope supporting the ladder rattled through the pulley, bringing up a light line – hardly more than a stout cord – and on this cord the cushions were raised. Cugel inspected them with disapproval; they were old and dusty, and not at all of the quality he had envisioned. Most certainly he would insist upon furnishings superior to this! Possibly the hetman intended these merely as a stop-gap until cushions of the requisite elegance could be provided. Cugel nodded: this was obviously the situation.

He looked around the horizon. Magnatz was nowhere to be seen. He swung his arms once or twice, paced back and forth, and went to look down at the plaza, where he expected to find artisans assembling the appurtenances he had ordered. But there was no such activity; the townspeople appeared to be going about their usual affairs. Cugel shrugged, and went to make another inspection of the horizon. As before, Magnatz was invisible.

Once more he surveyed the plaza. He frowned, squinted: was that his spouse Marlinka walking past in the company of a young man? He focused the optical device upon the supple shape: it was Marlinka indeed, and the young man who clasped her elbow with insolent intimacy

98

was the huntsman to whom she had at one time affianced. Cugel clamped his jaw in outrage. This of behavior could not continue! When Marlinka sented herself, he would speak emphatically upon ie subject.

The sun reached zenith; the cord quivered. Looking over the side Cugel saw that his noon repast was being hoisted in a basket, and he clapped his hands in anticipation. But the basket, when he lifted the cloth, contained only a half-loaf of bread, a chunk of tough meat and a flask of thin wine. Cugel stared at the sorry fare in shock, and decided to descend on the moment to set matters straight. He cleared his throat and called down for the ladder. No one appeared to hear him. He called more loudly. One or two of the folk looked up in mild curiosity, and passed on about their business. Cugel jerked angrily at the cord and hauled it over the pulley, but no heavy rope appeared nor a rope ladder. The light line was an endless loop, capable of supporting approximately the weight of a basket of food.

Thoughtfully Cugel sat back, and assessed the situation. Then, directing the optical device once more upon the plaza, he searched for the hetman, the one man to whom he might turn for satisfaction.

Late in the afternoon, Cugel chanced to observe the door to the tavern, just as the hetman came staggering forth, obviously much elevated by wine. Cugel called peremptorily down; the hetman stopped short, looked about for the source of the voice, shook his head in perplexity and continued across the plaza.

The sun slanted across Lake Vull; the whirlpools were spirals of maroon and black. Cugel's supper arrived: a dish of boiled leeks and a bowl of porridge. He inspected it with small interest, then went to the side of the cupola. 'Send up the ladder!' he called. 'Darkness omes! In the absence of light, it is futile to watch for Magnatz or anyone else!'

As before, his remarks passed unheeded. Firx suddenly seemed to take cognizance of the situation and visited several sharp twinges upon Cugel's vitals.

Cugel passed a fitful night. As merrymakers left the tavern Cugel called to them and made representations regarding his plight, but he might as well have saved his breath.

The sun appeared over the mountains. Cugel's morning meal was of fair quality, but by no means up to the standard described by Hylam Wiskode, the double-tongued hetman of Vull. In a rage, Cugel bellowed orders to those below, but was ignored. He drew a deep breath: it seemed then that he was cast upon his own resources. But what of this? Was he Cugel the Clever for nothing? And he considered various means for descending the tower.

The line by which his food ascended was far too light. If doubled and redoubled so that it bore his weight, it would yield, at most, a quarter of the distance to the ground. His clothes and leathers, if torn and knotted, might provide another twenty feet, leaving him dangling in mid-air. The stem of the tower provided no foothold. With appropriate tools and sufficient time he might be able to chisel a staircase down the outside of the tower, or even chip away the tower in its entirety, eventually reducing it to a short stump from which he might leap to earth. . . . The project was not feasible. Cugel slumped on the cushions in despair. Everything was now clear. He had been fooled. He was a prisoner. How long had the previous Watchman remained at his post? Sixty years? The prospect was by no means cheerful.

Firx, of like opinion, jabbed furiously with barb and prong, adding to Cugel's woes.

So passed days and nights. Cugel brooded long and darkly, and contemplated the folk of Vull with great revulsion. On occasion he considered ringing the great gong, as his predecessor had been driven to do – but, recalling the penalty, he restrained himself.

Cugel became familiar with every aspect of town, lake and landscape. In the morning heavy mists covered the lake; after two hours a breeze thrust them aside. The whirlpools sucked and groaned, swinging here and there, and the fishermen of Vull ventured hardly more than the length of their boats off-shore. Cugel grew to recognize all the villagers, and learned the personal habits of each. Marlinka, his perfidious spouse, crossed the plaza often, but seldom if ever thought to turn her glance upward. Cugel marked well the cottage where she lived and gave it constant surveillance through the optical device. If she dallied with the young huntsman, her discretion was remarkable, and Cugel's dark suspicions were never documented.

The food failed to improve in quality and not infrequently was forgotten altogether. Firx was persistently acrimonious, and Cugel paced the confines of the cupola with ever more frantic strides. Shortly after sundown, after a particularly agonizing admonishment by Firx, Cugel stopped short in his tracks. To descend the tower was a matter of simplicity! Why had he delayed so long? Cugel the Clever indeed!

He ripped into strips every fragment of cloth the cupola provided, and from the yield plaited a rope twenty feet long. Now he must wait till the town grew quiet: yet an hour or two.

Firx assailed him once more, and Cugel cried out. 'Peace, scorpion, tonight we escape this turret! Your acts are redundant!'

Firx gave over his demonstration, and Cugel went to

investigate the plaza. The night was cool and misty: ideal for his purposes, and the folk of Vull were early to bed.

Cugel cautiously raised the line on which his food was hoisted; doubled, redoubled and redoubled it again and so produced a cable amply strong to support him. He tied a loop on one end, and made the other fast to the pulley. After one last look around the horizon, he lowered himself over the side. He descended to the end of the cable, thrust himself into the loop and sat swaying some four hundred feet above the plaza. To one end of his twenty-foot rope he tied his shoe for a weight, and after several casts, flung a loop around the stem of the column, and pulled himself close. With infinite caution he slipped himself free and, using the loop around the column as a brake, slid slowly to the ground. He took himself quickly into the shadows and donned his shoes. Just as he rose to his feet the door to the tavern swung open and out reeled Hylam Wiskode, much the worse for drink. Cugel grinned unpleasantly and followed the staggering hetman into a side-street.

A single blow on the back of the head was enough; the hetman toppled into a ditch. Cugel was instantly upon him, and with deft fingers took his keys. Going now to the public repository, he opened the door, slipped inside and filled a sack with gems, coins, flasks of costly essences, relics, and the like.

Returning to the street, Cugel carried the sack to a dock beside the lake, where he hid it under a net. Now he proceeded to the cottage of his spouse Marlinka. Prowling beside the wall, he came to an open window, and stepping through found himself in her chamber.

She was awakened by his hands at her throat. When she tried to scream he cut off her wind. 'It is I,' he hissed, 'Cugel, your spouse! Arise and come with me. Your first sound will be your last!'

In great terror, the girl obeyed. At Cugel's order she threw a cloak about her shoulders and clasped sandals upon her feet. 'Where are we going?' she whispered in a tremulous voice.

'No matter. Come now – through the window. Make not a sound!'

Standing outside in the dark, Marlinka cast a horror-stricken glance toward the tower. 'Who is on watch? Who guards Vull from Magnatz?'

'No one is on watch,' said Cugel. 'The tower is empty!'

Her knees gave way; she sagged to the ground. 'Up!' said Cugel. 'Up! We must proceed!'

'But no one is on watch! This voids the spell the sorcerer cast upon Magnatz, who swore to return when vigilance ceased!'

Cugel lifted the girl to her feet. 'This is no concern of mine; I disclaim responsibility. Did you not seek to fool and victimize me? Where were my cushions? Where was the fine food? And my spouse – where were you?'

The girl wept into her hands, and Cugel led her to the dock. He pulled close a fisherman's boat, ordered her aboard, threw in his loot.

Untying the boat, he shipped oars and rowed out upon the lake. Marlinka was aghast. 'The whirlpools will drown us! Have you lost your reason?'

'Not at all! I have studied the whirlpools with care and know precisely the range of each.'

Out upon the face of the lake moved Cugel, counting each stroke of his oars, and watching the stars. 'Two hundred paces east . . . a hundred paces north . . . two hundred paces east . . . fifty paces south . . .'

So Cugel rowed while to right and left of them sounded the suck of whirling water. But the mist had gathered to blot out the stars and Cugel was forced to throw out the anchor. 'This is well enough,' he said. 'We are safe now, and there is much that lies between us.'

The girl shrank to her end of the boat. Cugel stepped astern and joined her. 'Here I am, your spouse! Are you not overjoyed that finally we are alone? My chamber at the inn was far more comfortable, but this boat will suffice.'

'No,' she whimpered. 'Do not touch me! The ceremony was meaningless, a trick to persuade you to serve as Watchman.'

'For three-score years perhaps, until I rang the gong from utter desperation?'

'It is not my doing! I am guilty only of merriment! But what will become of Vull? No one watches, and the spell is broken!'

'So much the worse for the faithless folk of Vull! They have lost their treasure, their most beautiful maiden, and when day breaks Magnatz will march upon them.'

Marlinka uttered a poignant cry, which was muffled in the mist. 'Never speak that cursed name!'

'Why not? I shall shout it across the water! I will inform Magnatz that the spell is gone, that now he may come for his revenge!'

'No, no, indeed not!'

'Then you must behave toward me as I expect.'

Weeping, the girl obeyed, and at last a wan red light filtering through the mist signaled dawn. Cugel stood up in the boat, but all landmarks were yet concealed.

Another hour passed; the sun was now aloft. The folk of Vull would discover that their Watchman was gone, and with him their treasure. Cugel chuckled, and now a breeze lifted the mists, revealing the landmarks he had memorized. He leapt to the bow and hauled on the anchor line, but to his annoyance the anchor had fouled itself.

He jerked, strained, and the line gave a trifle. Cugel pulled with all his strength. From below came a great bubbling. 'A whirlpool!' cried Marlinka in terror.

'No whirlpool here,' panted Cugel, and jerked once more. The line seemed to relax and Cugel hauled in the rope. Looking over the side, he found himself staring into an enormous pale face. The anchor had caught in a nostril. As he looked the eyes blinked open.

Cugel threw away the line, leapt for the oars and frantically rowed for the southern shore.

A hand as large as a house raised from the water, groping. Marlinka screamed. There was a great turbulence, a prodigious surge of water which flung the boat toward the shore like a chip, and Magnatz sat up in the center of Lake Vull.

From the village came the sound of the warning gong, a frenzied clanging.

Magnatz heaved himself to his knees, water and muck draining from his vast body. The anchor which had pierced his nostril still hung in place, and a thick black fluid issued from the wound. He raised a great arm and slapped petulantly at the boat. The impact threw up a wall of foam which engulfed the boat, spilled treasure, Cugel and the girl toppling through the dark depths of the lake.

Cugel kicked and thrust, and propelled himself to the seething surface. Magnatz had gained his feet and was looking toward Vull.

Cugel swam to the beach and staggered ashore. Marlinka had drowned, and was nowhere to be seen. Across the lake Magnatz was wading slowly toward the village.

Cugel waited no longer. He turned and ran with all speed up the mountainside.

CHAPTER FOUR

The Sorcerer Pharesm

The mountains were behind: the dark defiles, the tarns, the echoing stone heights – all now a sooty bulk to the north. For a time Cugel wandered a region of low rounded hills the color and texture of old wood, with groves of blue-black trees dense along the ridges, then came upon a faint trail which took him south by long swings and slants, and at last broke out over a vast dim plain. A half-mile to the right rose a line of tall cliffs, which instantly attracted his attention, bringing him a haunting pang of *déjà-vu*. He stared mystified. At some time in the past he had known these cliffs: how? when? His memory provided no response.

He settled himself upon a low lichen-covered rock to rest, but now Firx became impatient and inflicted a stimulating pang. Cugel leapt to his feet, groaning with weariness and shaking his fist to the southwest, the presumable direction of Almery. 'Iucounu, Iucounu! If I could repay a tenth of your offenses, the world would think me harsh!'

He set off down the trail, under the cliffs which had affected him with such poignant but impossible recollections. Far below spread the plain, filling three-quarters of the horizon with colors much like those of the lichened rock Cugel had just departed: black patches of woodland: a gray crumble where ruins filled an entire valley; nondescript streaks of gray-green, lavender, gray-brown; the leaden glint of two great rivers disappearing into the haze of distance.

Cugel's brief rest had only served to stiffen his joints; he limped, and the pouch chafed his hip. Even more distressing was the hunger gripping his belly. Another tally against Iucounu! True, the Laughing Magician had furnished an amulet converting such normally inedible substances as grass, wood, horn, hair, humus and the like into a nutritious paste. Unfortunately – and this was a measure of Iucounu's mordant humor – the paste retained the flavor of the native substance, and during his passage of the mountains Cugel had tasted little better than spurge, cullion, blackwort, oak-twigs and galls, and on one occasion, when all else had failed, certain refuse discovered in the cave of a bearded thawn. Cugel had eaten only minimally; his long spare frame had become gaunt; his cheekbones protruded like sponsons; the black eyebrows which once had crooked so jauntily now lay flat and dispirited. Truly, truly, Iucounu had much to answer for! And Cugel, as he proceeded, debated the exact quality of revenge he would take if ever he found his way back to Almery.

The trail swung down upon a wide stony flat where the wind had carved a thousand grotesque figures. Surveying the area, Cugel thought to perceive regularity among the eroded shapes, and halted to rub his long chin in appraisal. The pattern displayed an extreme subtlety – so subtle indeed that Cugel wondered if it had not been projected by his own mind. Moving closer, he discerned further complexities, and elaborations upon complexities: twists, spires, volutes; disks, saddles, wrenched spheres; torsons and flexions; spindles, cardioids, lanciform pinnacles: the most laborious, painstaking and intricate rock-carving conceivable, manifestly no random effort of the elements. Cugel frowned in perplexity, unable to imangine a motive for so complex an undertaking.

He went on and a moment later heard voices together with the clank of tools. He stopped short, listened cautiously, then proceeded to come upon a gang of about fifty men ranging in stature from three inches to well over twelve feet. Cugel approached on tentative feet, but after a glance the workers paid him no heed, continuing to chisel, grind, scrape, probe and polish with dedicated zeal.

Cugel watched for several minutes, then approached the overseer, a man three feet in height who stood at a lectern consulting the plans spread before him, comparing them to the work in progress by means of an ingenious optical device. He appeared to note everything at once, calling instructions, chiding, exhorting against error, instructing the least deft in the use of their tools. To exemplify his remarks he used a wonderfully extensible forefinger, which reached forth thirty feet to tap at a section of rock, to scratch a quick diagram, then as swiftly retract.

The foreman drew back a pace or two, temporarily satisfied with the work in progress, and Cugel came forward. 'What intricate effort is this and what is its object?'

'The work is as you see,' replied the foreman in a voice of penetrating compass. 'From natural rock we produce specified shapes, at the behest of the sorcerer Pharesm . . . Now then! Now then!' The cry was addressed to a man three feet taller than Cugel, who had been striking the stone with a pointed maul. 'I detect overconfidence!' The forefinger shot forth. 'Use great care at this juncture; note how the rock tends to cleave? Strike here a blow of the sixth intensity at the vertical, using a semi-clenched grip; at this point a fourth-intensity blow groin-wise; then employ a quarter-gauge bant-iron to remove the swange.'

With the work once more going correctly, he fell to studying his plans, shaking his head with a frown of dissatisfaction. 'Much too slow! The craftsmen toil as if in a drugged torpor, or else display a mulish stupidity. Only yesterday Dadio Fessadil, he of three ells with the green kerchief yonder, used a nineteen-gauge freezing-bar to groove the bead of a small inverted quatrefoil.'

Cugel shook his head in surprise, as if never had he heard of so egregious a blunder. And he asked: 'What prompts this inordinate rock-hewing?'

'I cannot say,' replied the foreman. 'The work has been in progress three hundred and eighteen years, but during this time Pharesm has never clarified his motives. They must be pointed and definite, for he makes a daily inspection and is quick to indicate errors.' Here he turned aside to consult with a man as tall as Cugel's knee, who voiced uncertainty as to the pitch of a certain volute. The foreman, consulting an index, resolved the matter; then he turned back to Cugel, this time with an air of frank appraisal.

'You appear both astute and deft; would you care to take employment? We lack several craftsmen of the half-ell category, or, if you prefer more forceful manifestations, we can nicely use an apprentice stone-breaker of sixteen-ells. Your stature is adjusted in either direction, and there is identical scope for advancement. As you see, I am a man of four ells. I reached the position of Stirker in one year, Molder of Forms in three, Assistant Chade in ten, and I have now served as Chief Chade for nineteen years. My predecessor was of two ells, and the Chief Chade before him was a ten-ell man.' He went on to enumerate advantages of the work, which included sustenance, shelter, narcotics of choice, nympharium privileges, a stipend starting at ten terces a day, various other benefits including Pharesm's services as diviner and exorciser. 'Additionally, Pharesm maintains a conservatory where all may enrich their intellects. I myself take instruction in Insect Identification, the Heraldry of the Kings of Old Gomaz, Unison Chanting, Practical Catalepsy and Orthodox Doctrine. You will never find master more generous than Pharesm the Sorcerer!'

109

Cugel restrained a smile for the Chief Chade's enthusiasm; still, his stomach was roiling with hunger and he did not reject the proffer out of hand. 'I have never before considered such a career,' he said. 'You cite advantages of which I was unaware.'

'True; they are not generally known.'

'I cannot immediately say yes or no. It is a decision of consequence which I feel I should consider in all its aspects.'

The Chief Chade gave a nod of profound agreement. 'We encourage deliberation in our craftsmen, when every stroke must achieve the desired effect. To repair an inaccuracy of as much as a fingernail's width the entire block must be removed, and a new block fitted into the socket of the old, whereupon all begins anew. Until the work has reached its previous stage nympharium privileges are denied to all. Hence, we wish no opportunistic or impulsive newcomers to the group.'

Firx, suddenly apprehending that Cugel proposed a delay, made representations of a most agonizing nature. Clasping his abdomen, Cugel took himself aside and, while the Chief Chade watched in perplexity, argued heatedly with Firx. 'How may I proceed without sustenance?' Firx's response was an incisive motion of the barbs. 'Impossible!' exclaimed Cugel. 'The amulet of Iucounu theoretically suffices, but I can stomach no more spurge; remember, if I fall dead in the trail, you will never rejoin your comrade in Iucounu's vats!'

Firx saw the justice of the argument and reluctantly became quiet. Cugel returned to the lectern, where the Chief Chade had been distracted by the discovery of a large tourmaline opposing the flow of a certain complicated helix. Finally Cugel was able to engage his attention. 'While I weigh the proffer of employment and the conflicting advantages of diminution versus elongation, I will need a couch on which to recline. I also wish to test the perquisites you describe, perhaps for the period of a day or more.'

'Your prudence is commendable,' declared the Chief Chade. 'The folk of today tend to commit themselves rashly to courses they later regret. It was not so in my youth, when sobriety and discretion prevailed. I will arrange for your admission into the compound, where you may verify each of my assertions. You will find Pharesm stern but just, and only the man who hacks the rock willynilly has cause to complain. But observe! here is Pharesm the Sorcerer on his daily inspection!'

Up the trail came a man of imposing stature wearing a voluminous white robe. His countenance was benign; his hair was like yellow down; his eyes were turned upward as if rapt in the contemplation of an ineffable sublimity. His arms were sedately folded, and he moved without motion of his legs. The workers, doffing their caps and bowing in unison, chanted a respectful salute, to which Pharesm returned an inclination of the head. Spying Cugel, he paused, made a swift survey of the work so far accomplished, then glided without haste to the lectern.

'All appears reasonably exact,' he told the Chief Chade. 'I believe the polish on the underside of Epi-projection 56-16 is uneven and I detect a minute chip on the secondary cinctor of the nineteenth spire. Neither circumstance seems of major import and I recommend no disciplinary action.'

'The deficiencies shall be repaired and the careless artisans reprimanded: this at the very least!' exclaimed the Chief Chade in an angry passion. 'Now I wish to introduce a possible recruit to our work-force. He claims no experience at the trade, and will deliberate before deciding to join our group. If he so elects, I envision the usual period as rubblegatherer, before he is entrusted with tool-sharpening and preliminary excavation.'

'Yes; this would accord with our usual practice. However. . .' Pharesm glided effortlessly forward, took Cugel's left hand and performed a swift divination upon the fingernails. His bland countenance became sober. 'I see contradictions of four varieties. Still it is clear that your optimum bent lies elsewhere than in the hewing and shaping of rock. I advise that you seek another and more compatible employment.'

'Well spoken!' cried the Chief Chade. 'Pharesm the Sorcerer demonstrates his infallible altruism! In order that I do not fall short of the mark I hereby withdraw my proffer of employment! Since no purpose can now be served by reclining upon a couch or testing the perquisites, you need waste no more irreplaceable time.'

Cugel made a sour face. 'So casual a divination might well be inaccurate.'

The Chief Chade extended his forefinger thirty feet vertically in outraged remonstrance, but Pharesm gave a placid nod. 'This is quite correct, and I will gladly perform a more comprehensive divination, though the process requires six to eight hours.'

'So long?' asked Cugel in astonishment.

'This is the barest minimum. First you are swathed head to foot in the intestines of fresh-killed owls, then immersed in a warm bath containing a number of secret organic substances. I must, of course, char the small toe of your left foot, and dilate your nose sufficiently to admit an explorer beetle, that he may study the conduits leading to and from your sensorium. But let us return to my divinatory, that we may commence the process in good time.'

Cugel pulled at his chin, torn this way and that. Finally he said, 'I am a cautious man, and must ponder even the advisability of undertaking such a divination; hence, I will require several days of calm and meditative somnolence.

Your compound and the adjacent nympharium appear to afford the conditions requisite to such a state; hence—'

Pharesm indulgently shook his head. 'Caution, like any other virtue, can be carried to an extreme. The divination must proceed at once.'

Cugel attempted to argue further but Pharesm was adamant, and presently glided off down the trail.

Cugel, disconsolately went to the side, considering first this stratagem, then that. The sun neared the zenith, and the workmen began to speculate as to the nature of the viands to be served for their mid-day meal. At last the Chief Chade signaled; all put down their tools and gathered about the cart which contained the repast.

Cugel jocularly called out that he might be persuaded to share the meal, but the Chief Chade would not hear of it. 'As in all of Pharesm's activities, an exactitude of consequence must prevail. It is an unthinkable discrepancy that fifty-four men should consume the food intended for fifty-three.'

Cugel could contrive no apposite reply, and sat in silence while the rock-hewers munched at meat pies, cheeses and salt fish. All ignored him save for one, a quarter-ell man whose generosity far exceeded his stature, and who undertook to reserve for Cugel a certain portion of his food. Cugel replied that he was not at all hungry, and rising to his feet wandered off through the project, hoping to discover some forgotten cache of food.

He prowled here and there, but the rubble-gatherers had removed every trace of substance extraneous to the pattern. With appetite unassuaged Cugel arrived at the center of the work where, sprawled on a carved disk, he spied a most peculiar creature: essentially a gelatinous globe swimming with luminous particles from which a number of transparent tubes or tentacles dwindled away to nothing. Cugel bent to examine the creature, which pulsed with a slow internal rhythm. He prodded it with his finger, and bright little flickers rippled away from the point of contact. Interesting: a creature of unique capabilities!

Removing a pin from his garments, he prodded a tentacle, which emitted a peevish pulse of light, while the golden flecks in its substance surged back and forth. More intrigued that ever, Cugel hitched himself close, and gave himself to experimentation, probing here and there, watching the angry flickers and sparkles with great amusement.

A new thought occurred to Cugel. The creature displayed qualities reminiscent of both coelenterate and echinoderm. A terrene nudibranch? A mollusc deprived of its shell? More importantly, was the creature edible?

Cugel brought forth his amulet and applied it to the central globe and to each of the tentacles. He heard neither chime nor buzz: the creature was non-poisonous. He unsheathed his knife and sought to excise one of the tentacles, but found the substance too resilient and tough to be cut. There was a brazier nearby, kept aglow for forging and sharpening the workers' tools. He lifted the creature by two of its tentacles, carried it to the brazier and arranged it over the fire. He toasted it carefully and, when he deemed it sufficiently cooked, sought to eat it. Finally, after various undignified efforts, he crammed the entire creature down his throat, finding it without taste or sensible nutritive volume.

The stone-carvers were returning to their work. With a significant glance for the foreman Cugel set off down the trail.

Not far distant was the dwelling of Pharesm the Sorcerer: a long low building of melted rock surmounted by eight oddly shaped domes of copper, mica and bright blue glass. Pharesm himself sat at leisure before the dwel-

114

ling, surveying the valley with a serene and all-inclusive magnanimity. He held up a hand in calm salute. 'I wish you pleasant travels and success in all future endeavors.'

'The sentiment is naturally valued,' said Cugel with some bitterness. 'You might however have rendered a more meaningful service by extending a share of your noon meal.'

Pharesm's placid benevolence was as before. 'This would have been an act of mistaken altruism. Too fulsome a generosity corrupts the recipient and stultifies his resource.'

Cugel gave a bitter laugh. 'I am a man of iron principle, and I will not complain, even though, lacking any better fare, I was forced to devour a great transparent insect which I found at the heart of your rock-carving.'

Pharesm swung about with a suddenly intent expression. 'A great transparent insect, you say?'

'Insect, epiphyte, mollusc – who knows? It resembled no creature I have yet seen, and its flavor even after carefully grilling at the brazier, was not distinctive.'

Pharesm floated seven feet into the air, to turn the full power of his gaze down at Cugel. He spoke in a low harsh voice: 'Describe this creature in detail!'

Wondering at Pharesm's severity, Cugel obeyed. 'It was thus and thus as to dimension.' He indicated with his hands. 'In color it was a gelatinous transparency shot with numberless golden specks. These flickered and pulsed when the creature was disturbed. The tentacles seemed to grow flimsy and disappear rather than terminate. The creature evinced a certain sullen determination, and ingestion proved difficult.'

Pharesm clutched at his head, hooking his fingers into the yellow down of his hair. He rolled his eyes upward and uttered a tragic cry. 'Ah! Five hundred years I have toiled to entice this creature, despairing, doubting, brooding by

115

night, yet never abandoning hope that my calculations were accurate and my great talisman cogent. Then, when finally it appears, you fall upon it for no other reason than to sate your repulsive gluttony!'

Cugel, somewhat daunted by Pharesm's wrath, asserted his absence of malicious intent. Pharesm would not be mollified. He pointed out that Cugel had committed trespass and hence had forfeited the option of pleading innocence. 'Your very existence is mischief, compounded by bringing the unpleasant fact to my notice. Benevolence prompted me to forebearance, which now I perceive for a grave mistake.'

'In this case,' stated Cugel with dignity, 'I will depart your presence at once. I wish you good fortune for the balance of the day, and now, farewell.'

'Not so fast,' said Pharesm in the coldest of voices. 'Exactitude has been disturbed; the wrong which has been committed demands a counter-act to validate the Law of Equipoise. I can define the gravity of your act in this manner: should I explode you on this instant into the most minute of your parts the atonement would measure one ten-millionth of your offense. A more stringent re-tribution becomes necessary.'

Cugel spoke in great distress. 'I understand that an act of consequence was performed, but remember! my participation was basically casual. I categorically declare first my absolute innocence, second my lack of criminal intent, and third my effusive apologies. And now, since I have many leagues to travel, I will—'

Pharesm made a peremptory gesture. Cugel fell silent. Pharesm drew a deep breath. 'You fail to understand the calamity you have visited upon me. I will explain, so that you may not be astounded by the rigors which await you. As I have adumbrated, the arrival of the creature was the culmination of my great effort. I determined its nature

116

through a perusal of forty-two thousand librams, all written in cryptic language: a task requiring a hundred years. During a second hundred years I evolved a pattern to draw it in upon itself and prepared exact specification. Next I assembled stone-cutters, and across a period of three hundred years gave solid form to my pattern. Since like subsumes like, the variates and inter-congeles create a suprapullulation of all areas, qualities and intervals into a crystorrhoid whorl, eventually exciting the ponentiation of a pro-ubietal chute. Today occurred the concatenation; the "creature" as you call it, pervolved upon itself; in your idiotic malice you devoured it.'

Cugel, with a trace of haughtiness, pointed out that the 'idiotic malice' to which the distraught sorcerer referred was in actuality simple hunger. 'In any event, what is so extraordinary about the "creature"? Others equally ugly may be found in the net of any fisherman.'

Pharesm drew himself to his full height, glared down at Cugel. 'The "creature",' he said in a grating voice, 'is TOTALITY. The central globe is all of space, viewed from the inverse. The tubes are vortices into various eras, and what terrible acts you have accomplished with your prodding and poking, your boiling and chewing, are impossible to imagine!'

'What of the effects of digestion?' inquired Cugel delicately. 'Will the various components of space, time and existence retain their identity after passing the length of my inner tract?'

'Bah. The concept is jejune. Enough to say that you have wreaked damage and created a serious tension in the ontological fabric. Inexorably you are required to restore equilibrium.'

Cugel held out his hands. 'Is it not possible a mistake has been made? That the "creature" was no more than pseudo-TOTALITY? Or is it conceivable that the "creature" may by some means be lured forth once more?'

117

'The first two theories are untenable. As to the last, I must confess that certain frantic expedients have been forming in my mind.' Pharesm made a sign, and Cugel's feet became attached to the soil. 'I must go to my divinatory and learn the full significance of the distressing events. In due course I will return.'

'At which time I will be feeble with hunger,' said Cugel fretfully. 'Indeed, a crust of bread and a bite of cheese would have averted all the events for which I am now reproached.'

'Silence!' thundered Pharesm. 'Do not forget that your penalty remains to be fixed; it is the height of impudent recklessness to hector a person already struggling to maintain his judicious calm!'

'Allow me to say this much,' replied Cugel. 'If you return from your divining to find me dead and desiccated here on the path, you will have wasted much time fixing upon a penalty.'

'The restoration of vitality is a small task,' said Pharesm. 'A variety of deaths by contrasting processes may well enter into your judgement.' He started toward his divinatory, then turned back and made an impatient gesture. 'Come, it is easier to feed you than return to the road.'

Cugel's feet were once more free and he followed Pharesm through a wide arch into the divinatory. In a broad room with splayed gray walls, illuminated by three-colored polyhedra, Cugel devoured the food Pharesm caused to appear. Meanwhile Pharesm secluded himself in his work-room, where he occupied himself with his divinations. As time passed Cugel grew restless, and on three occasions approached the arched entrance. On each occasion, a Presentment came to deter him, first in the shape of a leaping ghoul, next as a zig-zag blaze of energy, and finally as a score of glittering purple wasps.

Discouraged, Cugel went to a bench, and sat waiting with elbows on long legs, hands under his chin.

Pharesm at last reappeared, his robe wrinkled, the fine yellow down of his hair disordered into a multitude of small spikes. Cugel slowly rose to his feet.

'I have learned the whereabouts of TOTALITY,' said Pharesm, in a voice like the strokes of a great gong. 'In indignation, removing itself from your stomach, it has recoiled a million years into the past.'

Cugel gave his head a solemn shake. 'Allow me to offer my sympathy, and my counsel, which is: never despair! Perhaps the "creature" will choose to pass this way again.'

'An end to your chatter! TOTALITY must be recovered. Come.'

Cugel reluctantly followed Pharesm into a small room walled with blue tile, roofed with a tall cupola of blue and orange glass. Pharesm pointed to a black disk at the center of the floor. 'Stand there.'

Cugel glumly obeyed. 'In a certain sense, I feel that—'

'Silence!' Pharesm came forward. 'Notice this object!' He displayed an ivory sphere the size of two fists, carved in exceedingly fine detail. 'Here you see the pattern from which my great work is derived. It expresses the symbolic significance of NULLITY to which TOTALITY must necessarily attach itself, by Kratinjae's Second Law of Cryptorrhoid Affinities, with which you are possibly familiar.'

'Not in every aspect,' said Cugel. 'But may I ask your intentions?'

Pharesm's mouth moved in a cool smile. 'I am about to attempt one of the most cogent spells ever evolved: a spell so fractious, harsh, and coactive, that Phandaal, Ranking Sorcerer of Grand Motholam, barred its use. If I am able to control it, you will be propelled one million years into the past. There you will reside until you have accomplished your mission, when you may return.'

Cugel stepped quickly from the black disk. 'I am not the man for this mission, whatever it may be. I fervently urge the use of someone else!'

Pharesm ignored the expostulation. 'The mission of course, is to bring the symbol into contact with TOTALITY.' He brought forth a wad of tangled gray tissue. 'In order to facilitate your search, I endow you with this instrument which relates all possible vocables to every conceivable system of meaning.' He thrust the net into Cugel's ear, where it swiftly engaged itself with the nerve of consonant expression. 'Now,' said Pharesm, 'you need listen to a strange language for but three minutes when you become proficient in its use. And now, another article to enhance the prospect of success: this ring. Notice the jewel: should you approach to within a league of TOTALITY, darting lights within the gem will guide you. Is all clear?'

Cugel gave a reluctant nod. 'There is another matter to be considered. Assume that your calculations are incorrect and that TOTALITY has returned only nine hundred thousand years into the past: what then? Must I dwell out my life in this possibly barbarous era?'

Pharesm frowned in displeasure. 'Such a situation involves an error of ten percent. My system of reckoning seldom admits of deviation greater than one percent.'

Cugel began to make calculations, but now Pharesm signaled to the black disk. 'Back! And do not again move hence, or you will be the worse for it!'

Sweat oozing from his glands, knees quivering and sagging, Cugel returned to the place designated.

Pharesm retreated to the far end of the room, where he stepped into a coil of gold tubing, which sprang spiraling up to clasp his body. From a desk he took four black disks,

120

which he began to shuffle and juggle with such fantastic dexterity that they blurred in Cugel's sight. Pharesm at last flung the disks away; spinning and wheeling, they hung in the air, gradually drifting toward Cugel.

Pharesm next took up a white tube, pressed it tight against his lips and spoke an incantation. The tube swelled and bulged into a great globe. Pharesm twisted the end shut and, shouting a thunderous spell, hurled the globe at the spinning disks, and all exploded. Cugel was surrounded, seized, jerked in all directions outward, compressed with equal vehemence: the net result, a thrust in a direction contrary to all, with an impetus equivalent to the tide of a million years. Among dazzling lights and distorted visions Cugel was transported beyond his consciousness.

Cugel awoke in a glare of orange-gold sunlight, of a radiance he had never known before. He lay on his back looking up into a sky of warm blue, of lighter tone and softer texture than the indigo sky of his own time.

He tested arms and legs and, finding no damage, sat upright, then slowly rose to his feet, blinking in the unfamiliar radiance.

The topography had changed only slightly. The mountains to the north were taller and of harsher texture, and Cugel could not identify the way he had come (or, more properly, the way he would come). The site of Pharesm's project was now a low forest of feather-light green trees, on which hung clusters of red berries. The valley was as before, though the rivers flowed by different courses and three great cities were visible at varying distances. The air drifting up from the valley carried a strange tart fragrance mingled with an antique exhalation of molder and must, and it seemed to Cugel that a peculiar melancholy hung in the air; in fact, he thought to hear

121

music: a slow plaintive melody, so sad as to bring tears to his eyes. He searched for the source of the music, but it faded and disappeared even as he sought it, and only when he ceased to listen did it return.

For the first time Cugel looked toward the cliffs which rose to the west, and now the sense of *déja-vu* was stronger than ever. Cugel pulled at his chin in puzzlement. The time was a million years previous to that other occasion on which he had seen the cliffs, and hence, by definition, must be the first. But it was also the second time, for he well remembered his initial experience of the cliffs. On the other hand, the logic of time could not be contravened, and by such reckoning this view preceded the other. A paradox, thought Cugel: a puzzle indeed! Which experience had provided the background to the poignant sense of familiarity he had felt on both occasions?

. . . Cugel dismissed the subject as unprofitable and was starting to turn away when movement caught his eye. He looked back up the face of the cliffs, and the air was suddenly full and rich with the music he had heard before, music of anguish and exalted despair. Cugel stared in wonder. A great winged creature wearing white robes flapped on high along the face of the cliff. The wings were long, ribbed with black chitin, sheathed with gray membrane. Cugel watched in awe as it swooped into a cave high up in the face of the cliff.

A gong tolled, from a direction Cugel could not determine. Overtones shuddered across the air, and when they died the unheard music became almost audible. From far over the valley came one of the Winged Beings, carrying a human form, of what age and sex Cugel could not determine. It hovered beside the cliff and dropped its burden. Cugel thought to hear a faint cry and the music was sad, stately, sonorous. The body seemed to fall slowly down the great height and struck at last at the base of the cliff. The Winged Being, after dropping the body, glided to a high ledge, where it folded its wings and stood like a man, staring over the valley.

Cugel shrank back behind a rock. Had he been seen? He could not be sure. He heaved a deep sigh. This sad golden world of the past was not to his liking; the sooner he could leave the better. He examined the ring which Pharesm had furnished, but the gem shone like dull glass, with none of the darting glitters which would point the direction to TOTALITY. It was as Cugel feared. Pharesm had erred in his calculations and Cugel could never return to his own time.

The sound of flapping wings caused him to look into the sky. He shrank back into such concealment as the rock offered. The music of woe swelled and sighed away, as in the light of the setting sun the winged creature hovered beside the cliff and dropped its victim. Then it landed on a ledge with a great flapping of wings and entered a cave.

Cugel rose to his feet and ran crouching down the path through the amber dusk.

The path presently entered a grove of trees, and here Cugel paused to catch his breath, after which he proceeded more circumspectly. He crossed a path of cultivated ground on which stood a vacant hut. Cugel considered it as shelter for the night, but thought to see a dark shape watching from the interior and passed it by.

The trail led away from the cliffs, across rolling downs, and just before the twilight gave way to night Cugel came to a village standing on the banks of a pond.

Cugel approached warily, but was encouraged by the signs of tidiness and good husbandry. In a park beside the pond stood a pavilion possibly intended for music, miming or declamation; surrounding the park were small narrow houses with high gables, the ridges of which were raised in decorative scallops. Opposite the pond was a larger building, with an ornate front of woven wood and enameled plaques of red, blue and yellow. Three tall gables served as its roof, the central ridge supporting an intricate carved panel, while those to either side bore a series of small spherical blue lamps. At the front was a wide pergola sheltering benches, tables and an open space, all illuminated by red and green firefans. Here townsfolk took their ease, inhaling incense and drinking wine, while youths and maidens cavorted in an eccentric high-kicking dance, to the music of pipers and a concertina.

Emboldened by the placidity of the scene, Cugel approached. The villagers were of a type he had never before encountered, of no great stature, with generally large heads and long restless arms. Their skin was a rich pumpkin orange; their eyes and teeth were black; their hair, likewise black, hung smoothly down beside the faces of the men to terminate in a fringe of blue beads, while the women wound their hair around white rings and pegs, to arrived at a coiffure of no small complexity. The features were heavy at jaw and cheek-bone; the long wide-spaced eyes drooped in a droll manner at the outer corners. The noses and ears were long and were under considerable muscular control, endowing the faces with great vivacity. The men wore flounced black kirtles, brown surcoats, headgear consisting of a wide black disk, a black cylinder, another lesser disk, surmounted by a gilded ball. The women wore black trousers, brown jackets with enameled disks at the naval, and at each buttock a simulated tail of green or red plumes, possibly an indication as to marital status.

Cugel stepped into the light of the fire-fans; instantly all talk ceased. Noses became rigid, eyes stared, ears twisted about in curiosity. Cugel smiled to left and right, waved his hands in a debonair all-inclusive greeting, and took a seat at an empty table.

There were mutters of astonishment at the various tables, too quiet to reach Cugel's ears. Presently one of the elders arose and approaching Cugel's table spoke a sentence, which Cugel found unintelligible, for with insufficient scope, Pharesm's mesh as yet failed to yield meaning. Cugel smiled politely, held wide his hands in a gesture of well-meaning helplessness. The elder spoke once more, in a rather sharper voice, and again Cugel indicated his inability to understand. The elder gave his ears a sharp disapproving jerk and turned away. Cugel signaled to the proprietor, pointed to the bread and wine on a nearby table and signified his desire that the same be brought to him.

The proprietor voiced a query which, for all its unintelligibility, Cugel was able to interpret. He brought forth a gold coin, and, satisfied, the proprietor turned away.

Conversation recommenced at the various tables and before long the vocables conveyed meaning to Cugel. When he had eaten and drunk, he rose to his feet and walked to the table of the elder who had first spoken to him, where he bowed respectfully. 'Do I have permission to join you at your table?'

'Certainly; if you are so inclined. Sit.' The elder indicated a seat. 'From your behaviour I assumed that you were not only deaf and dumb, but also guilty of mental retardation. It is now clear, at least, that you hear and speak.'

'I profess rationality as well,' said Cugel. 'As a traveler from afar, ignorant of your customs, I thought it best to watch quietly a few moments, lest in error I commit a solecism.'

'Ingenious but peculiar,' was the elder's comment. 'Still, your conduct offers no explicit contradiction to orthodoxy. May I inquire the urgency which brings you to Farwan?'

Cugel glanced at his ring; the crystal was dull and lifeless: TOTALITY was clearly elsewhere. 'My home-land is uncultured; I travel that I may learn the modes and styles of more civilized folk.'

'Indeed!' The elder mulled the matter over for a moment, and nodded in qualified approval. 'Your garments and physiognomy are of a type unfamiliar to me; where is this homeland of yours?'

'It lies in a region remote,' said Cugel, 'that never till this instant had I knowledge of the land of Farwan!'

The elder flattened his ears in surprise. 'What? Glorious Farwan, unknown? The great cities Impergos, Tharuwe, Rhaverjand – all unheard of? What of the illustrious Sembers? Surely the fame of the Sembers has reached you? They expelled the star-pirates; they brought the sea to the Land of Platforms; the splendor of Padara Palace is beyond description!'

Cugel sadly shook his head. 'No rumor of this ex-traordinary magnificence has come to my ears.'

The elder gave his nose a saturnine twitch. Cugel was clearly a dolt. He said shortly, 'Matters are as I state.'

'I doubt nothing,' said Cugel. 'In fact I admit to ignor-ance. But tell me more, for I may be forced to abide long in this region. For instance, what of the Winged Beings that reside in the cliff? What manner of creature are they?'

The elder pointed toward the sky. 'If you had the eyes of a nocturnal titvit you might note a dark moon which reels around the earth, and which cannot be seen except when it casts its shadow upon the sun. The Winged Beings are denizens of this dark world and their ultimate nature is unknown. They serve the Great God Yelisea in this fashion: whenever comes the time for man or woman to die, the Winged Beings are informed by a despairing signal from the dying person's norn. They thereupon descend upon the unfortunate and convey him to their caves which in actuality constitute a magic opening into the blessed land Byssom.'

Cugel leaned back, eyebrows raised in a somewhat quizzical arch. 'Indeed, indeed,' he said, in a voice which the elder found insufficiently earnest.

'There can be no doubt as to the truth of the facts as I have stated them. Orthodoxy derives from this axiomatic foundation, and the two systems are mutually reinforcing: hence each is doubly validated.'

Cugel frowned. 'The matter undoubtedly goes as you aver – but are the Winged Beings consistently accurate in their choice of victim?'

The elder rapped the table in annoyance. 'The doctrine is irrefutable, for those whom the Winged Beings take never survive, even when they appear in the best of health. Admittedly the fall upon the rocks conduces toward death, but it is the mercy of Yelisea which sees fit to grant a speedy extinction, rather than the duration of a possibly agonizing canker. The system is wholly beneficent. The Winged Beings summon only the moribund which are then thrust through the cliff into the blessed land Byssom. Occasionally a heretic argues otherwise and in this case – but I am sure that you share the orthodox view?'

'Wholeheartedly,' Cugel asserted. 'The tenets of your belief are demonstrably accurate.' And he drank deep of his wine. Even as he set down the goblet a murmur of music whispered through the air: a concord infinitely sweet, infinitely melancholy. All sitting under the pergola became silent – though Cugel was unsure that he in fact had heard music.

The elder huddled forward a trifle, and drank from his own goblet. Only then did he glance up. 'The Winged Beings are passing over even now.'

Cugel pulled thoughtfully at his chin. 'How does one protect himself from the Winged Beings?'

The question was ill-put; the elder glared, an act which included the curling forward of his ears. 'If a person is about to die, the Winged Beings appear. If not, he need have no fear.'

Cugel nodded several times. 'You have clarified my perplexity. Tomorrow – since you and I are manifestly in the best of health – let us walk up the hill and saunter back and forth near the cliff.'

'No,' said the elder, 'and for this reason: the atmosphere at such an elevation is insalubrious; a person is likely to inhale a noxious fume, which entails damage to the health.'

'I comprehend perfectly,' said Cugel. 'Shall we abandon this dismal topic? For the nonce we are alive and concealed to some extent by the vines which shroud the pergola. Let us eat and drink and watch the merrymaking. The youths of the village dance with great agility.'

The elder drained his goblet and rose to his feet. 'You may do as you please; as for me, it is time for my Ritual Abasement, this act being an integral part of our belief.'

'I will perform something of a like nature by and by,' said Cugel. 'I wish you the enjoyment of your rite.'

The elder departed the pergola and Cugel was left by himself. Presently certain youths, attracted by curiosity, joined him, and Cugel explained his presence once again, though with less emphasis upon the barbaric crudity of his native land, for several girls had joined the group, and Cugel was stimulated by their exotic coloring and the vivacity of their attitudes. Much wine was served and Cugel was persuaded to attempt the kicking, jumping local dance, which he performed without discredit.

The exercise broght him into close proximity with an especially beguiling girl, who announced her name to be Zhiaml Vraz. At the conclusion of the dance, she put her arm around his waist, conducted him back to the table, and settled herself upon his lap. This act of familiarity excited no apparent disapproval among the others of the group, and Cugel was emboldened further. 'I have not yet arranged for a bed-chamber; perhaps I should do so before the hour grows late.'

The girl signaled the innkeeper. 'Perhaps you have reserved a chamber for this chisel-faced stranger?'

'Indeed; I will display it for his approval.'

He took Cugel to a pleasant chamber on the ground floor, furnished with couch, commode, rug and lamp. On one wall hung a tapestry woven in purple and black; on another was a representation of a peculiarly ugly baby which seemed trapped or compressed in a transparent globe. The room suited Cugel; he announced as much to the innkeeper and returned to the pergola, where now the merrymakers were commencing to disperse. The girl Zhiaml Vraz yet remained, and she welcomed Cugel with a warmth which undid the last vestige of his caution. After another goblet of wine, he leaned close to her ear. 'Perhaps I am over-prompt; perhaps I overindulge my vanity; perhaps I contravene the normal decorum of the village – but is there reason why we should not repair to my chamber, and there amuse ourselves?'

'None whatever,' the girl said. 'I am unwed and until this time may conduct myself as I wish, for this is our custom.'

'Excellent,' said Cugel. 'Do you care to precede me, or walk discreetly to the rear?'

'We shall go together; there is no need for furtiveness!'

Together they went to the chamber and performed a number of erotic exercises, after which Cugel collapsed into a sleep of utter exhaustion, for his day had been taxing.

During the middle hours he awoke to find Zhiaml Vraz departed from the chamber, a fact which in his drowsiness caused him no distress and he once more returned to sleep.

The sound of the door angrily flung ajar aroused him; he sat up on the couch to find the sun not yet arisen, and a deputation led by the elder regarding him with horror and disgust.

The elder pointed a long quivering finger through the gloom. 'I thought to detect heretical opinion; now the fact is known! Notice: he sleeps with neither headcovering nor devotional salve on his chin. The girl Zhiaml Vraz reports that at no time in their congress did the villain call out for the approval of Yelisea!'

'Heresy beyond a doubt!' declared the others of the deputation.

'What else could be expect of an outlander?' asked the elder contemptuously. 'Look! even now he refuses to make the sacred sign.'

'I do not know the sacred sign!' Cugel expostulated. 'I know nothing of your rites! This is not heresy, it is simple ignorance!'

'I cannot believe this,' said the elder. 'Only last night I outlined the nature of orthodoxy.'

'The situation is grievous,' said another in a voice of portentous melancholy. 'Heresy exists only through putrefaction of the Lobe of Correctitude.'

'This is an incurable and fatal mortification,' stated another, no less dolefully.

'True! Alas, too true!' sighed one who stood by the door. 'Unfortunate man!'

'Come!' called the elder. 'We must deal with the matter at once.'

'Do not trouble yourself,' said Cugel. 'Allow me to dress myself and I will depart the village never to return.'

'To spread your detestable doctrine elsewhere? By no means!'

And now Cugel was seized and hauled naked from the chamber. Out across the park he was marched, and to the

130

pavilion at the center. Several of the group erected an enclosure formed of wooden posts on the platform of the pavilion and into this enclosure Cugel was thrust. 'What do you do?' he cried out. 'I wish no part of your rites!'

He was ignored, and stood peering between the interstices of the enclosure while certain villagers sent aloft a large balloon of green paper buoyed by hot air, carrying three green fire-fans below.

Dawn showed sallow in the west. The villagers, with all arranged to their satisfaction, withdrew to the edge of the park. Cugel attempted to climb from the enclosure, but the wooden rods were of such dimension and spacing as to allow him no grip.

The sky lightened; high above burnt the green fire-fans. Cugel, hunched and in goose-flesh from the morning chill, walked back and forth the length of the enclosure. He stopped short, as from afar came the haunting music. It grew louder, seeming to reach the very threshold of audibility. High in the sky appeared a Winged Being, white robes trailing and flapping. Down it settled, and Cugel's joints became limp and loose.

The Winged Being hovered over the enclosure, dropped, enfolded Cugel in its white robe and endeavored to bear him aloft. But Cugel had seized a bar of the enclosure and the Winged Being flapped in vain. The bar creaked, groaned, cracked. Cugel fought free of the stifling cloak and tore at the bar with hysterical strength; it snapped and splintered. Cugel seized a fragment and stabbed at the Winged Being. The sharp stick punctured the white cloak, and the Winged Being buffeted Cugel with a wing. Cugel seized one of the chitin ribs and with a mighty effort twisted it around backward, so that the substance cracked and broke and the wing hung torn. The Winged Being, aghast, gave a great bound which carried both it and Cugel out upon

131

the pavilion, and now it hopped through the village trailing its broken wing.

Cugel ran behind belaboring it with a cudgel he had seized up. He glimpsed the villagers staring in awe; their mouths were wide and wet, and they might have been screaming but he heard nothing. The Winged Being hopped faster, up the trail toward the cliff, with Cugel wielding the cudgel with all his strength. The golden sun rose over the far mountains; the Winged Being suddenly turned to face Cugel, and Cugel felt the glare of its eyes, though the visage, if such there was, was concealed beneath the hood of the cloak. Abashed and panting, Cugel stood back, and now it occurred to him that adjust he stood almost defenseless should others drop on him from on high. So now he shouted an imprecation at the creature and turned back to the village.

All had fled. The village was deserted. Cugel laughed aloud. He went to the inn, dressed himself in his garments and buckled on his sword. He went out into the taproom and looking into the till, found a number of coins, which he transferred to his pouch, alongside the ivory representation of NULLITY. He returned outdoors: best to depart while none were on hand to detain him.

A flicker of light attracted his attention: the ring on his finger glinted with dozens of streaming sparks, and all pointed up the trail, toward the cliffs.

Cugel shook his head wearily, then checked the darting lights once again. Without ambiguity they directed him back the way he had come. Pharesm's calculations, after all, had been accurate. He had best act with decision, lest TOTALITY once more drift beyond his reach.

He delayed only long enough to find an axe, and hastened up the trail, following the glittering sparks of the ring.

Not far from where he had left it, he came upon the maimed Winged Being, now sitting on a rock beside the road, the hood drawn over its head. Cugel picked up a stone and heaved it at the creature, which collapsed into sudden dust, leaving only a tumble of white cloth to signal the fact of its existence.

Cugel continued up the road, keeping to such cover as offered itself, but to no avail. Overhead hovered Winged Beings, flapping and swooping. Cugel made play with the axe, striking at the wings, and the creatures flew high, circling above.

Cugel consulted the ring and was led on up the trail, with the Winged Beings hovering just above. The ring coruscated with the intensity of its message: there was TOTALITY, resting blandly on a rock!

Cugel restrained the cry of exultation which rose in his throat. He brought forth the ivory symbol of NULLITY, ran forward and applied it to the gelatinous central globe.

As Pharesm had asserted, adherence was instant. With the contact Cugel could feel the spell which bound him to the olden time dissolving.

A swoop, a buffet of great wings! Cugel was knocked to the ground. White cloth enveloped him, and with one hand holding NULLITY he was unable to swing his axe. This was now wrenched from his grasp. He released NULLITY, gripped a rock, kicked, somehow freed himself, and sprang for his axe. The Winged Being seized NULLITY, to which TOTALITY was attached, and bore both aloft and toward a cave high in the cliffs.

Great forces were pulling at Cugel, whirling in all directions at once. There was a roaring in his ears, a flutter of violet lights, and Cugel fell a million years into the future.

* * *

He recovered consciousness in the blue-tiled room with the sting of an aromatic liquor at his lips. Pharesm, bending over him, patted his face and poured more of the liquor into his mouth. 'Awake! Where is TOTALITY? How are you returned?'

Cugel pushed him aside, and sat up on the couch.

'TOTALITY!' roared Pharesm. 'Where is it? Where is my talisman?'

'I will explain,' said Cugel in a thick voice. 'I had it in my grasp, and it was wrenched away by winged creatures in the service of Great God Yelisea.'

'Tell me, tell me!'

Cugel recounted the circumstances which had led first to gaining and then losing that which Pharesm sought. As he talked, Pharesm's face became damp with grief, and his shoulders sagged. At last he marched Cugel outside, into the dim red light of late afternoon. Together they scrutinized the cliffs which now towered desolate and lifeless above them. 'To which cave did the creature fly?' asked Pharesm. 'Point it out, if you are able!'

Cugel pointed. 'There, or so it would seem. All was confusion, all a tumble of wings and white robes . . .'

'Remain here.' Pharesm went inside the workroom and presently returned. 'I give you light,' he said, and handed Cugel a cold white flame tied into a silver chain. 'Prepare yourself.'

At Cugel's feet he cast a pellet which broke into a vortex, and Cugel was carried dizzily aloft to that crumbling ledge which he had indicated to Pharesm. Nearby was the dark opening into a cave. Cugel turned the flame within. He saw a dusty passage, three strides wide and higher than he could reach. It led back into the cliff, twisting slightly to the side. It seemed barren of all life.

Holding the lamp before him, Cugel slowly moved along the passage, his heart thumping for dread of something he could not define. He stopped short: music? The memory of music? He listened and could hear nothing; but when he tried to step forward fear clamped his legs. He held high the lantern and peered down the dusty passage. Where did it lead? What lay beyond? Dusty cave? Demonland? The blessed land Byssom? Cugel slowly proceeded, every sense alert. On a ledge he spied a shrivelled brown spheroid: the talisman he had carried into the past. TOTALITY had long since disengaged itself and departed.

Cugel carefully lifted the object, which was brittle with the age of a million years, and returned to the ledge. The vortex, at a command from Pharesm, conveyed Cugel back to the ground.

Dreading the wrath of Pharesm, Cugel tendered the withered talisman.

Pharesm took it and held it between thumb and fore-finger. 'This was all?'

'There was nothing more.'

Pharesm let the object fall. It struck and instantly became dust. Pharesm looked at Cugel, took a deep breath, then turned with a gesture of unspeakable frustration and marched back to his divinatory.

Cugel gratefully moved off down the trail, past the work-men standing in an anxious group waiting for orders. They eyed Cugel sullenly and a two-ell man hurled a rock. Cugel shrugged and continued south along the trail. Presently he passed the site of the village, now a waste overgrown with gnarled old trees. The pond had disappeared and the ground was hard and dry. In the valley below were ruins, but none of these marked the sites of the ancient cities Impergos, Tharuwe and Rhaverjand, now gone beyond memory.

Cugel walked south. Behind him the cliffs merged with haze and presently were lost to view.

CHAPTER FIVE
The Pilgrims

1: At the Inn

For the better part of a day Cugel had traveled a dreary waste where nothing grew but salt-grass; then, only a few minutes before sunset, he arrived at the bank of a broad slow river, beside which ran a road. A half-mile to his right stood a tall structure of timber and dark brown stucco, evidently an inn. The sight gave Cugel vast satisfaction, for he had eaten nothing the whole of the day, and had spent the previous night in a tree. Ten minutes later he pushed open the heavy iron-bound door, and entered the inn.

He stood in a vestibule. To either side were diamond-paned casements, burnt lavender with age, where the setting sun scattered a thousand refractions. From the common room came the cheerful hum of voices, the clank of pottery and glass, the smell of ancient wood, waxed tile, leather and simmering cauldrons. Cugel stepped forward to find a score of men gathered about the fire, drinking wine and exchanging the large talk of travelers.

The landlord stood behind a counter: a stocky man hardly as tall as Cugel's shoulder, with a high-domed bald head and a black beard hanging a foot below his chin. His eyes were protuberant and heavy-lidded; his expression was as placid and calm as the flow of the river. At Cugel's request for accommodation he dubiously pulled at his nose. 'Already I am over-extended, with pilgrims upon the route to Erze Damath. Those you see upon the benches are not even half of all I must lodge this night. I will put down a pallet in the hall, if such will content you; I can do no more.'

Cugel gave a sigh of fretful dissatisfaction. 'This fails to meet my expectations. I strongly desire a private chamber with a couch of good quality, a window overlooking the river, a heavy carpet to muffle the songs and slogans of the pot-room.'

'I fear tht you will be disappointed,' said the landlord without emotion. 'The single chamber of this description is already occupied, by that man with the yellow beard sitting yonder: a certain Lodermulch, also traveling to Erze Damath.'

'Perhaps, on the plea of emergency, you might persuade him to vacate the chamber and occupy the pallet in my stead,' suggested Cugel.

'I doubt if he is capable of such abnegation,' the inn-keeper replied. 'But why not put the inquiry yourself? I, frankly, do not wish to broach the matter.'

Cugel, surveying Lodermulch's strongly-marked features, his muscular arms and the somewhat disdainful manner in which he listened to the talk of the pilgrims, was inclined to join the innkeeper in his assessment of Lodermulch's character, and made no move to press the request. 'It seems that I must occupy the pallet. Now, as to my supper: I require a fowl, suitably stuffed, trussed, roasted and garnished, accompanied by whatever side-dishes your kitchen affords.'

'My kitchen is overtaxed and you must eat lentils with the pilgrims,' said the landlord. 'A single fowl is on hand, and this again has been reserved to the order of Lodermulch, for his evening repast.'

Cugel shrugged in vexation. 'No matter. I will wash the dust of travel from my face, and then take a goblet of wine.'

'To the rear is flowing water and a trough occasionally used for this purpose. I furnish unguents, pungent oils and hot cloths at extra charge.'

'The water will suffice.' Cugel walked to the rear of the inn, where he found a basin. After washing he looked about and noticed at some small distance a shed, stoutly constructed of timber. He started back into the inn, then halted and once more examined the shed. He crossed the intervening area, opened the door and looked within; then, engrossed in thought, he returned to the common room. The landlord served him a mug of mulled wine, which he took to an inconspicuous bench.

Lodermulch had been asked his opinion of the so-called Funambulous Evangels, who, refusing to place their feet upon the ground, went about their tasks by tightrope. In a curt voice Lodermulch exposed the fallacies of this particular doctrine. 'They reckon the age of the earth at twenty-nine eons, rather than the customary twenty-three. They stipulate that for every square ell of soil two and one quarter million men have died and laid down their dust, thus creating a dank and ubiquitous mantle of lich-mold, upon which it is sacrilege to walk. The argument has a superficial plausibility, but consider: the dust of one desiccated corpse, spread over a square ell, affords a layer one thirty-third of an inch in depth. The total therefore represents almost one mile of compacted corpse-dust mantling the earth's surface, which is manifestly false.'

A member of the sect, who, without access to his customary ropes, walked in cumbersome ceremonial shoes, made an excited expostulation. 'You speak with neither logic nor comprehension! How can you be so absolute?'

Lodermulch raised his tufted eyebrows in surly displeasure. 'Must I really expatiate? At the ocean's shore, does a cliff one mile in altitude follow the demarcation between land and sea? No. Everywhere is inequality. Headlands extend into the water; more often beaches of pure white sand are found. Nowhere are the massive buttresses of gray-white tuff upon which the doctrines of your sect depend.'

'Inconsequential claptrap!' sputtered the Funambule.

'What is this?' demanded Lodermulch, expanding his massive chest. 'I am not accustomed to derision!'

'No derision, but hard and cold refutal of your dogmatism! We claim that a proportion of the dust is blown into the ocean, a portion hangs suspended in the air, a portion seeps through crevices into underground caverns, and another portion is absorbed by trees, grasses and certain insects, so that little more than a half-mile of ancestral sediment covers the earth upon which it is sacrilege to tread. Why are not the cliffs you mention everywhere visible? Because of that moistness exhaled and expelled by innumerable men of the past! This has raised the ocean an exact equivalence, so that no brink or precipice can be noted; and herein lies your fallacy.'

'Bah,' muttered Lodermulch, turning away. 'Somewhere there is a flaw in your concepts.'

'By no means!' asserted the evangel, with that fervor which distinguished his kind. 'Therefore, from respect to the dead, we walk aloft, on ropes and edges, and when we must travel, we use specially sanctified footgear.'

During the conversation Cugel had departed the room. Now a moon-faced stripling wearing the smock of a porter approached the group. 'You are the worthy Lodermulch?' he asked the person so designated.

Lodermulch squared about in his chair. 'I am he.'

'I bear a message, from one who has brought certain sums of money due to you. He waits in a small shed behind the inn.'

Lodermulch frowned increduously. 'You are certain that this person required Lodermulch, Provost of Barlig Township?'

'Indeed, sir, the name was specifically so.'

'And what man bore the message?'

'He was a tall man, wearing a voluminous hood, and described himself as one of your intimates.'

'Indeed,' ruminated Lodermulch. 'Tyzog, perhaps? Or conceivably Krednip. . .Why would they not approach me directly? No doubt there is some good reason.' He heaved his bulk erect. 'I suppose I must investigate.'

He stalked from the common room, circled the inn, and looked through the dim light toward the shed. 'Ho there!' he called. 'Tyzog? Krednip? Come forth!'

There was no response. Lodermulch went to peer into the shed. As soon as he had stepped within, Cugel came around from the rear, slammed shut the door, and threw bar and bolts.

Ignoring the muffled pounding and angry calls, Cugel returned into the inn. He sought out the innkeeper. 'An alteration in arrangements: Lodermulch has been called away. He will require neither his chamber nor his roast fowl and has kindly urged both upon me!'

The innkeeper pulled at his beard, went to the door, and looked up and down the road. Slowly he returned. 'Extraordinary! He has paid for both chamber and fowl, and made no representations regarding rebate.'

'We arranged a settlement to our mutual satisfaction. To recompense you for extra effort, I now pay an additional three terces.'

The innkeeper shrugged and took the coins. 'It is all the same to me. Come, I will lead you to the chamber.'

Cugel inspected the chamber and was well satisfied. Presently his supper was served. The roast fowl was beyond reproach, as were the additional dishes Lodermulch had ordered and which the landlord included with the meal.

Before retiring Cugel strolled behind the inn and satisfied himself that the bar at the door of the shed was in good order and that Lodermulch's hoarse calls were unlikely to attract attention. He rapped sharply on the door. 'Peace, Lodermulch!' he called out sternly. 'This is I, the innkeeper! Do not bellow so loudly; you will disturb my guests at their slumber.'

Without waiting for reply, Cugel returned to the common room, where he fell into conversation with the leader of the pilgrim band. This was Garstang, a man spare and taut, with a waxen skin, a fragile skull, hooded eyes and a meticulous nose so thin as to be translucent when impinged across a light. Addressing him as a man of experience and erudition, Cugel inquired the route to Almery, but Garstang tended to believe the region sheerly imaginary.

Cugel asserted otherwise. 'Almery is a region distinct; I vouch for this personally.'

'Your knowledge, then, is more profound than my own,' stated Garstang. 'This river is the Asc; the land to this side is Sudun, across is Lelias. To the south lies Erze Damath, where you would be wise to travel, thence perhaps west across the Silver Desert and the Songan Sea, where you might make new inquiry.'

'I will do as you suggest,' said Cugel.

'We, devout Gilfigites all, are bound for Erze Damath and the Lustral Rite at the Black Obelisk,' said Garstang. 'Since the route lies through wastes, we are banded together against the erbs and the gids. If you wish to join the group, to share both privileges and restrictions, you are welcome.'

'The privileges are self-evident,' said Cugel. 'As to the restrictions?'

'Merely to obey the commands of the leader, which is to say, myself, and contribute a share of the expenses.'

141

'I agree, without qualification,' said Cugel.

'Excellent! We march on the morrow at dawn.' Garstang pointed out certain other members of the group, which numbered fifty-seven. 'There is Vitz, locutor to our little band, and there sits Casmyre, the theoretician. The man with iron teeth is Arlo, and he of the blue hat and silver buckle is Voynod, a wizard of no small repute. Absent from the room is the estimable though agnostic Lodermulch, as well as the un-equivocally devout Subucule. Perhaps they seek to sway each other's convictions. The two who game with dice are Parso and Sayanave. There is Hant, there Cray.' Garstang named several others, citing their attributes. At last Cugel, pleading fatigue, repaired to his chamber. He relaxed upon the couch and at once fell asleep.

During the small hours he was subjected to a disturbance. Lodermulch, digging into the floor of the shed, then burrowing under the wall, had secured his freedom, and went at once to the inn. First he tried the door to Cugel's chamber, which Cugel had been at pains to lock.

'Who is there?' called Cugel.

'Open! It is I, Lodermulch. This is the chamber where I wish to sleep!'

'By no means,' declared Cugel. 'I paid a princely sum to secure a bed, and was even forced to wait while the landlord evicted a previous tenant. Be off with you now; I suspect that you are drunk; if you wish further revelry, rouse the wine-steward.'

Lodermulch stamped away. Cugel lay back once more.

Presently he heard the thud of blows, and the land-lord's cry as Lodermulch seized his beard. Lodermulch was eventually thrust from the inn, by the joint efforts of the innkeeper, his spouse, the porter, the pot-boy and others; whereupon Cugel gratefully returned to sleep.

Before dawn the pilgrims, together with Cugel, arose and took their breakfast. The innkeeper seemed somewhat sullen of mood, and displayed bruises, but he put no questions to Cugel, who in his turn initiated no conversation.

After breakfast the pilgrims assembled in the road, where they were joined by Lodermulch, who had spent the night pacing up and down the road.

Garstang made a count of the group, then blew a great blast on his whistle. The pilgrims marched forward, across the bridge, and set off along the south bank of the Asc toward Erze Damath.

2: *The Raft on the River*

For three days the pilgrims proceeded beside the Asc, at night sleeping behind a barricade evoked by the wizard Voynod from a circlet of ivory slivers: a precaution of necessity, for beyond the bars, barely visible by the rays of the fire, were creatures anxious to join the company: deodands softly pleading, erbs shifting posture back and forth from four feet to two, comfortable in neither style. Once a gid attempted to leap the barricade; on another occasion three hoons joined to thrust against the posts – backing off, racing forward, to strike with grunts of effort, while from within the pilgrims watched in fascination.

Cugel stepped close, to touch a flaming brand to one of the heaving shapes, and elicited a scream of fury. A great gray arm snatched through the gap; Cugel jumped back for his life. The barricade held and presently the creatures fell to quarreling and departed.

On the evening of the third day the party came to the confluence of the Asc with a great slow river which Garstang identified as the Scamander. Nearby stood a forest of tall baldamas, pines and spinth oaks. With the help of local woodcutters trees were felled, trimmed and conveyed to the water's edge, where a raft was fabricated. With all the pilgrims aboard, the raft was poled out into the current, where it drifted downstream in ease and silence.

For five days the raft moved on the broad Scamander, sometimes almost out of sight of the banks, sometimes gliding close beside the reeds which lined the shore. With nothing better to do, the pilgrims engaged in lengthy disputations, and the diversity of opinion upon every issue was remarkable. As often as not the talk explored metaphysical arcana, or the subtleties of Gilfigite principle.

Subucle, the most devout of the pilgrims, stated his credo in detail. Essentially he professed the orthodox Gilfigite theosophy, in which Zo Zam, the eight-headed deity, after creating cosmos, struck off his toe, which then became Gilfig, while the drops of blood dispersed to form the eight races of mankind. Roremaund, a skeptic, attacked the doctrine: 'Who created this hypothetical "creator" of yours? Another "creator"? Far simpler merely to presuppose the end product: in this case, a blinking sun and a dying earth!' To which Subucule cited the Gilfigite Text in crushing refutal.

One named Bluner staunchly propounded his own creed. He believed the sun to be a cell in the corpus of a great deity, who had created the cosmos in a process analogous to the growth of a lichen along a rock.

Subucule considered the thesis over-elaborate: 'If the sun were a cell, what then becomes the nature of the earth?'

'An animalcule deriving nutriment,' replied Bluner. 'Such dependencies are known elsewhere and need not evoke astonishment.'

'What then attacks the sun?' demanded Vitz in scorn. 'Another animalcule similar to earth?'

Bluner began a detailed exposition of his organon, but before long was interrupted by Pralixus, a tall thin man with piercing green eyes. 'Listen to me; I know all; my doctrine is simplicity itself. A vast number of conditions are possible, and there are an even greater number of impossibilities. Our cosmos is a possible condition: it exists. Why? Time is infinite, which is to say that every possible condition must come to pass. Since we reside in this particular possibility and know of no other, we arrogate to ourselves the quality of singleness. In truth, any universe which is possible sooner or later, not once but many times, will exist.'

'I tend to a similar doctrine, though a devout Gilfigite,' stated Casmyre the theoretician. 'My philosophy presupposes a succession of creators, each absolute in his own right. To paraphrase the learned Pralixus, if a deity is possible, it must exist! Only impossible deities will not exist! The eight-headed Zo Zam who struck off his Divine Toe is possible, and hence exists, as is attested by the Gilfigite Texts!'

Subucule blinked, opened his mouth to speak, then closed it once more. Roremaund, the skeptic, turned away to inspect the waters of the Scamander.

Garstang, sitting to the side, smiled thoughtfully. 'And you, Cugel the Clever, for once you are reticent. What is your belief?'

'It is somewhat inchoate,' Cugel admitted. 'I have assimilated a variety of viewpoints, each authoritative in its own right: from the priests at the Temple of Teleologues; from a bewitched bird who plucked messages from a box; from a a fasting anchorite who drank a bottle of pink elixir which I offered him in jest. The resulting visions were contradictory but of great profundity. My world-scheme, hence, is syncretic.'

'Interesting,' said Garstang. 'Lodermulch, what of you?'

'Ha,' growled Lodermulch. 'Notice this rent in my garment; I am at a loss to explain its presence! I am even more puzzled by the existence of the universe.'

Others spoke. Voynod the wizard defined the known cosmos as the shadow of a region ruled by ghosts, themselves dependent for existence upon the psychic energies of men. The devout Subucule denounced this scheme as contrary to the Protocols of Gilfig.

The argument continued at length. Cugel and one or two others including Lodermulch became bored and instituted a game of chance, using dice and cards and counters. The stakes, originally nominal, began to grow. Lodermulch at first won scantily, then lost ever greater sums, while Cugel won stake after stake. Lodermulch presently flung down the dice and seizing Cugel's elbow shook it, to dislodge several additional dice from the cuff of his jacket. 'Well then!' bawled Lodermulch, 'what have we here? I thought to detect knavery, and here is justification! Return my money on the instant!'

'How can you say so?' demanded Cugel. 'Where have you demonstrated chicanery? I carry dice – what of that? Am I required to throw my property into the Scamander, before engaging in a game? You demean my reputation!'

'I care nothing for this,' retorted Lodermulch. 'I merely wish the return of my money.'

'Impossible,' said Cugel. 'For all your bluster you have proved no malfeasance.'

'Proof?' roared Lodermulch. 'Need there be further? Notice these dice, all askew, some with identical markings

146

on three sides, others rolling only with great effort, so heavy are they at one edge.'

'Curios only,' explained Cugel. He indicated Voynod the wizard, who had been watching. 'Here is a man as keen of eye as he is agile of brain; ask if any illicit transaction was evident.'

'None was evident,' stated Voynod. 'In my estimation Lodermulch has made an over-hasty accusation.'

Garstang came forward, and heard the controversy. He spoke in a voice both judicious and conciliatory: 'Trust is essential in a company such as ours, comrades and devout Gilfigites all. There can be no question of malice or deceit! Surely, Lodermulch, you have misjudged our friend, Cugel!'

Lodermulch laughed harshly. 'If this is conduct characteristic of the devout, I am fortunate not to have fallen in with ordinary folk!' With this remark, he took himself to a corner of the raft, where he seated himself and fixed Cugel with a glance of menace and loathing.

Garstang shook his head in distress. 'I fear Lodermulch has been offended. Perhaps, Cugel, if in a spirit of amity you were to return his gold—'

Cugel made a firm refusal. 'It is a matter of principle. Lodermulch has assailed my most valuable possession, which is to say, my honor.'

'Your nicety is commendable,' said Garstang, 'and Lodermulch has behaved tactlessly. Still, for the sake of good-fellowship – no? Well, I cannot argue the point. Ha hum. Always small troubles to fret us.' Shaking his head, he departed.

Cugel gathered his winnings, together with the dice which Lodermulch had dislodged from his sleeve. 'An unsettling incident,' he told Voynod. 'A boor, this Lodermulch! He has offended everyone; all have quit the game.'

'Perhaps because all the money is in your possession,' Voynod suggested.

Cugel examined his winnings with an air of surprise. 'I never suspected that they were so substantial! Perhaps you will accept this sum to spare me the effort of carrying it?'

Voynod acquiesced and a share of the winnings changed hands.

Not long after, while the raft floated placidly along the river, the sun gave an alarming pulse. A purple film formed upon the surface like tarnish, then dissolved. Certain of the pilgrims ran back and forth in alarm, crying, 'The sun goes dark! Prepare for the chill!'

Garstang, however, held up his hands in reassurance. 'Calm, all! The quaver has departed, the sun is as before!'

'Think!' urged Subucule with great earnestness. 'Would Gilfig allow this cataclysm, even while we travel to worship at the Black Obelisk?'

The group became quiet, though each had his personal interpretation of the event. Vitz, the locutor, saw an analogy to the blurring of vision, which might be cured by vigorous blinking. Voynod declared, 'If all goes well at Erze Damath, I plan to dedicate the next four years of life to a scheme for replenishing the vigor of the sun!' Lodermulch merely made an offensive statement to the effect that for all of him the sun could go dark, with the pilgrims forced to grope their way to the Lustral Rites.

But the sun shone on as before. The raft drifted along the great Scamander, where the banks were now so low and devoid of vegetation as to seem distant dark lines. The day passed and the sun seemed to settle into the river itself, projecting a great maroon glare which gradually went dull and dark as the sun vanished.

In the twilight a fire was built around which the pilgrims gathered to eat their supper. There was discussion of the sun's alarming flicker, and much speculation along eschatolgoical lines. Subucule relinquished all responsibility for life, death, the future and past to Gilfig. Haxt, however, declared that he would feel easier if Gilfig had heretofore displayed a more expert control over the affairs of the world. For a period the talk became intense. Subucule accused Haxt of superficiality, while Haxt used such words as 'credulity' and 'blind abasement'. Garstang intervened to point out that as yet all facts were not known, and that the Lustral Rites at the Black Obelisk might clarify the situation.

The next morning a great weir was noted ahead: a line of stout poles obstructing navigation of the river. At one area only was passage possible, and even this gap was closed by a heavy iron chain. The pilgrims allowed the raft to float close to this gap, then dropped the stone which served as an anchor. From a nearby hut appeared a zealot, long of hair and gaunt of limb, wearing tattered black robes and flourishing an iron staff. He sprang out along the weir to gaze threateningly down at those aboard the raft. 'Go back, go back!' he shouted. 'The passage of the river is under my control; I permit none to go by!'

Garstang stepped forward. 'I beg your indulgence! We are a group of pilgrims, bound for the Lustral Rites at Erze Damath. If necessary we will pay a fee to pass the weir, though we trust that in your generosity you will remit the toll.'

The zealot gave a cry of harsh laughter and waved his iron staff. 'My fee may not be remitted! I demand the life of the most evil in your company – unless one among you can to my satisfaction demonstrate his virtue!' And legs astraddle, black robe flapping in the wind, he stood glaring down at the raft.

Among the pilgrims was a stir of uneasiness, and all looked furtively at one another. There was a mutter, which presently became a confusion of assertions and claims. Casmyre's strident tones at last rang forth. 'It cannot be I who am most evil! My life has been clement and austere and during the gambling I ignored an ignoble advantage.'

Another called out, 'I am even more virtuous, who eat only dry pulses for fear of taking life.'

Another: 'I am even of greater nicety, for I subsist solely upon the discarded husks of these same pulses, and bark which has fallen from trees, for fear of destroying even vegetative vitality.'

Another: 'My stomach refuses vegetable matter, but I uphold the same exalted ideals and allow only carrion to pass my lips.'

Another: 'I once swam on a lake of fire to notify an old woman that the calamity she dreaded was unlikely to occur.'

Cugel declared: 'My life is incessant humility, and I am unswerving in my dedication to justice and equivalence, even though I fare the worse for my pains.'

Voynod was no less staunch: 'I am a wizard, true, but I devote my skill only to the amelioration of public woe.'

Now it was Garstang's turn: 'My virtue is of the quintessential sort, being distilled from the erudition of the ages. How can I be other than virtuous? I am dispassionate to the ordinary motives of mankind.'

Finally all had spoken save Lodermulch, who stood to the side, a sour grin on his face. Voynod pointed a finger. 'Speak, Lodermulch! Prove your virtue, or else be judged most evil, with the consequent forfeit of your life!'

Lodermulch laughed. He turned and made a great jump which carried him to an outlying member of the weir. He scrambled to the parapet, drew his sword and threatened the zealot. 'We are all evil together, you as well as we, for enforcing this absurd condition. Relax the chain, or prepare to face my sword.'

The zealot flung high his arms. 'My condition is fulfilled; you, Lodermulch, have demonstrated your virtue. The raft may proceed. In addition, since you employ your sword in the defense of honor, I now bestow upon you this salve which when applied to your blade enables it to slice steel or rock as easily as butter. Away, then, and may all profit by the lustral devotions!'

Lodermulch accepted the salve and returned to the raft. The chain was relaxed and the raft slid without hindrance past the weir.

Garstang approached Lodermulch to voice measured approval for his act. He added a caution: 'In this case an impulsive, indeed almost insubordinate, act redounded to the general benefit. If a similar circumstance arises in the future, it would be well to take counsel with others of proved sagacity: myself, Casmyre, Voynod or Subucule.'

Lodermulch grunted indifferently. 'As you wish, so long as the delay involves me in no personal inconvenience.' And Garstang was forced to be content with this.

The other pilgrims eyed Lodermulch with dissatisfaction, and drew themselves apart, so that Lodermulch sat by himself at the forward part of the raft.

Afternoon came, then sunset, evening and night; when morning arrived it was seen that Lodermulch had disappeared.

There was general puzzlement. Garstang made inquiries, but none could throw light upon the mystery, and there was no general consensus as to what in fact had occasioned the disappearance.

Strangely enough, the departure of the unpopular Lodermulch failed to restore the original cheer and fellowship to the group. Thereafter each of the pilgrims sat dourly silent, casting glances to left and right; there were no further games, nor philosophical discussions, and Garstang's announcement that Erze Damath lay a single day's journey ahead aroused no great enthusiasm.

3: Erze Damath

On the last night aboard the raft a semblance of the old camaraderie returned. Vitz the locutor performed a number of vocal exercises and Cugel demonstrated a high-kneed capering dance typical of the lobster fishermen of Kauchique, where he had passed his youth. Voynod in his turn performed a few simple metamorphoses, and then displayed a small silver ring. He signaled Haxt. 'Touch this with your tongue, press it to your forehead, then look through.'

'I see a procession!' exclaimed Haxt. 'Men and women by the hundreds, and thousands, marching past. My mother and my father walk before, then my grandparents – but who are the others?'

'Your ancestors,' declared Voynod, 'each in his characteristic costume, back to the primordial homunculus from which all of us are derived.' He retrieved the ring, and reaching into his pouch brought forth a dull blue and green gem.

'Watch now, as I fling this jewel into the Scamander!' And he tossed the gem off to the side. It flickered through the air and splashed into the dark water. 'Now, I merely fold forth my palm, and the gem returns!' And indeed, as the company watched there was a wet sparkle across the firelight and upon Voynod's palm rested the gem. 'With this gem a man need never fear penury. True, it is of no great value, but he can sell it repeatedly . . .

'What else shall I show you? This small amulet perhaps. Frankly an erotic appurtenance, it arouses intense emotion in that person toward whom the potency is directed. One must be cautious in its use; and indeed, I have here an indispensable ancillary: a periapt in the shape of a ram's head, fashioned to the order of Emperor Dalmasmius the Tender, that he might not injure the sensibilities of any of his ten thousand concubines. . . What else can I display? Here: my wand, which instantly affixes any object to any other. I keep it carefully sheathed so that I do not inadvertently weld trouser to buttock or pouch to fingertip. The object has many uses. What else? Let us see . . . Ah, here! A horn of singular quality. When thrust into the mouth of a corpse, it stimulates the utterance of twenty final words. Inserted into the cadaver's ear it allows the transmission of information into the lifeless brain. . . What have we here? Yes, indeed: a small device which has brought much pleasure!' And Voynod displayed a doll which performed a heroic declamation, sang a somewhat raffish song and engaged in repartee with Cugel, who squatted close in front, watching all with great attentiveness.

At last Voynod tired of his display, and the pilgrims one by one reposed themselves to sleep.

Cugel lay awake, hands behind his head, staring up at the stars thinking of Voynod's unexpectedly large collection of thaumaturgical instruments and devices.

When satisfied that all were asleep, he arose to his feet and inspected the sleeping form of Voynod. The pouch was securely locked and tucked under Voynod's arm, much as Cugel had expected. Going to the little pantry where stores were kept, he secured a quantity of lard, which he mixed with flour to produce a white salve. From a fragment of heavy paper he folded a small box, which he filled with the salve. He then returned to his couch.

On the following morning he contrived that Voynod, as if by accident, should see him anointing his sword blade with the salve.

Voynod became instantly horrified. 'It cannot be! I am astounded! Alas, poor Lodermulch!'

Cugel signaled him to silence. 'What are you saying?' he muttered. 'I merely protect my sword against rust.'

Voynod shook his head with inexorable determination. 'All is clear! For the sake of gain you have murdered Lodermulch! I have no choice but to lodge an information with the thief-takers at Erze Damath!'

Cugel made an imploring gesture. 'Do not be hasty! You have mistaken all; I am innocent!'

Voynod, a tall saturnine man with purple flush under his eyes, a long chin and a tall pinched forehead, held up his hand. 'I have never been one to tolerate homicide. The principle of equivalence must in this case apply, and a rigorous requital is necessary. At minimum, the evil-doer may never profit by his act!'

'You refer to the salve?' inquired Cugel delicately.

'Precisely,' said Voynod. 'Justice demands no less.'

'You are a stern man,' exclaimed Cugel in distress. 'I have no choice but to submit to your judgement.'

Voynod extended his hand. 'The salve, then, and since you are obviously overcome by remorse I will say no more of the matter.'

Cugel pursed his lips reflectively. 'So be it. I have already anointed my sword. Therefore I will sacrifice the remainder of the salve in exchange for your erotic appurtenance and its ancillary, together with several lesser talismans.'

'Do I hear correctly?' stormed Voynod. 'Your arrogance transcends all! Such effectuants are beyond value!'

Cugel shrugged. 'This salve is by no means an ordinary article of commerce.'

After dispute Cugel relinquished the salve in return for a tube which projected blue concentrate to a distance of fifty paces, together with a scroll listing eighteen phases of

154

the Laganetic Cycle; and with these items he was forced to be content.

Not long afterward the outlying ruins of Erze Damath appeared upon the western banks: ancient villas now toppled and forlorn among overgrown gardens.

The pilgrims plied poles to urge the raft toward the shore. In the distance appeared the tip of the Black Obelisk, at which all emitted a glad cry. The raft moved slantwise across the Scamander and was presently docked at one of the crumbling old jetties.

The pilgrims scrambled ashore, to gather round Garstang, who addressed the group: 'It is with vast satisfaction that I find myself discharged of responsibility. Behold! The holy city where Gilfig issued the Gneustic Dogma! where he scourged Kazue and denounced Enxis the Witch! Not impossibly the sacred feet have trod this very soil!' Garstang made a dramatic gesture toward the ground, and the pilgrims, looking downward, shuffled their feet uneasily. 'Be that as it may, we are here and each of us must feel relief. The way was tedious and not without peril. Fifty-nine set forth from Pholgus Valley. Bamish and Randol were taken by grues at Sagma Field; by the bridge across the Asc Cugel joined us; upon the Scamander we lost Lodermulch. Now we muster fifty-seven, comrades all, tried and true, and it is a sad thing to dissolve our association, which we all will remember forever!

Two days hence the Lustral Rites begin. We are in good time. Those who have not disbursed all their funds gaming' – here Garstang turned a sharp glance toward Cugel – 'may seek comfortable inns at which to house themselves. The impoverished must fare as best they can. Now our journey is at its end; we herewith disband and go our own ways, though all will necessarily meet two days hence at the Black Obelisk. Farewell until this time!'

155

The pilgrims now dispersed, some walking along the banks of the Scamander toward a nearby inn, others turning aside and proceeding into the city proper.

Cugel approached Voynod. 'I am strange to this region, as you are aware; perhaps you can recommend an inn of large comfort at small cost.'

'Indeed,' said Voynod. 'I am bound for just such an inn: the Old Dastric Empire Hostelry, which occupies the precincts of a former palace. Unless conditions have changed, sumptuous luxury and exquisite viands are offered at no great cost.'

The prospect met with Cugel's approval; the two set out through the avenues of old Erze Damath, past clusters of stucco huts, then across a region where no buildings stood and the avenues created a vacant checkerboard, then into a district of great mansions still currently in use: these set back among intricate gardens. The folk of Erze Damath were handsome enough, if somewhat swarthier than the folk of Almery. The men wore only black: tight trousers and vests with black pompoms; the women were splendid in gowns of yellow, red, orange and magenta, and their slippers gleamed with orange and black sequins. Blue and green were rare, being unlucky colors, and purple signified death.

The women displayed tall plumes in their hair, while the men wore jaunty black disks, their scalps protruding through a central hole. A resinous balsam seemed very much the fashion, and everyone Cugel met exuded a waft of aloes or myrrh or carcynth. All in all the folk of Erze Damath seemed no less cultivated than those of Kauchique, and rather more vital than the listless citizens of Azenomei.

Ahead appeared the Old Dastric Empire Hostelry, not far from the Black Obelisk itself. To the dissatisfaction of both Cugel and Voynod, the premises were completely

156

occupied, and the attendant refused them admittance. 'The Lustral Rites have attracted all manner of devout folk,' he explained. 'You will be fortunate to secure lodging of any kind.'

So it proved: from inn to inn went Cugel and Voynod, to be turned away in every case. Finally, on the western outskirts of the city, at the very edge of the Silver Desert, they were received by a large tavern of somewhat disreputable appearance: the Inn of the Green Lamp.

'Until ten minutes ago I could not have housed you,' stated the landlord, 'but thief-takers apprehended two persons who lodged here, naming them footpads and congenital rogues.'

'I trust this is not the general tendency of your clientele?' inquired Voynod.

'Who is to say?' replied the innkeeper. 'It is my business to provide food and drink and lodging, no more. Ruffians and deviants must eat, drink, and sleep, no less than savants and zealots. All have passed on occasion through my doors, and, after all, what do I know of you?'

Dusk was falling and without further ado Cugel and Voynod housed themselves at the Sign of the Green Lamp. After refreshing themselves they repaired to the common room for their evening meal. This was a hall of considerable extent, with age-blackened beams, a floor of dark brown tile, and various posts and columns of scarred wood, each supporting a lamp. The clientele was various, as the landlord had intimated, displaying a dozen costumes and complexions. Desert-men lean as snakes, wearing leather smocks, sat on one hand; on the other were four with white faces and silky red top-knots who uttered never a word. Along a counter to the back sat a group of bravos in brown trousers, black capes and leather berets, each with a spherical jewel dangling by a gold chain from his ear.

Cugel and Voynod consumed a meal of fair quality, though somewhat rudely served, then sat drinking wine and considering how to pass the evening. Voynod decided to rehearse cries of passion and devotion frenzies to be exhibited at the Lustral Rites. Cugel thereupon besought him to lend his talisman of erotic stimulation. 'The women of Erze Damath show to good advantage, and with the help of the talisman I will extend my knowledge of their capabilities.'

'By no means,' said Voynod, hugging his pouch close to his side. 'My reasons need no amplification.'

Cugel put on a sullen scowl. Voynod was a man whose grandiose personal conceptions seemed particularly farfetched and distasteful, by reason of his unhealthy, gaunt and saturnine appearance.

Voynod drained his mug, with a meticulous frugality Cugel found additionally irritating, and rose to his feet. 'I will now retire to my chamber.'

As he turned away a bravo swaggering across the room jostled him. Voynod snapped an acrimonious instruction, which the bravo did not choose to ignore. 'How dare you use such words to me! Draw and defend yourself, or I cut your nose from your face!' And the bravo snatched forth his blade.

'As you will,' said Voynod. 'One moment until I find my sword.' With a wink at Cugel he annointed his blade with the salve, then turned to the bravo. 'Prepare for death, my good fellow!' He leapt grandly forward. The bravo, noting Voynod's preparations, and understanding that he faced magic, stood numb with terror. With a flourish Voynod ran him through, and wiped his blade on the bravo's hat.

The dead man's companions at the counter started to their feet, but halted as Voynod with great aplomb turned to face them. 'Take care, you dunghill cocks! Notice the

158

fate of your fellow! He died by the power of my magic blade, which is of inexorable metal and cuts rock and steel like butter. Behold!' And Voynod struck out at a pillar. The blade, striking an iron bracket, broke into a dozen pieces. Voynod stood non-plussed, but the bravo's companions surged forward.

'What then of your magic blade? Our blades are ordinary steel but bite deep!' And in a moment Voynod was cut to bits.

The bravos now turned upon Cugel. 'What of you? Do you wish to share the fate of your comrade?'

'By no means!' stated Cugel. 'This man was but my servant, carrying my pouch. I am a magician; observe this tube! I will project blue concentrate at the first man to threaten me!'

The bravos shrugged and turned away. Cugel secured Voynod's pouch, then gestured to the landlord. 'Be so good as to remove these corpses; then bring a further mug of spiced wine.'

'What of your comrade's account?' demanded the landlord testily.

'I will settle it in full, have no fear.'

The corpses were carried to the rear compound: Cugel consumed a last mug of wine, then retired to his chamber, where he spread the contents of Voynod's pouch upon the table. The money went into his purse; the talismans, amulets and instruments he packed into his own pouch; the salve he tossed aside. Content with the day's work, he reclined upon the couch, and was soon asleep.

On the following day Cugel roamed the city, climbing the tallest of the eight hills. The vista which spread before him was both bleak and magnificent. To right and left rolled the great Scamander. The avenues of the city marked off square blocks of ruins, empty wastes, the stucco huts of the poor and the palaces of the rich. Erze

Damath was the largest city of Cugel's experience, far vaster than any of Almery or Ascolais, though now the greater part lay tumbled in moldering ruin.

Returning to the central section, Cugel sought out the booth of a professional geographer, and after paying a fee inquired the most secure and expeditious route to Almery.

The sage gave no hasty nor ill-considered answer, but brought forth several charts and directories. After profound deliberation he turned to Cugel. 'This is my counsel. Follow the Scamander north to the Asc, proceed along the Asc until you encounter a bridge of six piers. Here turn your face to the north, proceed across the Mountains of Magnatz, whereupon you will find before you that forest known as the Great Erm. Fare westward through this forest and approach the shore of the Northern Sea. Here you must build a coracle and entrust yourself to the force of the wind and current. If by chance you should reach the Land of the Falling Wall, then it is a comparatively easy journey south to Almery.'

Cugel made an impatient gesture. 'In essence this is the way I came. Is there no other route?'

'Indeed there is. A rash man might choose to risk the Silver Desert, whereupon he would find the Songan Sea, across which lie the impassable wastes of a region contiguous to East Almery.'

'Well then, this seems feasible. How may I cross the Silver desert? Are there caravans?'

'To what purpose? There are none to buy the goods thus conveyed – only bandits who prefer to preempt the merchandise. A minimum force of forty men is necessary to intimidate the bandits.'

Cugel departed the booth. At a nearby tavern he drank a flask of wine and considered how best to raise a force of forty men. The pilgrims, of course, numbered fifty-six – no, fifty-five, what with the death of Voynod. Still, such a band would serve very well. . . .

Cugel drank more wine and considered further.

At last he paid his score and turned his steps to the Black Obelisk. 'Obelisk' perhaps was a misnomer, the object being a great fang of solid black stone rearing a hundred feet above the city. At the base five statues had been carved, each facing a different direction, each the Prime Adept of some particular creed. Gilfig faced to the south, his four hands presenting symbols, his feet resting upon the necks of ecstatic suppliants, with toes elongated and curled upward, to indicate elegance and delicacy.

Cugel sought information of a nearby attendant. 'Who, in regard to the Black Obelisk, is Chief Hierarch, and where may he be found?'

'Precursor Hulm is that individual,' said the attendant and indicated a splendid structure nearby. 'Within that gem-encrusted structure his sanctum may be found.'

Cugel proceeded to the building indicated and after many vehement declarations was ushered into the presence of Precursor Hulm: a man of middle years, somewhat stocky and round of face. Cugel gestured to the under-hierophant who so reluctantly had brought him hither. 'Go; my message is for the Precursor alone.'

The Precursor gave a signal; the hierophant departed. Cugel hitched himself forward. 'I may talk without fear of being overheard?'

'Such is the case.'

'First of all,' said Cugel, 'know that I am a powerful wizard. Behold: a tube which projects blue concentrate! And here, a screed listing eighteen phases of the Laganetic Cycle! And this instrument: a horn which allows the dead to speak, and used in another fashion, allows information to be conveyed into the dead brain! I possess other marvels galore!'

'Interesting indeed,' murmured the Precursor.

'My second disclosure is this: at one time I served as incense-blender at the Temple of Teleologues in a far land, where I learned that each of the sacred images was constructed so that the priests, in case of urgency, might perform acts purporting to be those of the divinity itself.'

'Why should this not be the case?' inquired the Precursor benignly. 'The divinity, controlling every aspect of existence, persuades the priests to perform such acts.'

Cugel assented to the proposition. 'I therefore assume that the images carved into the Black Obelisk are somewhat similar?'

The Precursor smiled. 'To which of the five do you specifically refer?'

'Specifically to the representation of Gilfig.'

The Precursor's eyes went vague; he seemed to reflect.

Cugel indicated the various talismans and instruments. 'In return for a service I will donate certain of these contrivances to the care of this office.'

'What is the service?'

Cugel explained in detail, and the Precursor nodded thoughtfully. 'Once more, if you will demonstrate your magic goods.'

Cugel did so.

'These are all of your devices?'

Cugel reluctantly displayed the erotic stimulator and explained the function of the ancillary talisman. The Precursor nodded his head, briskly this time. 'I believe that we can reach agreement; all is as omnipotent Gilfig desires.'

'We are agreed, then?'

'We are agreed!'

The following morning the group of fifty-five pilgrims assembled at the Black Obelisk. They prostrated themselves before the image of Gilfig, and prepared to proceed with their devotions. Suddenly the eyes of the image flashed fire and the mouth opened. 'Pilgrims!' came a brazen voice. 'Go forth to do my bidding! Across the Silver Desert you must travel, to the shore of the Songan Sea! Here you will find a fane, before which you must abase yourselves. Go! Across the Silver Desert, with all despatch!'

The voice quieted. Garstang spoke in a trembling voice. 'We hear, O Gilfig! We obey!'

At this moment Cugel leapt forward. 'I also have heard this marvel! I too will make the journey! Come, let us set forth!'

'Not so fast,' said Garstang. 'We cannot run skipping and bounding like dervishes. Supplies will be needed, as well as beasts of burden. To this end funds are required. Who then will subscribe?'

'I offer two hundred terces!' 'And I, sixty terces, the sum of my wealth!' 'I, who lost ninety terces gaming with Cugel, possess only forty terces, which I hereby contribute.' So it went, and even Cugel turned sixty-five terces into the common fund.

'Good,' said Garstang. 'Tomorrow then I will make arrangements, and the following day, if all goes well, we depart Erze Damath by the Old West Gate!'

4: The Silver Desert and the Songan Sea

In the morning Garstang, with the assistance of Cugel and Casmyre, went forth to procure the necessary equipage. They were directed to an outfitting yard, situated on one of the now-vacant areas bounded by the boulevards of the old city. A wall of mud brick mingled with fragments of carved stone surrounded a compound, whence issued sounds: crying, calls, deep bellows, throaty growls, barks,

163

screams and roars, and a stong multiphase odor, combined of ammonia, ensilage, a dozen sorts of dung, the taint of old meat, general acridity.

Passing through a portal, the travelers entered an office overlooking the central yard, where pens, cages and stockades held beasts of so great variety as to astound Cugel.

The yard-keeper came forward: a tall, yellow-skinned man, much scarred, lacking his nose and one ear. He wore a gown of gray leather belted at the waist and a tall conical black hat with flaring ear-flaps.

Garstang stated the purpose of the visit. 'We are pilgrims who must journey across the Silver Desert, and wish to hire pack-beasts. We number fifty or more, and anticipate a journey of twenty days in each direction with perhaps five days spent at our devotions: let this information be a guide in your thinking. Naturally we expect only the staunchest, most industrious and amenable beasts at your disposal.'

'All this is very well,' stated the keeper, 'but my price for hire is identical to my price for sale, so you might as well have the full benefit of your money, in the form of title to the beasts concerned in the transaction.'

'And the price?' inquired Casmyre.

'This depends upon your choice; each beast commands a different value.'

Garstang, who had been surveying the compound, shook his head ruefully. 'I confess to puzzlement. Each beast is of a different sort, and none seem to fit any well-defined categories.'

The keeper admitted that such was the case. 'If you care to listen, I can explain all. The tale is of a continuing fascination, and will assist you in the management of your beasts.'

'We will doubly profit to hear you, then,' said Garstang

gracefully, though Cugel was making motions of impatience.

The keeper went to a shelf and took forth a leather-bound folio. 'In a past eon Mad King Kutt ordained a menagerie like none before, for his private amazement and the stupefaction of the world. His wizard, Follinense, therefore produced a group of beasts and teratoids unique, combining the wildest variety of plasms; to the result that you see.'

'The menagerie has persisted so long?' asked Garstang in wonder.

'Indeed not. Nothing of Mad King Kutt is extant save the legend, and a casebook of the wizard Follinense' –here he tapped the leather folio – 'which describes his bizarre systemology. For instance—' He opened the folio. 'Well . . . hmmm. Here is a statement, somewhat less explicit than others, in which he analyzes the half-men, little more than a brief set of notes:

"*Gid: hybrid of man, gargoyle, whorl, leaping insect.*
Deodand: wolverine, basilisk, man.
Erb: bear, man, lank-lizard, demon.
Grue: man, ocular bat, the unusual hoon.
Leucomorph: unknown.
Bazil: felinodore, man (wasp?)."'

Casmyre clapped his hands in astonishment. 'Did Follinense then create these creatures, to the subsequent disadvantage of humanity?'

'Surely not,' said Garstang. 'It seems more an exercise in idle musing. Twice he admits to wonder.'

'Such is my opinion, in this present case,' stated the keeper, 'though elsewhere he is less dubious.'

'How are the creatures before us then connected with the menagerie?' inquired Casmyre.

The keeper shrugged. 'Another of the Mad King's jocularities. He loosed the entire assemblage upon the countryside, to the general disturbance. The creatures, endowed with an eclectic fecundity, became more rather than less bizarre, and now they roam the Plain of Oparona and Blanwalt Forest in great numbers.'

'So then, what of us?' demanded Cugel. 'We wish pack-animals, docile and frugal of habit, rather than freaks and curiosities, no matter how edifying.'

'Certain of my ample stock are capable of this function,' said the keeper with dignity. 'These command the highest prices. On the other hand, for a single terce you may own a long-necked big-bellied creature of astounding voracity.'

'The price is attractive,' said Garstang with regret. 'Unfortunately, we need beasts to carry food and water across the Silver Desert.'

'In this case we must be more pointed.' The keeper fell to studying his charges. 'The tall beast on two legs is perhaps less ferocious than he appears . . .'

Eventually a selection of beasts numbering fifteen was made, and a price agreed upon. The keeper brought them to the gate; Garstang, Cugel and Casmyre took possession and led the fifteen ill-matched creatures at a sedate pace through the streets of Erze Damath, to the West Gate. Here Cugel was left in charge, while Garstang and Casmyre went to purchase stores and other necessaries.

By nightfall all preparations were made, and on the following morning, when the first maroon ray of sunlight struck the Black Obelisk, the pilgrims set forth. The beasts carried panniers of food and bladders of water; the pilgrims all wore new shoes and broad-brimmed hats. Garstang had been unable to hire a guide, but had secured a chart from the geographer, though it indicated no more than a small circle labeled 'Erze Damath' and a larger area marked 'Songan Sea'.

Cugel was given one of the beasts to lead, a twelve-legged creature twenty feet in length, with a small foolishly grinning child's head and tawny fur covering all. Cugel found the task irking, for the beast blew a reeking breath upon his neck, and several times pressed so close as to tread on his heels.

Of the fifty-seven pilgrims who had disembarked from the raft, forty-nine departed for the fane on the shores of the Songan Sea, and the number was almost at once reduced to forty-eight. A certain Tokharin, stepping off the trail to answer a call of nature, was stung by a monster scorpion, and ran northward in great leaps, screaming hoarsely, until presently he disappeared from view.

The day passed with no further incident. The land was a dry gray waste, scattered with flints, supporting only ironweed. To the south was a range of low hills, and Cugel thought to perceive one or two shapes standing motionless along the crest. At sunset the caravan halted; and Cugel, recalling the bandits who reputedly inhabited the area, persuaded Garstang to post two sentries: Lippelt and Mirch-Masen.

In the morning they were gone, leaving no trace, and the pilgrims were alarmed and oppressed. They stood in a nervous cluster looking in all directions. The desert lay flat and dim in the dark low light of dawn. To the south were a few hills, only their smooth top surfaces illuminated; elsewhere the land lay flat to the horizon.

Presently the caravan started off, and now there were but forty-six. Cugel, as before, was put in charge of the long many-legged beast, who now engaged in the practice of butting its grinning face into Cugel's shoulder blades.

The day passed without incident; miles ahead became miles behind. First marched Garstang, with a staff, then came Vitz and Casmyre, followed by several others. Then came the pack-beasts, each with its particular silhouette:

one low and sinuous; another tall and bifurcate, almost of human conformation, except for its head, which was small and squat like the shell of a horseshoe crab. Another, convex of back, seemed to bounce or prance on its six stiff legs; another was like a horse sheathed in white feathers. Behind the packbeasts straggled the remaining pilgrims, with Bluner characteristically walking to the rear, in accordance with the exaggerated humility to which he was prone. At the camp that evening Cugel brought forth the expansible fence, once the property of Voynod, and enclosed the group in a stout stockade.

The following day the pilgrims crossed a range of low mountains, and here they suffered attack by bandits, but it seemed no more than an exploratory skirmish, and the sole casualty was Haxt, who suffered a wound in the heel. But a more serious affair occurred two hours later. As they passed a slope a boulder became dislodged, to roll through the caravan, killing a packbeast, as well as Andle the Funambulous Evangel and Roremaund the Skeptic. During the night Haxt died also, evidently poisoned by the weapon which had wounded him.

With grave faces the pilgrims set forth, and almost at once were attacked from ambush by the bandits. Luckily the pilgrims were alert, and the bandits were routed with a dozen dead, while the pilgrims lost only Cray and Magasthen.

Now there was grumbling and long looks turned eastward toward Erze Damath. Garstang rallied the flagging spirits: 'We are Gilfigites; Gilfig spoke! On the shores of the Songan Sea we will seek the sacred fane! Gilfig is allwise and all-merciful; those who fall in his service are instantly transported to paradisiacal Gamamere! Pilgrims! To the west!'

Taking heart, the caravan once more set forth, and the day passed without further incident. During the night, however, three of the pack-beasts slipped their tethers and decamped, and Garstang was forced to announce short rations for all.

During the seventh day's march, Thilfox ate a handful of poison berries and died in spasms, whereupon his brother Vitz, the locutor, went raving mad and ran up the line of pack-beasts, blaspheming Gilfig and slashing water bladders with his knife, until Cugel finally killed him.

Two days later the haggard band came upon a spring. In spite of Garstang's warning, Sayanave and Arlo flung themselves down and drank in great gulps. Almost at once they clutched their bellies, gagged and choked, their lips the color of sand, and presently they were dead.

A week later fifteen men and four beasts came over the rise to look out across the placid waters of the Songan Sea. Cugel had survived, as well as Garstang, Casmyre and Subucule. Before them lay a marsh, fed by a small stream. Cugel tested the water with that amulet bestowed upon him by Iucounu, and pronounced it safe. All drank to repletion, ate reeds converted to a nutritious if insipid substance by the same amulet, then slept.

Cugel, aroused by a sense of peril, jumped up, to note a sinister stir among the reeds. He roused his fellows, and all readied their weapons; but whatever had caused the motion took alarm and retired. The time was middle afternoon; the pilgrims walked down to the bleak shore to take stock of the situation. They looked north and south but found no trace of the fane. Tempers flared; there was a quarrel which Garstang was able to quell only by dint of the utmost persuasiveness.

Then Balch, who had wandered up the beach, returned in great excitement: 'A village!'

All set forth in hope and eagerness, but the village, when the pilgrims approached, proved a poor thing indeed, a huddle of reed huts inhabited by lizard people

169

who bared their teeth and lashed sinewy blue tails in defiance. The pilgrims moved off down the beach and sat on hummocks watching the low surf of the Songan Sea.

Garstang, frail and bent with the privations he had suffered, was the first to speak. He attempted to infuse his voice with cheer. 'We have arrived, we have triumphed over the terrible Silver Desert! Now we need only locate the fane and perform our devotions; we may then return to Erze Damath and a future of assured bliss!'

'All very well,' grumbled Balch, 'but where may the fane be found? To right and left is the same bleak beach!'

'We must put our trust in the guidance of Gilfig!' declared Subucule. He scratched an arrow upon a bit of wood, and touched it with his holy ribbon. He called, 'Gilfig, O Gilfig! Guide us to the fane! I hereby toss high a marked pointer!' And he flung the chip high into the air. When it alighted, the arrow pointed south. 'South we must fare!' cried Garstang. 'South to the fane!'

But Balch and certain others refused to respond. 'Do you not see that we are fatigued to the point of death? In my opinion Gilfig should have guided our steps to the fane, instead of abandoning us to uncertainty!'

'Gilfig has guided us indeed!' responded Subucule. 'Did you not notice the direction of the arrow?'

Balch gave a croak of sardonic laughter. 'Any stick thrown high must come down, and it will point south as easily as north.'

Subucule drew back in horror. 'You blaspheme Gilfig!'

'Not at all; I am not sure that Gilfig heard your instruction, or perhaps you gave him insufficient time to react. Toss up the stick one hundred times; if it points south on each occasion, I will march south in haste.'

'Very well,' said Subucule. He once again called upon Gilfig and threw up the chip, but when it struck the ground the arrow pointed north.

Balch said nothing. Subucule blinked, then grew red in the face. 'Gilfig has no time for games. He directed us once, and deemed it sufficient.'

'I am unconvinced,' said Balch.

'And I.'

'And I.'

Garstang held up his arms imploringly. 'We have come far; we have toiled together, rejoiced together, fought and suffered together – let us not now fall in dissidence!'

Balch and the others only shrugged. 'We will not plunge blindly south.'

'What will you do, then? Go north? Or return to Erze Damath?'

'Erze Damath? Without food and only four pack-beasts? Bah!'

'Then let us fare south in search of the fane.'

Balch gave another mulish shrug, at which Subucule became angry. 'So be it! Those who fare south to this side, those who cast in with Balch to that!'

Garstang, Cugel and Casmyre joined Subucule; the others stayed with Balch, a group numbering eleven, and now they fell to whispering among themselves, while the four faithful pilgrims watched in apprehension.

The eleven jumped to their feet. 'Farewell.'

'Where do you go?' asked Garstang.

'No matter. Seek your fane if you must; we go about our own affairs.' With the briefest of farewells they marched to the village of the lizard folk, where they slaughtered the males, filed the teeth of the females, dressed them in garments of reeds, and installed themselves as lords of the village.

Garstang, Subucule, Casmyre and Cugel meanwhile traveled south along the shore. At nightfall they pitched camp and dined upon molluscs and crabs. In the morn-

171

ing they found that the four remaining packbeasts had departed, and now they were alone.

'It is the will of Gilfig,' said Subucule. 'We need only find the fane and die!'

'Courage!' muttered Garstang. 'Let us not give way to despair!'

'What else is left? Will we ever see Pholgus Valley again?'

'Who knows? Let us first perform our devotions at the fane.'

With that they proceeded, and marched the remainder of the day. By nightfall they were too tired to do more than slump to the sand of the beach.

The sea spread before them, flat as a table, so calm that the setting sun cast only its exact image rather than a trail. Clams and crabs once more provided a meager supper, after which they composed themselves to sleep on the beach.

Somewhat after the first hours of night Cugel was awakened by a sound of music. Starting up, he looked across the water to find that a ghostly city had come into existence. Slender towers reared into the sky, lit by glittering motes of white light which drifted slowly up and down, back and forth. On the promenades sauntered the gayest of crowds, wearing pale luminous garments and blowing horns of delicate sound. A barge piled with silken cushions, moved by an enormous sail of cornflower silk, drifted past. Lamps at the bow and stern-post illuminated a deck thronged with merrymakers: some singing and playing lutes, others drinking from goblets.

Cugel ached to share their joy. He struggled to his knees, and called out. The merrymakers put down their instruments and stared at him, but now the barge had drifted past, tugged by the great blue sail. Presently the city flickered and vanished, leaving only the dark night sky.

Cugel stared into the night, his throat aching with a sorrow he had never known before. To his surprise he found himself standing at the edge of the water. Nearby were Subucule, Garstang and Casmyre. All gazed at each other through the dark, but exchanged no words. All returned up the beach, where presently they fell asleep on the sand.

Throughout the next day, there was little conversation, and even a mutual avoidance, as if each of the four wished to be alone with his thoughts. From time to time one or the other looked half-heartedly toward the south, but no one seemed in a mood to leave the spot, and no one spoke of departure.

The day passed while the pilgrims rested in a half-torpor. Sunset came, and night; but none of the group sought to sleep.

During the middle evening the ghost city reappeared, and tonight a fête was in progress. Fireworks of a wonderful intricacy bloomed in the sky: laces, nets, starbursts of red and green and blue and silver. Along the promenade came a parade, with ghost-maidens dressed in iridescent garments, ghost-musicians in voluminous garments of red and orange and capering ghost-harlequins. For hours the sound of revelry drifted across the water, and Cugel went out to stand knee-deep, and here he watched until the fête quieted and the city dimmed. As he turned away, the others followed him back up the shore.

On the following day all were weak from hunger and thirst. In a croaking voice Cugel muttered that they must proceed. Garstang nodded and said huskily, 'To the fane, the fane of Gilfig!'

Subucule nodded. The cheeks of his once plump face were haggard; his eyes were filmed and clouded. 'Yes,' he wheezed. 'We have rested; we must go on.'

Casmyre nodded dully. 'To the fane!'

But none set forth to the south. Cugel wandered up the fore-shore and seated himself to wait for nightfall. Looking to his right, he saw a human skeleton resting in a posture not dissimilar to his own. Shuddering, Cugel turned to the left, and here was a second skeleton, this one broken by time and the seasons, and beyond yet another, this a mere heap of bones.

Cugel rose to his feet and ran tottering to the others. 'Quick!' he called. 'While strength yet remains to us! To the south! Come, before we die, like those others whose bones rest above!'

'Yes, yes,' mumbled Garstang. 'To the fane.' And he heaved himself to his feet. 'Come!' he called to the others. 'We fare south!'

Subucule raised himself erect, but Casmyre, after a listless attempt, fell back. 'Here I stay,' he said. 'When you reach the fane, intercede for me with Gilfig; explain that the entrancement overcame the strength of my body.'

Garstang wished to remain and plead, but Cugel pointed to the setting sun. 'If we wait till darkness, we are lost! Tomorrow our strength will be gone!'

Subucule took Garstang's arm. 'We must be away, before nightfall.'

Garstang made a final plea to Casmyre. 'My friend and fellow, gather your strength. Together we have come, from far Pholgus Valley, by raft down the Scamander, and across the dreadful desert! Must we part before attaining the fane?'

'Come to the fane!' croaked Cugel.

But Casmyre turned his face away. Cugel and Subucule led Garstang away, with tears coursing down his withered cheeks; and they staggered south along the beach, averting their eyes from the clear smooth face of the sea.

The old sun set and cast up a fan of color. A high scatter of cloud-flakes glowed halcyon yellow on a strange bronze-brown sky. The city now appeared, and never had it seemed more magnificent, with spires catching the light of sunset. Along the promenade walked youths and maidens with flowers in their hair, and sometimes they paused to stare at the three who walked along the beach. Sunset faded; white lights shone from the city, and music wafted across the water. For a long time it followed the three pilgrims, at last fading into the distance and dying. The sea lay blank to the west, reflecting a few last umber and orange glimmers.

About this time the pilgrims found a stream of fresh water, with berries and wild plums growing nearby, and here they rested the night. In the morning Cugel trapped a fish and caught crabs along the beach. Strengthened, the three continued south, always seeking ahead for the fane, which now Cugel had almost come to expect, so intense was the feeling of Garstang and Subucule. Indeed, as the days passed, it was the devout Subucule who began to despair, to question the sincerity of Gilfig's command, to doubt the essential virtue of Gilfig himself. 'What is gained by this agonizing pilgrimage? Does Gilfig doubt our devotion? Surely we proved ourselves by attendance at the Lustral Rite; why has he sent us so far?'

'The ways of Gilfig are inscrutable,' said Garstang. 'We have come so far; we must seek on and on and on!'

Subucule stopped short, to look back the way they had come. 'Here is my proposal. At this spot let us erect an altar of stones, which becomes our fane; let us then perform a rite. With Gilfig's requirement satisfied, we may turn our faces to the north, to the village where our fellows reside. Here, happily, we may recapture the pack-beasts, replenish our stores, and set forth across the desert, perhaps to arrive once more at Erze Damath.'

Garstang hesitated. 'There is much to recommend your proposal. And yet—'

'A boat!' cried Cugel. He pointed to the sea where a half-mile offshore floated a fishing boat propelled by a square sail hanging from a long limber yard. It passed behind a headland which rose a mile south of where the pilgrims stood, and now Cugel indicated a village along the shore.

'Excellent!' declared Garstang. 'These folk may be fellow Gilfigites, and this village the site of the fane! Let us proceed!'

Subucule still was reluctant. 'Could knowledge of the sacred texts have penetrated so far?'

'Caution is the watchword,' said Cugel. 'We must reconnoiter with great care.' And he led the way through a forest of tamarisk and larch, to where they could look down into the village. The huts were rudely constructed of black stone and housed a folk of ferocious aspect. Black hair in spikes surrounded the round clay-colored faces; coarse black bristles grew off the burly shoulders like epaulettes. Fangs protruded from the mouths of male and female alike and all spoke in harsh growling shouts. Cugel, Garstang and Subucule drew back with the utmost caution, and, hidden among the trees, conferred in low voices.

Garstang at last was discouraged and found nothing more to hope for. 'I am exhausted, spiritually as well as physically; perhaps here is where I die.'

Subucule looked to the north. 'I return to take my chances on the Silver Desert. If all goes well, I will arrive once more at Erze Damath, or even Pholgus Valley.'

Garstang turned to Cugel. 'And what of you, since the fane of Gilfig is nowhere to be found?'

Cugel pointed to a dock at which a number of boats were moored. 'My destination is Almery, across the Songan Sea. I propose to commandeer a boat and sail to the west.'

'I then bid you farewell,' said Subucule. 'Garstang, will you come?'

Garstang shook his head. 'It is too far. I would surely die on the desert. I will cross the sea with Cugel and take the Word of Gilfig to the folk of Almery.'

'Farewell, then, to you as well,' said Subucule. Then he turned swiftly, to hide the emotion in his face, and started north.

Cugel and Garstang watched the sturdy form recede into the distance and disappear. Then they turned to a consideration of the dock. Garstang was dubious. 'The boats seem seaworthy enough, but to "commandeer" is to "steal": an act specifically discountenanced by Gilfig.'

'No difficulty exists,' said Cugel. 'I will place gold coins upon the dock, to a fair valuation of the boat.'

Garstang gave a dubious assent. 'What then of food and water?'

'After securing the boat, we will proceed along the coast until we are able to secure supplies, after which we sail due west.'

To this Garstang assented and the two fell to examining the boats, comparing one against the other. The final selection was a staunch craft some ten or twelve paces long, of ample beam, with a small cabin.

At dusk they stole down to the dock. All was quiet: the fishermen had returned to the village. Garstang boarded the craft and reported all in good order. Cugel began casting off the lines, when from the end of the dock came a savage outcry and a dozen of the burly villagers came lumbering forth.

'We are lost!' cried Cugel. 'Run for your life, or better, swim!'

'Impossible,' declared Garstang. 'If this is death, I will meet it with what dignity I am able!' And he climbed up on the dock.

In short order they were surrounded by folk of all ages, attracted by the commotion. One, an elder of the village, inquired in a stern voice, 'What do you here, skulking on our dock, and preparing to steal a boat?'

'Our motive is simplicity itself,' said Cugel. 'We wish to cross the sea.'

'What?' roared the elder. 'How is that possible? The boat carries neither food nor water, and is poorly equipped. Why did you not approach us and make your needs known?'

Cugel blinked and exchanged a glance with Garstang. He shrugged. 'I will be candid. Your appearance caused us such alarm that we did not dare.'

The remark evoked mingled amusement and surprise in the crowd. The spokesman said, 'All of us are puzzled; explain if you will.'

'Very well,' said Cugel. 'May I be absolutely frank?'

'By all means!'

'Certain aspects of your appearance impress us as feral and barbarous: your protruding fangs, the black mane which surrounds your faces, the cacophony of your speech – to name only a few items.'

The villagers laughed incredulously. 'What nonsense!' they cried. 'Our teeth are long that we may tear the coarse fish on which we subsist. We wear our hair thus to repel a certain noxious insect, and since we are all rather deaf, we possibly tend to shout. Essentially we are a gentle and kindly folk.'

'Exactly,' said the elder, 'and in order to demonstrate this, tomorrow we shall provision our best boat and send you forth with hopes and good wishes. Tonight there shall be a feast in your honor!'

'Here is a village of true saintliness,' declared Garstang. 'Are you by chance worshippers of Gilfig?'

'No; we prostrate ourselves before the fish-god Yob,

178

who seems as efficacious as any. But come, let us ascend to the village. We must make preparations for the feast.'

They climbed steps hewn in the rock of the cliff, which gave upon an area illuminated by a dozen flaring torches. The elder indicated a hut more commodious than the others: 'This is where you shall rest the night; I will sleep elsewhere.'

Garstang again was moved to comment upon the benevolence of the fisher-folk, at which the elder bowed his head. 'We try to achieve a spiritual unity. Indeed, we symbolize this ideal in the main dish of our ceremonial feasts.' He turned, clapping his hands. 'Let us prepare!'

A great cauldron was hung over a tripod; a block and a cleaver were arranged, and now each of the villagers, marching past the block, chopped off a finger and cast it into the pot.

The elder explained, 'By this simple rite, which naturally you are expected to join, we demonstrate our common heritage and our mutual dependence. Come, let us step into the line.' And Cugel and Garstang had no choice but to excise fingers and cast them into the pot with the others.

The feast continued long into the night. In the morning the villagers were as good as their word. An especially seaworthy boat was provided and loaded with stores, including food left over from the previous night's feast.

The villagers gathered on the dock. Cugel and Garstang voiced their gratitude, then Cugel hoisted the sail and Garstang threw off the mooring lines. A wind filled the sail and the boat moved out on the face of the Songan Sea. Gradually the shore became one with the murk of distance, and the two were alone, with only the black metallic shimmer of the water to all sides.

Noon came, and the boat moved in an elemental emptiness: water below, air above; silence in all directions. The afternoon was long and torpid, unreal as a dream; and

179

the melancholy grandeur of sunset was followed by a dusk the color of watered wine.

The wind seemed to freshen and all night they steered west. At dawn the wind died and with sails flapping idly both Cugel and Garstang slept.

Eight times the cycle was repeated. On the morning of the ninth day a low coastline was sighted ahead. During the middle afternoon they drove the prow of their boat through gentle surf up on a wide white beach. 'This then is Almery?' asked Garstang.

'So I believe,' said Cugel, 'but which quarter I am uncertain. Azenomei may lie to north, west or south. If the forest yonder is that which shrouds East Almery, we would do well to pass to the side, as it bears an evil reputation.'

Garstang pointed down the shore. 'Notice: another village. If the folk here are like those across the sea, they will help us on our way. Come, let us make our wants known.'

Cugel hung back. 'It might be wise to reconnoiter, as before.'

'To what end?' asked Garstang. 'On that occasion we were only misled and confused.' He led the way down the beach toward the village. As they approached they could see folk moving across the central plaza: a graceful golden-haired people, who spoke to each other in voices like music.

Garstang advanced joyfully, expecting a welcome even more expansive than that they had received on the other shore; but the villagers ran forward and caught them under nets; 'Why do you do this?' called Garstang. 'We are strangers and intend no harm!'

'You are strangers; just so,' spoke the tallest of the golden-haired villagers. 'We worship that inexorable god known as Dangott. Strangers are automatically heretics,

180

and so are fed to the sacred apes.' With that they began to drag Cugel and Garstang over the sharp stones of the fore-shore while the beautiful children of the village danced joyfully to either side.

Cugel managed to bring forth the tube he had secured from Voynod and expelled blue concentrate at the villagers. Aghast, they toppled to the ground and Cugel was able to extricate himself from the net. Drawing his sword, he leapt forward to cut Garstang free, but now the villagers rallied. Cugel once more employed his tube, and the villagers fled in dismal agony.

'Go, Cugel,' spoke Garstang. 'I am an old man, of little vitality. Take to your heels; seek safety, with all my good wishes.'

'This normally would be my impulse,' Cugel conceded. 'But these people have stimulated me to quixotic folly; so clamber from the net; we retreat together.' Once more he wrought dismay with the blue projection, while Garstang freed himself, and the two fled along the beach.

The villagers pursued with harpoons. Their first cast pierced Garstang through the back. He fell without a sound. Cugel swung about and aimed the tube, but the spell was exhausted and only a limpid exudation appeared. The villagers drew back their arms to hurl a second volley; Cugel shouted a curse, dodged and ducked, and the harpoons plunged past him into the sand of the beach.

Cugel shook his fist a final time, then took to his heels and fled into the forest.

CHAPTER SIX

The Cave in the Forest

Through the Old Forest came Cugel, step by furtive step, pausing often to listen for breaking twig or quiet footfall or even the exhalation of a breath. His caution, though it made for slow progress, was neither theoretical nor impractical; others wandered the forest with anxieties and yearnings greatly at odds with his own. All one terrible dusk he had fled and finally outdistanced a pair of deodands; on another occasion he had stopped short at the very brink of a glade where a leucomorph had stood musing: whereupon Cugel had become more diffident and furtive than ever, skulking from tree to tree, peering and listening, darting across open spaces with an extravagantly delicate gait, as if contact with the ground pained his feet.

During a middle afternoon he came upon a small dank glade surrounded by black mandours, tall and portentuous as hooded monks. A few red rays slanting into the glade, illumined a single twisted quince tree, where hung a strip of parchment. Standing back in the shadows Cugel studied the glade at length, then stepping forward took the parchment. In crabbed characters a message was indicated:

Zaraides the Sage makes a generous offer! He who finds this message may request and obtain an hour of judicious counsel at no charge. Into a nearby hillock opens a cave; the Sage will be found within.

Cugel studied the parchment with puzzlement. A large question hung in the air: why should Zaraides give forth

182

his lore with such casual largesse? The purportedly free was seldom as represented; in one guise or another the Law of Equivalence must prevail. If Zaraides offered counsel – dismissing the premise of absolute altruism – he expected some commodity in return: at minimum an inflation of self-esteem, or knowledge regarding distant events, or polite attention at a recitation of odes, or some such service. And Cugel re-read the message, his skepticism, if anything augmented. He would have flung the parchment aside had not he felt a real and urgent need for information: specifically knowledge regarding the most secure route to the manse of Iucounu, together with a method for rendering the Laughing Magician helpless.

Cugel looked all about, seeking the hillock to which Zaraides referred. Across the glade the ground seemed to rise, and lifting his eyes Cugel noticed gnarled limbs and clotted foliage on high, as if a number of daobados grew on lofty ground.

With maximum vigilance Cugel proceeded through the forest, and presently was halted by a sudden upthrust of gray rock crowned with trees and vines: undoubtedly the hillock in question.

Cugel stood pulling at his chin, showing his teeth in a grimace of doubt. He listened: quiet, utter and complete. Keeping to the shadows, he continued around the hillock, and presently came upon the cave: an arched opening into the rock as high as a man, as wide as his outstretched arms. Above hung a placard printed in untidy characters:

ENTER: ALL ARE WELCOME!

Cugel looked this way and that. No sight nor sound in the forest. He took a few careful steps forward, peered into the cave, and found only darkness.

183

Cugel drew back. In spite of the genial urgency of the sign, he felt no inclination to thrust himself forward, and squatting on his haunches he watched the cave intently.

Fifteen minutes passed. Cugel shifted his position; and now, to the right, he spied a man approaching, using a caution hardly less elaborate than his own. The newcomer was of medium stature and wore the rude garments of a peasant: gray trousers, a rust-coloured blouse, a cocked brown hat with bill thrust forward. He had a round, somewhat coarse face, with a stub of a nose, small eyes set far apart, a heavy chin bestubbled with a fuscous growth. Clutched in his hand was a parchment like that which Cugel had found.

Cugel rose to his feet. The newcomer halted, then came forward. 'You are Zaraides? If so, know me for Fabeln the herbalist; I seek a rich growth of wild leeks. Further, my daughter moons and languishes, and will no longer carry panniers; therefore—'

Cugel held up his hand. 'You err; Zaraides keeps to his cave.'

Fabeln narrowed his eyes craftily. 'Who then are you?'

'I am Cugel: like yourself, a seeker after enlightenment.'

Fabeln nodded in full comprehension. 'You have consulted Zaraides? He is accurate and trustworthy? He demands no fee as his prospectus purports?'

'Correct in every detail,' said Cugel. 'Zaraides, who is apparently omniscient, speaks from the sheer joy of transmitting information. My perplexities are resolved.'

Fabeln inspected him sidelong. 'Why then do you wait beside the cave?'

'I also am a herbalist, and I formulate new questions, specifically in regard to a nearby glade profuse with wild leeks.'

184

'Indeed!' ejaculated Fabeln, snapping his fingers in agitation. 'Formulate with care, and while you arrange your phrases, I will step within and inquire regarding the lassitude of my daughter.'

'As you will,' said Cugel. 'Still, if you care to delay, I will be only a short time composing my question.'

Fabeln made a jovial gesture. 'In this short period, I will be into the cave, out and away, for I am a man swift to the point of brusqueness.'

Cugel bowed. 'In that case, proceed.'

'I will be brief.' And Fabeln strode into the cave. 'Zaraides?' he called. 'Where is Zaraides the Sage? I am Fabeln; I wish to make certain inquiries. Zaraides? Be so good as to come forth!' His voice became muffled. Cugel, listening intently, heard the opening and closing of a door, and then there was silence. Thoughtfully he composed himself to wait.

Minutes passed . . . and an hour. The red sun moved down the afternoon sky and passed behind the hillock. Cugel became restive. Where was Fabeln? He cocked his head: once more the opening and closing of a door? Indeed, and here was Fabeln: all then was well!

Fabeln looked forth from the cave. 'Where is Cugel the herbalist?' He spoke in a harsh brusque voice. 'Zaraides will not sit down to the banquet nor will he discuss leeks, except in the most general terms, until you present yourself.'

'A banquet?' asked Cugel with interest. 'Does the bounty of Zaraides extend so far?'

'Indeed: did you not notice the tapestried hall, the carved goblets, the silver tureen?' Fabeln spoke with a certain saturnine emphasis which puzzled Cugel. 'But come; I am in haste, and do not care to wait. If you already have dined, I will so inform Zaraides.'

'By no means,' said Cugel, with dignity. 'I would burn

with humiliation thus to slight Zaraides. Lead on; I follow.'

'Come, then.' Fabeln turned; Cugel followed him into the cave, where his nostrils were assailed by a revolting odor. He paused. 'I seem to notice a stench – one which affects me unpleasantly.'

'I noticed the same,' said Fabeln. 'But through the door and the foul odor is no more!'

'I trust as much,' said Cugel peevishly. 'It would destroy my appetite. Where then—'

As he spoke he was swarmed upon by small quick bodies, clammy of skin and tainted with the odor he found so detestable. There was a clamor of high-pitched voices; his sword and pouch were snatched; a door was opened; Cugel was pitched into a low burrow. In the light of a flickering yellow flame he saw his captors: creatures half his height, pallid of skin, pointed of face, with ears on the tops of their heads. They walked with a slight forward hunch, and their knees seemed pointed opposite to those of true men, and their feet, in sandals, seemed very soft and supple.

Cugel looked about in bewilderment. Nearby crouched Fabeln, regarding him with loathing mingled with malicious satisfaction. Cugel saw now that a metal band encircled Fabeln's neck, to which was connected a long metal chain. At the far end of the burrow huddled an old man with long white hair, likewise fitted with collar and chain. Even as Cugel looked about him, the rat-people clamped a collar to his own neck. 'Hold off!' exclaimed Cugel in consternation. 'What does this mean? I deplore such treatment!'

The rat-folk gave him a shove and ran away. Cugel saw that long squamous tails depended from their pointed rumps, which protruded peculiarly from the black smocks which they wore.

The door closed; the three men were alone.

Cugel turned angrily upon Fabeln. 'You tricked me; you led me to capture! This is a serious offense!'

Fabeln gave a bitter laugh. 'No less serious than the deceit you practiced upon me! By your knavish trick, I was taken; I therefore ensured that you should not escape.'

'This is inhuman malice!' roared Cugel. 'I shall see to it that you receive your just desserts!'

'Bah,' said Fabeln. 'Do not annoy me with your complaints. In any event, I did not lure you into the cave from malice alone.'

'No? You have a further perverse motive?'

'It is simple: the rat-folk are nothing if not clever! Whoever entices two others into the cave wins his own freedom. You represent one item to my account; I need furnish a second and I go free. Is this not correct, Zaraides?'

'Only in a broad sense,' replied the old man. 'You may not tally this man to your account; if justice were absolute you and he would fulfill my score; did not my parchments bring you to the cave?'

'But not within!' declared Fabeln. 'Here lies the careful distinction which must be made! The rat-folk concur, and hence you have not been released.'

'In this case,' said Cugel, 'I hereby claim you as an item upon my score, since I sent you into the cave to test the circumstances to be encountered.'

Fabeln shrugged. 'This is a matter you must take up with the rat-folk.' He frowned and blinked his small eyes. 'Why should I not claim myself as a credit to my own account? It is a point worth asserting.'

'Not so, not so,' came a shrill voice from behind a grate. 'We tally only those items provided after impoundment. Fabeln is tallied to no one's account. He however is adjudged one item: namely, the person of Cugel. Zaraides has a score of null.'

Cugel felt the collar at his neck. 'What if we fail to provide two items?'

'A month is your time; no more. If you fail in this month, you are devoured.'

Fabeln spoke in a voice of sober calculation. 'I believe that I am as good as free. At no great distance my daughter waits. She is suddenly impatient with wild leeks and hence redundant to my household. It is fitting that by her agency I am released.' And Fabeln nodded with ponderous satisfaction.

'It will be interesting to watch your methods,' Cugel remarked. 'Precisely where is she to be found and how will she be summoned?'

Fabeln's expression became both cunning and rancorous. 'I tell you nothing! If you wish to tally items, devise the means yourself!'

Zaraides gestured to a board where lay strips of parchment. 'I tie persuasive messages to winged seeds, which are then liberated into the forest. The method is of questionable utility, luring passersby to the mouth of the cave, but enticing them no further. I fear that I have only five days to live. If only I had my librams, my folios, my work-books! What spells, what spells! I would rive this warren end to end; I would convert each of these man-rodents into a blaze of green fire. I would punish Fabeln for cheating me . . . Hmmm. The Gyrator? Lugwiler's Dismal Itch?'

'The Spell of Forlorn Encystment has its advocates,' Cugel suggested.

Zaraides nodded. 'The idea has much to recommend it . . . But this is an idle dream: my spells were snatched away and conveyed to some secret place.'

Fabeln snorted and turned aside. From behind the grate

came a shrill admonition: 'Regrets and excuses are poor substitutes for items upon your score. Emulate Fabeln! Already he boasts one item and plans a second on the morrow! This is the sort we capture by choice!'

'I captured him!' asserted Cugel. 'Have you no probity? I sent him into the cave; he should be credited to my account!'

Zaraides cried out in vehement protest. 'By no means! Cugel distorts the case! If pure justice were done, both Cugel and Fabeln should be tallied to my score!'

'All is as before!' called out the shrill voice.

Zaraides threw up his hands and went to writing parchments with furious zeal. Fabeln hunched himself on a stool and sat in placid reflection. Cugel, in crawling past, kicked a leg from the stool and Fabeln fell to the floor. He rose and sprang at Cugel, who threw the stool at him.

'Order!' called the shrill voice. 'Order or penalties will be inflicted!'

'Cugel dislodged the stool, to send me sprawling,' complained Fabeln. 'Why is he not punished?'

'The sheerest mischance,' stated Cugel. 'In my opinion the irascible Fabeln should be placed incommunicado, for at least two, or more properly, three weeks.'

Fabeln began to sputter, but the shrill voice behind the grate enjoined an impartial silence upon all.

Food was presently brought, a coarse porridge of offensive odor. After the meal all were forced to crawl to a constricted burrow on a somewhat lower level, where they were chained to the wall. Cugel fell into a troubled sleep, to be awakened by a call through the door to Fabeln: 'The message has been delivered – it was read with great attention.'

Good news!' came Fabeln's voice. 'Tomorrow I shall walk the forest a free man!'

189

'Silence,' croaked Zaraides from the dark. 'Must I daily write parchments for everyone's benefit but my own, only to lie awake by night to your vile gloating?'

'Ha ha!' chortled Fabeln. 'Hear the voice of the in-effectual wizard!'

'Alas for my lost librams!' groaned Zaraides. 'You would sing a vastly different tune!'

'In what quarter are they to be found?' inquired Cugel cautiously.

'As to that, you must ask these foul murids; they seized me unawares.'

Fabeln raised his head to complain. 'Do you intend to exchange reminiscences the whole night through? I wish to sleep.'

Zaraides, infuriated, began to upbraid Fabeln in so violent a manner that the rat-folk ran into the burrow and dragged him away, leaving Cugel and Fabeln alone.

In the morning Fabeln ate his porridge with great rapidity. 'Now then,' he called to the grating, 'detach this collar, that I may go forth to summon the second of my tallies, Cugel being the first.'

'Bah,' muttered Cugel. 'Infamous!'

The rat-folk, paying no heed to Fabeln's protests, adjusted the collar even more tightly around his neck, affixed the chain and pulled him forth on hands and knees, and Cugel was left alone.

He tried to sit erect, but the damp dirt pressed on his neck, and he slumped back down on his elbows. 'Cursed rat-creatures! Somehow I must evade them! Unlike Fabeln, I have no household to draw from, and the efficacy of Zaraides' parchments is questionable . . . Conceivably, however, others may wander close, in the fashion of Fabeln and myself.' He turned to the gate, behind which sat the sharp-eyed monitor. 'In order to recruit the required two items, I wish to wait outside the cave.'

'This is permitted,' announced the monitor. 'Supervision must of course be rigid.'

'Supervision is understandable,' agreed Cugel. 'I request however that the chain and collar be removed from my neck. With a constraint so evident, even the most credulous will turn away.'

'There is something in what you say,' admitted the monitor. 'But what is there to prevent you from taking to your heels?'

Cugel gave a somewhat labored laugh. 'Do I seem one to betray a trust? Further, why should I do so, when I can easily procure tally after tally for my score?'

'We shall make certain adjustments.' A moment later a number of the rat-folk swarmed into the burrow. The collar was loosened from Cugel's neck, his right leg was seized and a silver pin driven through his ankle, to which, while Cugel called out in anguish, a chain was secured.

'The chain is now inconspicuous,' stated one of his captors. 'You may now stand before the cave and attract passers-by as best you may.'

Still groaning in pain, Cugel crawled up through the burrow and into the cave-mouth, where Fabeln sat, a chain about his neck, awaiting the arrival of his daughter. 'Where do you go?' he asked suspiciously.

'I go to pace before the cave, to attract passers-by and direct them within!'

Fabeln gave a sour grunt, and peered off through the trees.

Cugel went to stand before the cave-mouth. He looked in all directions, then gave a melodious call. 'Does anyone walk near?'

He received no reply, and began to pace back and forth, the chain jingling along the ground.

Movement through the trees: the flutter of yellow and green cloth, and here came Fabeln's daughter, carrying a

191

basket and an axe. At the sight of Cugel she paused, then hesitantly approached. 'I seek Fabeln, who has requested certain articles.'

'I will take them,' said Cugel, reaching for the axe, but the rat-folk were alert and hauled him quickly back into the cave. 'She must place the axe on that far rock,' they hissed into Cugel's ear. 'Go forth and so inform her.'

Cugel limped forth once more. The girl looked at him in puzzlement. 'Why did you leap back in that fashion?'

'I will tell you,' said Cugel, 'and it is an odd matter, but first you must place your basket and axe on that rock yonder, where the true Fabeln will presently arrive.'

From within the cave came a mutter of angry protest, quickly stifled.

'What was that sound?' inquired the girl.

'Do with the axe as I require, and I will make all known.'

The girl, puzzled, took axe and basket to the designated spot, then returned. 'Now, where is Fabeln?'

'Fabeln is dead,' said Cugel. 'His body is currently possessed by a malicious spirit; do not on any grounds heed it: this is my warning.'

At this Fabeln gave a great groan, and called from the cave. 'He lies, he lies. Come hither, into the cave!'

Cugel held up a hand in restraint. 'By no means. Be cautious!'

The girl peered in wonder and fear toward the cave, where now Fabeln appeared, making the most earnest gesticulations. The girl drew back. 'Come, come!' cried Fabeln. 'Enter the cave!'

The girl shook her head, and Fabeln in a fury attempted to tear loose his chain. The rat-folk dragged him hastily back into the shadows, where Fabeln fought so vigorously the rat-folk were obliged to kill him and drag his body back into the burrow.

Cugel listened attentively, then turned to the girl and nodded. 'All is now well. Fabeln left certain valuables in my care; if you will step within the cave, I will relinquish them to you.'

The girl shook her head in bewilderment. 'Fabeln owned nothing of value!'

'Be good enough to inspect the objects.' Cugel courteously motioned her to the cave. She stepped forward, peered within, and instantly the rat-folk seized her and dragged her down into the burrow.

'This is item one on my score,' called Cugel within. 'Do not neglect to record it!'

'The tally is duly noted,' came a voice from within. 'One more such and you go free.'

The remainder of the day Cugel paced back and forth before the cave, looking this way and that through the trees, but saw no one. At nightfall he was drawn back into the cave and pent in the low-level burrow where he had passed the previous night. Now it was occupied by Fabeln's daughter. Naked, bruised, vacant-eyed, she stared at him fixedly. Cugel attempted an exchange of conversation, but she seemed bereft of speech.

The evening porridge was served. While Cugel ate, he watched the girl surreptitiously. She was by no means uncomely, though now bedraggled and soiled. Cugel crawled closer, but the odor of the rat-folk was so strong that his lust diminished, and he drew back.

During the night there was furtive sound in the burrow: a scraping, scratching, grating sound. Cugel, blinking sleepily, raised on an elbow, to see a section of the floor tilt stealthily ajar, allowing a seep of smoky yellow light to play on the girl. Cugel cried out; into the burrow rushed rat-folk carrying tridents, but it was too late: the girl had been stolen.

The rat-folk were intensely angry. They raised the stone, screamed curses and abuse into the gap. Others poured into the hole, with further vituperation. One aggrievedly explained the situation to Cugel. 'Other beings live below; they cheat us at every turn. Someday we will exact revenge; our patience is not inexhaustible! This night you must sleep elsewhere lest they make another sortie.' He loosened Cugel's chain, but now was called by those who cemented the hole in the floor.

Cugel moved quietly to the entrance, and when the attention of all were distracted he slipped out into the passage. Gathering up the chain, he crawled in that direction which he thought led to the surface, but encountering a side-passage became confused. The tunnel turned downward and, becoming narrow, constricted his shoulders; then it diminished in height, pressing down on him from above, so that he was forced to writhe forward, jerking himself by his elbows.

His absence was discovered; from behind came squeals of rage, as the rat-folk rushed this way and that.

The passage made a sharp twist, at an angle into which Cugel found it impossible to twist his body. Writhing and jerking, he squeezed himself into a new posture, and now could no longer move. He exhaled and with eyes starting from his head, lunged about and up, and drew himself into a passage more open. In a niche he came upon a fire-ball, which he carried with him.

The rat-folk were approaching, screaming injunctions. Cugel thrust himself into a side-passage which opened into a store-room. The first objects to meet his eye were his sword and pouch.

The rat-folk rushed into the room with tridents. Cugel hacked and slashed and drove them squealing back into the corridor. Here they gathered, darting back and forth, calling shrill threats in at Cugel. Occasionally one would rush forward to gnash its teeth and flourish its trident, but when Cugel killed two of these, they drew back to confer in low tones.

Cugel took occasion to thrust certain heavy cases against the entrance, thus affording himself a moment's respite.

The rat-folk pressed forward, kicking and shoving. Cugel thrust his blade through a chink, eliciting a wail of intense distress.

One spoke: 'Cugel, come forth! We are a kindly folk and bear no malice. You have one item upon your score, and shortly no doubt will secure another, and thus go free. Why discommode us all? There is no reason why, in an essentially inconvenient relationship, we should not adopt an attitude of camaraderie. Come forth, then, and we will provide meat for your morning porridge.'

Cugel spoke politely. 'At the moment I am too distraught to think clearly. Did I hear you say that you planned to set me free without further charge or difficulty?'

There was a whispered conversation in the corridor, then came the response. 'There was indeed a statement to that effect. You are hereby declared free, to come and go as you wish. Unblock the entrance, cast down your sword, and come forth!'

'What guarantee can you offer me?' asked Cugel, listening intently at the blocked entrance.

There were shrill chattering whispers, then the reply: 'No guarantee is necessary. We now retire. Come forth, walk along the corridor to your freedom.'

Cugel made no response. Holding aloft the fire-ball, he turned to inspect the store-room, which contained a great store of articles of clothing, weapons and tools. In that bin which he had pushed against the entrance he noticed a group of leather-bound librams. On the face of the first was printed:

ZARAIDES THE WIZARD
His Work-book: Beware!

The rat-folk called once more, in gentle voices: 'Cugel, dear Cugel, why have you not come forth?'

'I rest; I recover my strength,' said Cugel. He took forth the libram, turned the pages, and found an index.

'Come forth, Cugel!' came a command, somewhat sterner. 'We have here a pot of noxious vapor which we propose to discharge into the chamber where you so obdurately seclude yourself. Come forth, or it shall be the worse for you!'

'Patience,' called Cugel. 'Allow me time to collect my wits!'

'While you collect your wits we ready the pot of acid in which we plan to immerse your head.'

'Just so, just so,' said Cugel absently, engrossed in the work-book. There was a scraping sound and a tube was thrust into the chamber. Cugel took hold of the tube and twisted it so that it pointed back into the corridor.

'Speak, Cugel!' came the portentous order. 'Will you come forth or shall we send a great gust of vile gas into the chamber?'

'You lack that capability,' said Cugel. 'I refuse to come forth.'

'You shall see! Let the gas exude!'

The tube pulsed and hissed; from the corridor came a cry of vast dismay. The hissing ceased.

Cugel, not finding what he sought in the work-book, drew forth a tome. This bore the title:

ZARAIDES THE WIZARD
His Compendium of Spells
Beware!

Cugel opened and read; finding an appropriate spell, he held the fire-ball close the better to encompass the activating syllables. There were four lines of words, thirty-one syllables in all. Cugel forced them into his brain, where they lay like stones.

A sound behind him? Into the chamber from another portal came the rat-folk. Crouching low, white faces twitching, ears down, they crept forward, tridents leveled.

Cugel menaced them with his sword, then chanted that spell known as the Inside Out and Over, while the rat-folk stared aghast. There came a great tearing sound: a convulsive lift and twist as the passages everted, spewing all through the forest. Rat-folk ran squealing back and forth, and there were also running white things whose nature Cugel could not distinguish by starlight. Rat-folk and the white creatures grappled and tore ferociously at each other, and the forest was filled with snarling and gnashing, shrill screams and small voices raised in outcry.

Cugel moved quietly away, and in a bilberry thicket waited out the night.

When dawn arrived he returned cautiously to the hillock, hoping to possess himself of Zaraides' compendium and work-book. There was great litter, and many small corpses, but the articles he sought were not to be found. Regretfully Cugel turned away and presently came upon Fabeln's daughter sitting among the ferns. When he approached, she squeaked at him. Cugel pursed his lips and shook his head in disapproval. He led her to a nearby stream and attempted to wash her, but at the first opportunity she disengaged herself and hid under a rock.

CHAPTER SEVEN

The Manse of Iucounu

The spell known as the Inside Out and Over was of derivation so remote as to be forgotten. An unknown Cloud-rider of the Twenty-first Eon had construed an archaic version; the half-legendary Basile Blackweb had refined its contours, a process continued by Veronifer the Bland, who had added a reinforcing resonance. Archemand of Glaere had annotated fourteen of its pervulsions: Phandaal had listed it in the "A," or "Perfected," category of his monumental catalogue. In this fashion it had reached the workbook of Zaraides the Sage, where Cugel, immured under a hillock, had found it and spoken it forth.

Now, once more searching through the multifarious litter of the spell's aftermath, Cugel found articles of every description: garments new and old; jerkins, vests and cloaks; antique tabards; breeches flared after the new taste of Kauchique, or fringed and tasseled in the style of Old Romarth, or pied and gored in the extravagant Andromach mode. There were boots and sandals and hats of every description; plumes, panaches, emblems and crests; old tools and broken weapons; bangles and trinkets; tarnished filigrees, crusted cameos; gemstones which Cugel could not refrain from gathering and which perhaps delayed him from finding that which he sought: the work-books of Zaraides, which had been scattered with the rest.

Cugel searched at length. He found silver bowls, ivory spoons, porcelain vases, gnawed bones and shining teeth of many sorts, these glittering like pearls among the leaves – but nowhere the tomes and folios which might have helped him overcome Iucounu the Laughing Magician. Even now Iucounu's creature of coercion, Firx, clamped serrated members upon Cugel's liver. Cugel finally called out: 'I merely seek the most direct route to Azenomei; you will soon rejoin your comrade in Iucounu's vat! Meanwhile take your ease; are you in such an agony of haste?' At which Firx sullenly relaxed his pressure.

Cugel wandered disconsolately back and forth, looking among branches and under roots, squinting up the forest aisles, kicking among the ferns and mosses. Then at the base of a stump he saw that which he sought: a number of folios and librams, gathered into a neat stack. Upon the stump sat Zaraides.

Cugel stepped forward, pinch-mouthed with disappointment. Zaraides surveyed him with a serene countenance. 'You appear to seek some misplaced object. The loss, I trust, is not serious?'

Cugel gave his head a terse shake. 'A few trifles have gone astray. Let them molder among the leaves.'

'By no means!' declared Zaraides. 'Describe the loss; I will send forth a searching oscillation. You will have your property within moments!'

Cugel demurred. 'I would not impose such a trivial business upon you. Let us consider other matters.' He indicated the stack of tomes, upon which Zaraides had now placed his feet. 'Happily your own property is secure.'

Zaraides nodded with placid satisfaction. 'All is now well; I am concerned only with that imbalance which distorts our relationship.' He held up his hand as Cugel stood back. 'There is no cause for alarm; in fact, quite the reverse. Your acts averted my death; the Law of Equivalences has been disturbed and I must contrive a

199

reciprocity.' He combed his beard with his fingers. 'The requital unfortunately must be largely symbolic. I could well fulfill the totality of your desires and still not nudge the scale against the weight of the service you have performed, even if unwittingly, for me.'

Cugel became somewhat more cheerful, but now Firx, once again impatient, made a new demonstration. Clasping his abdomen, Cugel cried out, 'Preliminary to all, be good enough to extract the creature which lacerates my vitals, a certain Firx.'

Zaraides raised his eyebrows. 'What manner of creature is this?'

'A detestable object from a far star. It resembles a tangle, a thicket, a web of white spines, barbs and claws.'

'A matter of no great difficulty,' said Zaraides. 'These creatures are susceptible to a rather primitive method of extirpation. Come; my dwelling lies at no great distance.'

Zaraides stepped down from the stump, gathered his compendia and flung them into the air; all lofted high to float swiftly over the treetops and out of sight. Cugel watched them go with sadness.

'You marvel?' inquired Zaraides. 'It is nothing: the simplest of procedures and a curb on the zeal of thieves and footpads. Let us set forth; we must expel this creature which causes you such distress.'

He led the way through the trees. Cugel came after, but now Firx, belatedly sensing that all was not to his advantage, made a furious protest. Cugel, bending double, jumping sidewise, forced himself to totter and run after Zaraides, who marched without so much as a backward glance.

In the branches of an enormous daobado Zaraides had his dwelling. Stairs rose to a heavy drooping bough which led to a rustic portico. Cugel crawled up the staircase, along the bough, and into a great square room. The

200

furnishings were at once simple and luxurious. Windows looked in all directions over the forest; a thick rug patterned in black, brown and yellow covered the floor.

Zaraides beckoned Cugel into his workroom. 'We will abate this nuisance at once.'

Cugel stumbled after him and at a gesture settled upon a glass pedestal.

Zaraides brought a screen of zinc strips which he placed at Cugel's back. 'This is to inform Firx that a trained wizard is at hand: creatures of his sort are highly antipathetic to zinc. Now then, a simple potion: sulfur, aquastel, tincture of zyche; certain herbs: bournade, hilp, cassas, though these latter are perhaps not essential. Drink, if you will . . . Firx, come forth! Hence, you extraterrestrial pest! Remove! Or I dust Cugel's entire interior with sulfur and pierce him with zinc rods! Come forth! What? Must I flush you forth with aquastel? Come forth; return to Achernar as best you may!'

At this Firx angrily relinquished his grip and issued from Cugel's chest: a tangle of white nerves and tendrils, each with its claw or barb. Zaraides captured the creature in a zinc basin which he covered with a mesh of zinc.

Cugel, who had lost consciousness, awoke to find Zaraides serenely affable, awaiting his recovery. 'You are a lucky man,' Zaraides told him. 'The treatment was only barely in time. It is the tendency of this maleficent incubus to extend its prongs everywhere through the body, until it clamps upon the brain; then you and Firx are one and the same. How did you become infected with the creature?'

Cugel gave a small grimace of distaste. 'It was at the hands of Iucounu the Laughing Magician. You know him?' For Zaraides had allowed his eyebrows to arch high.

201

'Mainly by his reputation for humor and grotesquerie,' replied the sage.

'He is nothing less than a buffoon!' exclaimed Cugel. 'For a fancied slight he threw me to the north of the world, where the sun wheels low and casts no more heat than a lamp. Iucounu must have his joke, but now I will have a joke of my own! You have announced your effusive gratitude, and so, before proceeding to the main body of my desires, we will take a suitable revenge upon Iucounu.'

Zaraides nodded thoughtfully and ran his fingers through his beard. 'I will advise you. Iucounu is a vain and sensitive man. His most vulnerable spot is his self-esteem. Turn your back on him, take yourself to another quarter! This act of proud disdain will strike a pang more exquisite than any other discomfort you might devise.'

Cugel frowned. 'The reprisal seems rather too abstract. If you will be good enough to summon a demon, I will give him his instructions in regard to Iucounu. The business will then be at an end, and we can discuss other matters.'

Zaraides shook his head. 'All is not so simple. Iucounu, himself devious, is not apt to be taken unawares. He would instantly learn who instigated the assault, and the relations of distant cordiality we have enjoyed would be at an end.'

'Pah!' scoffed Cugel. 'Does Zaraides the Sage fear to identify himself with the cause of justice? Does he blink and draw aside from one so timid and vacillating as Iucounu?'

'In a word – yes,' said Zaraides. 'At any instant the sun may go dark; I do not care to pass these last hours exchanging jests with Iucounu, whose humor is much more elaborate than my own. So now, attend. In one minute I must concern myself with certain important duties. As a final signal of gratitude I will transfer you to whatever locale you choose. Where shall it be?'

'If this is your best, take me then to Azenomei, at the juncture of the Xzan with the Scaum!'

'As you wish. Be so good as to step upon this stage. Hold out your hands thus . . . Draw your breath deep, and during the passage neither inhale nor exhale . . . Are you ready?'

Cugel assented. Zaraides drew back and called a spell. Cugel was jerked up and away. An instant later the ground touched his feet and he found himself walking the main concourse of Azenomei.

He drew a deep breath. 'After all the trials, all the vicissitudes, I am once again in Azenomei!' And, shaking his head in wonder, he looked about him. The ancient structures, the terraces overlooking the river, the market: all were as before. Not far distant was the booth of Fianosther. Turning his back to avoid recognition, he sauntered away.

'Now what?' he ruminated. 'First, new garments, then the comforts of an inn, where I may weigh every aspect of my present condition. When one wishes to laugh with Iucounu, he should embark upon the project with all caution.'

Two hours later, bathed, shorn, refreshed, and wearing new garments of black, green and red, Cugel sat in the common room of the River Inn with a plate of spiced sausages and a flask of green wine.

'This matter of a just settlement poses problems of extreme delicacy,' he mused. 'I must move with care!'

He poured wine from the flagon, and ate several of the sausages. Then he opened his pouch and withdrew a small object wrapped carefully in soft cloth: the violet cusp which Iucounu wished as a match for the one already in his possession. He raised the cusp to his eye, but stopped short: it would display the surroundings in an illusion so favorable that he might never wish to remove it. And

203

now, as he contemplated the glossy surface, there entered his mind a program so ingenious, so theoretically effective and yet of such small hazard, that he instantly abandoned the search for a better.

Essentially, the scheme was simple. He would present himself to Iucounu and tender the cusp, or more accurately, a cusp of similar appearance. Iucounu would compare it with that which he already owned, in order to test the efficacy of the coupled pair, and inevitably look through both. The discord between the real and the false would jar his brain and render him helpless, whereupon Cugel could take such measures as seemed profitable.

Where was the flaw in the plan? Cugel could see none. If Iucounu discovered the substitution, Cugel need only utter an apology and produce the real cusp, and so lull Iucounu's suspicions. All in all, the probabilities of success seemed excellent.

Cugel finished his sausages in leisure, ordered a second flagon of wine, and observed with pleasure the view across the Xzan. There was no need for haste; indeed, while dealing with Iucounu, impulsiveness was a serious mistake, as he had already learned.

On the following day, still finding no fault in his plan, he visited a glass-blower whose workroom was established on the banks of the Scaum a mile to the east of Azenomei, in a copse of fluttering yellow bilibobs.

The glass-blower examined the cusp. 'An exact duplicate, of identical shape and color? No small task, with a violet so pure and rich. Such a color is most difficult to work into glass; there is no specific stain; all must be a matter of guess and hazard. Still – I will prepare a melt. We shall see, we shall see.'

After several trials he produced a glass of the requisite hue, from which he fashioned a cusp superficially indistinguishable from the magic lens.

'Excellent!' declared Cugel. 'And now, as to your fee?'

'Such a cusp of violet glass I value at a hundred terces,' replied the glass-blower in a casual manner.

'What?' cried Cugel in outrage. 'Do I appear so gullible? The charge is excessive.'

The glass-blower replaced his tools, swages and crucibles, showing no concern for Cugel's indignation. 'The universe evinces no true stability. All fluctuates, cycles, ebbs and flows; all is pervaded with mutability. My fees, which are immanent with the cosmos, obey the same laws and vary according to the anxiety of the customer.'

Cugel drew back in displeasure, at which the glass-blower reached forth and possessed himself of both cusps. Cugel exclaimed: 'What do you intend?'

'I return the glass to the crucible; what else?'

'And what of that cusp which is my property?'

'I retain it as a memento of our conversation.'

'Hold!' Cugel drew a deep breath. 'I might pay your exorbitant fee if the new cusp were as clear and perfect as the old.'

The glass-blower inspected first one, then the other. 'To my eye they are identical.'

'Of what focus?' Cugel challenged. 'Hold both to your vision, look through both, then say as much!'

The glass-blower raised both cusps to his eyes. One allowed a view into the Overworld, the other transmitted a view of Reality. Stunned by the discord, the glass-blower swayed and would have fallen had not Cugel, in an effort to protect the cusps, supported him, and guided him to a bench.

Taking the cusps, Cugel tossed three terces to the worktable. 'All is mutability, and thus your hundred terces has fluctuated to three.'

205

The glass-blower, too dazed to make sensible reply, mumbled and struggled to raise his hand, but Cugel strode from the studio and away.

He returned to the inn. Here he donned his old garments, stained and torn by much harsh treatment, and set forth along the banks of the Xzan.

As he walked he rehearsed the approaching confrontation, trying to anticipate every possible contingency. Ahead, the sunlight glinted through spiral green glass towers: the manse of Iucounu!

Cugel halted to gaze up at the eccentric structure. How many times during his journey had he envisioned himself standing here, with Iucounu the Laughing Magician close at hand!

He climbed the winding way of dark brown tile, and every step increased the tautness of his nerves. He approached the front door, and saw on the heavy panel an object which he had failed to notice previously: a visage carved in ancient wood, a gaunt face pinched of cheek and jaw, the eyes aghast, the lips drawn back, the mouth wide in a yell of despair or perhaps defiance.

With his hand raised to rap at the door, Cugel felt a chill settle on his soul. He drew back from the haggard wooden countenance, turning to follow the gaze of the blind eyes – across the Xzan and away over the dim bare hills, rolling and heaving as far as vision could reach. He reviewed his plan of operations. Was there a flaw? Danger to himself? None was apparent. If Iucounu discovered the substitution Cugel could always plead error and produce the genuine cusp. Great advantage was to be gained at small risk! Cugel turned back and rapped on the heavy panel.

A minute passed. Slowly the portal swung open. A flow of cool air issued forth, carrying a bitter odor which Cugel could not identify. The sunlight slanting across his shoulder passed through the portal and fell upon the stone floor. Cugel peered uncertainly into the vestibule, reluctant to enter without an express invitation. 'Iucounu!' he called. 'Come forth, that I may enter your manse! I wish no further unjust accusations!'

Within was a stir, a slow sound of feet. From a room to the side came Iucounu, and Cugel thought to detect a change in his countenance. The great soft yellow head seemed looser than before: the jowls sagged, the nose hung like a stalactite, the chin was little more than a pimple below the great twitching mouth.

Iucounu wore a square brown hat with each of the corners tipped up, a blouse of brown and black diaper, loose pantaloons of a heavy dark brown stuff with black embroidery – a handsome set of garments which Iucounu wore without grace, as if they were strange to him, and uncomfortable; and indeed, he gave Cugel a greeting which Cugel found odd. 'Well, fellow, what is your purpose? You will never learn to walk ceilings standing on your hands.' And Iucounu hid his mouth with his hands to conceal a snicker.

Cugel raised his eyebrows in surprise and doubt. 'This is not my purpose. I have come on an errand of vast import: namely to report that the mission I undertook on your behalf is satisfactorily terminated.'

'Excellent!' cried Iucounu. 'You may now tender me the keys to the bread locker.'

'Bread locker?' Cugel stared in surprise. Was Iucounu mad? 'I am Cugel, whom you sent north on a mission. I have returned with the magic cusp affording a view into the Overworld!'

'Of course, of course!' cried Iucounu. '"Brzm-szzst." I fear I am vague, among so many contrasting situations; nothing is quite as before. But now I welcome you, Cugel, of course! All is clear. You have gone forth, you have

207

returned! How is friend Firx? Well, I trust? I have longed for his companionship. An excellent fellow, Firx!'

Cugel acquiesced with no great fervor. 'Yes, Firx has been a friend indeed, an unflagging source of encouragement.'

'Excellent! Step within! I must provide refreshment! What is your preference: "sz-mzsm" or "szk-zsm"?'

Cugel eyed Iucounu askance. His demeanor was more than peculiar. 'I am familiar with neither of the items you mention, and hence will decline both with gratitude. But observe! The magic violet cusp!' And Cugel displayed the glass fabrication which he had procured only a few hours previously.

'Excellent!' declared Iucounu. 'You have done well, and your transgressions – now I recall all, having sorted among the various circumstances – are hereby declared nullified. But give me the cusp! I must put it to trial!'

'Of course,' said Cugel. 'I respectfully suggest, that in order to comprehend the full splendor of the Overworld, you bring forth your own cusp and look through both simultaneously. This is the only appropriate method.'

'True, how true! My cusp; now where did that stubborn rascal conceal it?'

'"Stubborn rascal"?' inquired Cugel. 'Has someone been misarranging your valuables?'

'In a manner of speaking.' Iucounu gave a wild titter, and kicked up both feet far to the side, falling heavily to the floor, from where he addressed the astounded Cugel. 'It is all one, and no longer of consequence, since all must now transpire in the "mnz" pattern. Yes. I will shortly consult with Firx.'

'On a previous occasion,' said Cugel patiently, 'you procured your cusp from a cabinet in that chamber yonder.'

'Silence!' commanded Iucounu in sudden annoyance.

He hauled himself to his feet. '"Szsz"! I am well aware as to where the cusp is stored. All is completely coordinated! Follow me. We shall learn the essence of the Overworld at once!' He emitted a bray of immoderate laughter, at which Cugel stared in new astonishment.

Iucounu shuffled into the side-chamber and returned with the case containing his magic cusp. He made an imperious gesture to Cugel. 'Stand exactly at this spot. Do not move, as you value Firx!'

Cugel bowed obediently. Iucounu took forth his cusp. 'Now – the new object!'

Cugel tendered the glass cusp. 'To your eyes, both together, that you may enjoy the full glory of the Overworld!'

'Yes! This is as it shall be!' Iucounu lifted the two cusps and applied them to his eyes. Cugel, expecting him to fall paralyzed by the discord, reached for the cord he had brought to tie the insensible savant; but Iucounu showed no signs of helplessness. He peered this way and that, chortling in a peculiar fashion. 'Splendid! Superb! A vista of pure pleasure!' He removed the cusps and placed them carefully in the case. Cugel watched glumly.

'I am much pleased,' said Iucounu, making a sinuous gesture of hands and arms, which further bewildered Cugel. 'Yes,' Iucounu continued, 'you have done well, and the insensate wickedness of your offense is hereby remitted. Now all that remains is the delivery of my indispensible Firx, and to this end I must place you in a vat. You will be submerged in an appropriate liquid for approximately twenty-six hours, which may well suffice to tempt Firx forth.'

Cugel grimaced. How was one to reason with a magician not only droll and irascible, but also bereft? 'Such an immersion might well affect me adversely,' he pointed out cautiously. 'Far wiser to allow Firx a period of further perambulation.'

Iucounu seemed favorably impressed by the suggestion, and expressed his delight by means of an extremely intricate jig, which he performed with agility remarkable in a man of Iucounu's short limbs and somewhat corpulent body. He concluded the demonstration with a great leap into the air, alighting on his neck and shoulders, arms and legs waving like those of an overturned beetle. Cugel watched in fascination, wondering whether Iucounu was alive or dead.

But Iucounu, blinking somewhat, nimbly gained an upright posture. 'I must perfect the exact pressures and thrusts,' he ruminated. 'Otherwise there is impingement. The eluctance here is of a different order than of "ssz-pntz".' He emitted another great chortle, throwing back his head, and looking into the open mouth Cugel saw, rather than a tongue, a white claw. Instantly he apprehended the reason for Iucounu's bizarre conduct. In some fashion a creature like Firx had inserted itself into Iucounu's body, and had taken possession of his brain.

Cugel rubbed his chin with interest. A situation of marvel! He applied himself to concentrated thought. Essential to know was whether the creature retained Iucounu's mastery of magic. Cugel said, 'Your wisdom astounds me! I am filled with admiration! Have you added to your collection of thaumaturgical curios?'

'No; there is ample at hand,' declared the creature, speaking through Iucounu's mouth. 'But now I feel the need for relaxation. The evolution I performed a moment or so ago has made quietude necessary.'

'A simple matter,' said Cugel. 'The most effective means to this end is to clamp with extreme intensity upon the Lobe of Directive Volition.'

'Indeed?' inquired the creature. 'I will attempt as much; let me see: this is the Lobe of Antithesis and here, the Convolvement of Subliminal Configuration. . . "Szzm."

Much here puzzles me; it was never thus on Achernar.' The creature gave Cugel a sharp look to see if the slip had been noticed. But Cugel put on an attitude of lackadaisical boredom; and the creature continued to sort through the various elements of Iucounu's brain. 'Ah yes, here: the Lobe of Directive Volition. Now, a sudden vigorous pressure.'

Iucounu's face became taut, the muscles sagged, and the corpulent body crumpled to the floor. Cugel leapt forward and in a trice bound Iucounu's arms and legs and affixed an adhesive pad across the big mouth.

Now Cugel performed a joyful caper of his own. All was well! Iucounu, his manse and his great collection of magical adjuncts were at his disposal! Cugel considered the helpless hulk and started to drag it outside where he might conveniently strike off the great yellow head, but the recollection of the numerous indignities, discomforts and humiliations he had suffered at Iucounu's hands gave him pause. Should Iucounu attain oblivion so swiftly, with neither cognition nor remorse? By no means!

Cugel pulled the still body out into the hall, and sat on a nearby bench to consider.

Presently the body stirred, opened its eyes, made an effort to arise, and, finding this impossible, turned to examine Cugel first in surprise, then outrage. From the mouth came peremptory sounds which Cugel acknowledged with a noncommittal sign.

Presently he arose to his feet, examined the bonds and the mouth-plaster, made all doubly secure, then set about a cautious inspection of the manse, alert for traps, lures or deadfalls which the whimsical Iucounu might have established in order to outwit or beguile intruders. He was especially vigilant during his inspection of Iucounu's workroom, probing everywhere with a long rod, but if Iucounu had set forth snares or beguilements, none were evident.

Looking along Iucounu's shelves, Cugel found sulfur, aquastel, tincture of zyche and herbs from which he prepared a viscous yellow elixir. He dragged the flaccid body into the workroom, administered the potion, called orders and persuasions and finally, with Iucounu an even more intense yellow from ingested sulfur, with aquastel steaming from his ears, with Cugel panting and perspiring from his own exertions, the creature from Achernar clawed free of the heaving body. Cugel caught it in a great stone mortar, crushed it to a paste with an iron pestle, dissolved all with spirits of vitriol, added aromatic mernaunce and poured the resultant slime down a drain.

Iucounu, presently returning to consciousness, fixed Cugel with a glare of disturbing intensity. Cugel administered an exhalation of raptogen and the Laughing Magician, rolling his eyes upward, returned to a state of apathy.

Cugel sat back to rest. A problem existed: how best to restrain Iucounu while he made his representations. Finally, after looking through one or two manuals, he sealed Iucounu's mouth with a daub of juncturing compound, secured his vitality with an uncomplicated spell, then pent him in a tall glass tube, which he suspended from a chain in the vestibule.

This accomplished, and Iucounu once more conscious, Cugel stood back with an affable grin. 'At last, Iucounu, matters begin to right themselves. Do you recall the indignities you visited upon me? How gross they were! I vowed that you would regret the circumstance! I now begin to validate the vow. Do I make myself clear?'

The expression distorting Iucounu's face was an adequate response.

Cugel seated himself with a goblet of Iucounu's best yellow wine. 'I intend to pursue the matter in this wise: I shall calculate the sum of those hardships I have endured, including such almost incommensurable qualities as chills, cold draughts, insults, pangs of apprehension, uncertainties, bleak despairs, horrors and disgusts, and other indescribable miseries, not the least of which the ministrations of the unspeakable Firx. From this total I will subtract for my initial indiscretion, and possibly one or two further ameliorations, leaving an imposing balance of retribution. Luckily, you are Iucounu the Laughing Magician: you will certainly derive a wry impersonal amusement from the situation.' Cugel turned an inquiring glance up at Iucounu, but the returning gaze was anything but jocular.

'A final question,' said Cugel. 'Have you arranged any traps or lures in which I might be destroyed or immobilized? One blink will express "no"; two, "yes".'

Iucounu merely gazed contemptuously from the tube.

Cugel sighed. 'I see that I must conduct myself warily.'

Taking his wine into the great hall, he began to familiarize himself with the collection of magical instruments, artifacts, talismans and curios: now, for all practical purposes, his own property. Iucounu's gaze followed him everywhere with anxious hope that was by no means reassuring.

Days went by and Iucounu's trap, if such existed, remained unsprung, and Cugel at last came to believe that none existed. During this time he applied himself to Iucounu's tomes and folios, but with disappointing results. Certain of the tomes were written in archaic tongues, indecipherable script or arcane terminology; others described phenomena beyond his comprehension; others exuded a waft of such urgent danger that Cugel instantly clamped shut the covers.

One or two of the work-books he found susceptible to his understanding. These he studied with great diligence, cramming syllable after wrenching syllable into his mind, where they rolled and pressed and distended his temples. Presently he was able to encompass a few of the most simple and primitive spells, certain of which he tested upon Iucounu: notably Lugwiler's Dismal Itch. But by and large Cugel was disappointed by what seemed a lack of innate competence. Accomplished magicians could encompass three or even four of the most powerful effectuants; for Cugel, attaining even a single spell was a task of extraordinary difficulty. One day, while applying a spatial transposition upon a satin cushion, he inverted certain of the pervulsions and was himself hurled backward into the vestibule. Annoyed by Iucounu's smirk, Cugel carried the tube to the front of the manse and affixed a pair of brackets upon which he hung lamps, which thereafter illuminated the area before the manse during the hours of night.

A month passed, and Cugel became somewhat more confident in his occupancy of the manse. Peasants of a nearby village brought him produce, and in return Cugel performed what small services he was able. On one occasion the father of Jince, the maiden who served as arranger of his bed-chamber, lost a valuable buckle in a deep cistern, and implored Cugel to bring it forth. Cugel readily agreed, and lowered the tube containing Iucounu into the cistern. Iucounu finally indicated the location of the buckle, which was then recovered with a grapple.

The episode set Cugel to devising other uses for Iucounu. At the Azenomei Fair a 'Contest of Grotesques' had been arranged. Cugel entered Iucounu in the competition, and while he failed to win the prime award, his grimaces were unforgettable and attracted much comment.

At the fair Cugel encountered Fianosther, the dealer in talismans and magical adjuncts who had originally sent Cugel to Iucounu's manse. Fianosther looked in jocular surprise from Cugel to the tube containing Iucounu, which Cugel was transporting back to the manse in a cart. 'Cugel! Cugel the Clever!' exclaimed Fianosther. 'Rumor then speaks accurately! You are now lord of Iucounu's manse, and of his great collection of instruments and curios!'

Cugel at first pretended not to recognize Fianosther, then spoke in the coolest of voices. 'Quite true,' he said. 'Iucounu has chosen to participate less actively in the affairs of the world, as you see. Nonetheless, the manse is a warren of traps and deadfalls; several famished beasts stalk the grounds by night, and I have established a spell of intense violence to guard each entrance.'

Fianosther seemed not to notice Cugel's distant manner. Rubbing his plump hands, he inquired, 'Since you now control a vast collection of curios, will you sell certain of the less choice items?'

'I have neither the need nor inclination to do so,' said Cugel. 'Iucounu's coffers contain gold to last till the sun goes dark.' And both men, after the habit of time, looked up to gauge the color of the moribund star.

Fianosther made a gracious sign. 'In this case, I wish you a good day, and you as well.' The last was addressed to Iucounu, who returned only a surly glare.

Returning to the manse, Cugel brought Iucounu into the vestibule; then, making his way to the roof, he leaned on a parapet and gazed over the expanse of hills which rolled away like swells on a sea. For the hundredth time he pondered Iucounu's peculiar failure of foresight; by no means must he, Cugel, fall into similar error. And he looked about with an eye to defense.

Above rose the spiral green glass towers; below slanted the steep ridges and gables which Iucounu had deemed esthetically correct. Only the face of the ancient keep offered an easy method of access to the manse. Along the

slanting outer abutments Cugel arranged sheets of soap-
stone in such a manner that anyone climbing to the parapets must step on these and slide to his doom. Had Iucounu
taken a similar precaution – so Cugel reflected – instead
of arranging the oversubtle crystal maze, he would not now
be looking forth from the tall glass tube.

Other defenses must also be perfected: namely those
resources to be derived from Iucounu's shelves.

Returning to the great hall, he consumed the repast set
forth by Jince and Skivvee, his two comely stewardesses,
then immediately applied himself to his studies. Tonight
they concerned themselves with the Spell of Forlorn Encystment, a reprisal perhaps more favored in earlier eons
than the present, and the Agency of Far Despatch, by
which Iucounu had transported him to the northern wastes.
Both spells were of no small power; both required a bold
and absolutely precise control, which Cugel at first feared
he would never be able to supply. Nevertheless he persisted, and at last felt able to encompass either the one or
the other, at need.

Two days later it was as Cugel had expected: a rap at the
front door which, when Cugel flung wide the portal, indicated the unwelcome presence of Fianosther.

'Good day,' said Cugel cheerlessly. 'I am indisposed, and
must request that you instantly depart.'

Fianosther made a bland gesture. 'A report of your
distressing illness reached me, and such was my concern
that I hastened here with an opiate. Allow me to step
within' – so saying he thrust his portly figure past
Cugel – 'and I will decant the specific dose.'

'I suffer from a spiritual malaise,' said Cugel
meaningfully, 'which manifests itself in outbursts of vicious
rage. I implore you to depart, lest, in an uncontrollable
spasm, I cut you in three pieces with my sword, or worse,
invoke magic.'

Fianosther winced uneasily, but continued in a voice of unquenchable optimism. 'I likewise carry a potion against this disorder.' He brought forth a black flask. 'Take a single swallow and your anxieties will be no more.'

Cugel grasped the pommel of his sword. 'It seems that I must speak without ambiguity. I command you: depart, and never return! I understand your purpose and I warn you that you will find me a less indulgent enemy than was Iucounu! So now, be off! Or I inflict upon you the Spell of the Macroid Toe, whereupon the signalized member swells to the proportions of a house.'

'Thus and so,' cried Fianosther in a fury. 'The mask is torn aside! Cugel the Clever stands revealed as an ingrate! Ask yourself: who urged you to pillage the manse of Iucounu? It was I, and by every standard of honest conduct I should be entitled to a share of Iucounu's wealth!'

Cugel snatched forth his blade. 'I have heard enough; now I act.'

'Hold!' And Fianosther raised high the black flask. 'I need only hurl this bottle to the flor to unloose a purulence, to which I am immune. Stand back, then!'

But Cugel, infuriated, lunged, to thrust his blade through the upraised arm. Fianosther called out in woe, and flung the black bottle into the air. Cugel leapt to catch it with great dexterity; but meanwhile, Fianosther, jumping forward, struck him a blow, so that Cugel staggered back and collided with the glass tube containing Iucounu. It toppled to the stone and shattered; Iucounu crept painfully away from the fragments.

'Ha ha!' laughed Fianosther. 'Matters now move in a different direction!'

'By no means!' called Cugel, bringing forth a tube of blue concentrate which he had found among Iucounu's instruments.

Iucounu strove with a sliver of glass to cut the seal on

217

his lips. Cugel projected a waft of blue concentrate and Iucounu gave a great tight-lipped moan of distress. 'Drop the glass!' ordered Cugel. 'Turn about to the wall.' He threatened Fianosther. 'You as well!'

With great care he bound the arms of his enemies, then stepping into the great hall possessed himself of the work-book which he had been studying.

'And now – both outside!' he ordered. 'Move with alacrity! Events will now proceed to a definite condition!'

He forced the two to walk to a flat area behind the manse, and stood them somewhat apart. 'Fianosther, your doom is well-merited. For your deceit, avarice and odious mannerisms I now visit upon you the Spell of Forlorn Encystment!

Fianosther wailed piteously, and collapsed to his knees. Cugel took no heed. Consulting the work-book, he encompassed the spell; then, pointing and naming Fianosther, he spoke the dreadful syllables.

But Fianosther, rather than sinking into the earth, crouched as before. Cugel hastily consulted the work-book and saw that in error he had transposed a pair of pervulsions, thereby reversing the quality of the spell. Indeed, even as he understood the mistake, to all sides there were small sounds, and previous victims across the eons were now erupted from a depth of forty-five miles, and discharged upon the surface. Here they lay, blinking in glazed astonishment; though a few lay rigid, too slugg-ish to react. Their garments had fallen to dust, though the more recently encysted still wore a rag or two. Presently all but the most dazed and rigid made tentative motions, feeling the air, groping at the sky, marveling at the sun.

Cugel uttered a harsh laugh. 'I seem to have performed incorrectly. But no matter. I shall not do so a second time. Iucounu, your penalty shall be commensurate with your offense, no more, no less! You flung me willy-nilly to the

218

northern wastes, to a land where the sun slants low across the south. I shall do the same for you. You inflicted me with Firx; I will inflict you with Fianosther. Together you may plod the tundras, penetrate the Great Erm, win past the Mountains of Magnatz. Do not plead; put forward no excuses: in this case I am obdurate. Stand quietly unless you wish a further infliction of blue ruin!'

So now Cugel applied himself to the Agency of Far Despatch, and established the activating sounds carefully within his mind. 'Prepare yourselves,' he called, 'and farewell!'

With that he sang forth the spell, hesitating at only one pervulsion where uncertainty overcame him. But all was well. From on high came a thud and a guttural outcry, as a coursing demon was halted in mid-flight.

'Appear, appear!' called Cugel. 'The destruction is as before: to the shore of the northern sea, where the cargo must be delivered alive and secure! Appear! Seize the designated persons and carry them in accordance with the command!'

A great flapping buffeted the air; a black shape with a hideous visage peered down. It lowered a talon; Cugel was lifted and carried off to the north, betrayed a second time by a misplaced pervulsion.

For a day and a night the demon flew, grumbling and moaning. Somewhat after dawn Cugel was cast down on a beach and the demon thundered off through the sky.

There was silence. To right and left spread the gray beach. Behind rose the foreshore with a few clumps of salt-grass and spinifex. A few yards up the beach lay the splintered cage in which once before Cugel had been delivered to this same spot. With head bowed and arms clasped around his knees, Cugel sat looking out across the sea.

The world's greatest science fiction authors
now available in Panther Books

Robert Silverberg

Earth's Other Shadow	£1.50	☐
The World Inside	£1.50	☐
Tower of Glass	£1.50	☐
Recalled to Life	£1.50	☐
Invaders from Earth	£1.50	☐
Master of Life and Death	£1.50	☐

J G Ballard

The Crystal World	75p	☐
The Drought	£1.50	☐
Hello America	£1.50	☐
The Disaster Area	£1.50	☐
Crash	£1.50	☐
Low-Flying Aircraft	75p	☐
The Atrocity Exhibition	£1.50	☐
The Venus Hunters	£1.50	☐
The Unlimited Dream Company	£1.25	☐
Concrete Island	60p	☐

Philip Mann

The Eye of the Queen	£1.95	☐

To order direct from the publisher just tick the titles you want
and fill in the order form.

The world's greatest science fiction authors now available in Panther Books

Ursula K LeGuin

The Dispossessed	£1.95	☐
The Lathe of Heaven	£1.95	☐
City of Illusions	£1.25	☐
Malafrena	£1.95	☐
Threshold	£1.25	☐

Short Stories

Orsinian Tales	£1.50	☐
The Wind's Twelve Quarters (Volume 1)	£1.25	☐
The Wind's Twelve Quarters (Volume 2)	£1.25	☐

Ursula K LeGuin and Others

The Eye of the Heron	£1.95	☐

A E van Vogt

The Undercover Aliens	£1.50	☐
Rogue Ship	£1.50	☐
The Mind Cage	75p	☐
The Voyage of the Space Beagle	£1.50	☐
The Book of Ptath	£1.50	☐
The War Against the Rull	£1.50	☐
Away and Beyond	£1.50	☐
Destination Universe!	£1.50	☐
Planets for Sale	85p	☐

To order direct from the publisher just tick the titles you want
and fill in the order form.   SF481

The world's greatest science fiction authors now available in Panther Books

Frederik Pohl

The Man Who Ate the World	£1.25	☐
Survival Kit	£1.25	☐
Drunkard's Walk	£1.25	☐
Man Plus	£1.25	☐
The Age of the Pussyfoot	£1.25	☐
Jem	£1.50	☐
The Gold at the Starbow's End	40p	☐
The Way the Future Was (Autobiography)	£2.50	☐

Harlan Ellison

The Time of the Eye	£1.25	☐
All the Sounds of Fear	£1.25	☐
Shatterday	£1.95	☐

Jack Vance

Trullion: Alastor 2262	85p	☐
The Houses of Iszm	65p	☐
The Five Gold Bands	95p	☐
The Blue World	60p	☐
The Pnume	50p	☐
Servants of the Wankh	40p	☐
City of the Chasch	40p	☐
Lyonesse	£2.50	☐

To order direct from the publisher just tick the titles you want
and fill in the order form.

All these books are available at your local bookshop or newsagent, or can be ordered direct from the publisher.

To order direct from the publisher just tick the titles you want and fill in the form below.

Name_____

Address _____

_____

Send to:
Panther Cash Sales
PO Box 11, Falmouth, Cornwall TR10 9EN.

Please enclose remittance to the value of the cover price plus:

UK 45p for the first book, 20p for the second book plus 14p per copy for each additional book ordered to a maximum charge of £1.63.

BFPO and Eire 45p for the first book, 20p for the second book plus 14p per copy for the next 7 books, thereafter 8p per book.

Overseas 75p for the first book and 21p for each additional book.